Dusty Bluebells

Angeline King

LOTTERY FUNDED

For Liam, Eliza and Christopher,
with Love

By Angeline King

Snugville Street

A Belfast Tale

Children of Latharna

Irish Dancing: The Festival Story

Part One

A Hallowed Eve
October 1945

Maisie looked beyond her own reflection in the window pane. Eight o'clock had passed and not a soul was to be seen on the street, not so much as a beggar seeking a ha'penny for a rhyme. There had been no crackling of squibs under the door or through the keyhole, no oranges, nuts, pastries, barm-bracks or fireworks for at least four years. And now that the war was over, Hallowe'en was to slip by in a storm.

Jamesina must have had a word with God about the weather. She had been witness to Maisie's preparations that morning and had chastised her younger sister for wasting good food on the devil's party, but Maisie had been saving the odd spoonful of sugar and butter here and there, and she had plucked the apples for her tart straight from her friend's garden. She had wanted to recreate the old ways of halleve nicht, when tales of ghosts and ghouls enlivened young faces replete with the bounty of harvest.

Maisie's reflection disappeared as a bright light dashed across the black street, and the sound of wind came up so close that she stopped and wondered if it was her sister rapping the window to admonish the first rhymer.

"It's only a motor," said Leonard as Maisie lifted the lace curtain to see the Waterloo Road speckled in yellow rain.

"It'll be for you," she said. "The road to Glenoe must be cleared for the dance."

Leonard's eyes beamed as he placed the makings of his cigarette onto the floor.

"Model A Ford," he said, his eyes clutching the body of the car. "She's a beauty."

Maisie tutted and followed him out the front door and down the path. It was his dream to own a motor as much as it was his dream to have a child, but tinkering with motors up the back lane and playing in three different bands in dance halls around the country meant that every inch towards the one dream added a yard's distance to the other.

She looked into the car and wondered if the ghosts and ghouls of Hallowe'en had arrived, after all. On the driver's side sat a man trussed up in high collars and a Fedora, his red silk tie clashing with his skin. Even in the warm yellow glow, he was all pale, sweat and swank. Beside him lounged a woman in black, her eyes tucked underneath eyebrows that had been plucked into semi-circles, her lipstick as stark as the red tie on the man with the Fedora hat. Maisie looked at Leonard and wondered if it was the woman who impressed the easy gait upon him, but assured herself that it could only have been the Model A Ford, for a more tasteless critter, Maisie had never seen.

"Good Evening. I'm looking for Mrs Gourley," said the woman, slurring the surname with her blood-red lips.

"Yes, I'm Mrs Gourley," replied Maisie, staring at the Punch and Judy cheeks.

Maisie could never bring herself to paint her face. When Jamesina had got herself into trouble up Pauper's Loanen at the age of sixteen, the rounded stomach was deemed to be symptomatic of burning corks for eyeliner by the fire. "No daughter of mine…" Maisie's mother had heralded as she forbade her second and third daughters from partaking in such devilish practices.

"I'm Esther," came a confident voice as a hand reached out to Maisie. "Esther McCallum," she added. "Could I speak to you please? It's aboot the boy."

"What boy?" said Maisie, checking the back of the car where blackness moved, silence swayed and two watery eyes rippled like buoys in the lough. She turned to the front again. There was plenty of room between the suave couple to fit the tiny shoulders set in the small corner. What in the name of goodness was the child doing stowed away like a suitcase?

A soft sniffle came from the boot of the car. Leonard opened the passenger door and Esther propelled herself onto the road. "Oot ye get," she hurled into the back as she buttoned up her coat and tidied away her polite posturing. "And stap thon greetin and gurnin, wud ye! Honest God's truth! Weans!" she said, as though she and Maisie shared the same affected pain of motherhood.

Esther was smaller than her long, fine face suggested and she was now lugging a short arm out of the boot of the car. Maisie cocked her head and assessed the whisper of a boy, who was all bones and white skin in the headlights. His narrow shoulders jumped at the clack of a door opening and closing and Maisie, without thinking, reached out her hand and took his mort cold fingers in her own. She knelt down and looked him in the eye. "How do you do?" she asked.

A smile shivered at the corners of his lips.

Twit twoos and whistles emerged from the shadows. "Come on over," laughed Maisie, knowing that every soul within a mile would want to take a look at the motor. Esther had a coy smile as she looked at the young men gathering around. Leonard winked towards Maisie and tapped the roof of the car. "She's a fine yin," he said and Maisie took it to be testimony of his interest in the car and not the woman.

"Daniel will need the lavatory," said Esther.

"Well, you'd better come in then," directed Maisie, holding

Daniel's hand tightly. Esther led the way and Maisie wondered what trick God had planned to push such a squib through her door. A holy eve. That's what Reverend Greer from the Parochial School had called Hallowe'en.

A holy eve, when souls move from one world to the next.

Esther loitered in the threshold between the kitchen and scullery, the golden fire swaddling her bird-like frame as Maisie took Daniel and into the back yard. Maisie looked over her shoulder to see Esther through the scullery window — her head twitching and turning and taking it all in.

She opened the door to the lavatory and pulled the cord. A gust of wind wafted the electric bulb hooked to the corrugated roof. "You take your time now," said Maisie. "And rap the door if you need help."

Eyes peered around the door seconds after a tinkle of sound. "Come on," directed Maisie. "Let's get ye oot o the cowl."

She lathered his hands in soap and rinsed them under the cool water taps. She led him to the kitchen. "Sit yersel down by the fire and warm them hands,' she said. She took a heated brick and wrapped it in a blanket. "Take this, son."

Daniel didn't speak. She brushed back a long wisp of fair hair from his cheek and took in the hard contours of his face.

"It's as weel for some," rang a note of aggression from the scullery next door.

"I beg your pardon?" replied Maisie, indignant that a slight should occur in her own home.

"It's as well for some," repeated Esther, surveying the apple tart and fresh soda farls on the bench. "The wean's starvin. He hasnae had a bite tae eat since Stranraer."

Maisie walked to the larder in the scullery and measured out a bowl of porridge. "He'll need something warm," she said to Esther, whose eyes were stealing the distempered flowers on the walls and gripping each square of clean oilcloth at her feet.

Maisie poured the water over the porridge, pausing by Esther on her way to the stove. "Who are you, and why are you here?"

"Who am I? Ye mean ye dinnae know your ain freen?" Esther laughed bitterly and circled her foot on the oilcloth. "Leonard didnae know me neither, did ye?"

Maisie flinched. What had Leonard to do with this woman?

"Who are you?" she repeated, stern this time, fearful that some unearthed ghost might unsettle a night that felt less hallowed as each second was extracted from it.

"Esther Gibson."

"You said McCallum."

"Aye, I was murried the day."

"I don't know any Esther Gibson."

"You don't know any Esther Gibson?" she smiled, imitating Maisie's authoritative tone. "Naw, I suppose ye wouldnae hae heard o Esther Gibson. Did Tam Gourley no mention me?"

"Tam's dead."

"Good riddance to him."

Maisie blinked. Her brother-in-law had died on the Normandy beaches. He had died a hero.

"Did your husband no tell ye aboot the young girl sent up to the country to look after his widowed da? I scrubbed for thon oul blirt morning, noon and night. I cleaned oot his pot and his gutter and much mair forbye. They took me oot o school when I was eleven til tend tae him. And God knows I cried when I seen them dry toilets in Broughshane. I hadnae much on Mill Street, but there was porcelain in the yard. And your Leonard's brother — Tam. Well, Tam took care of me."

Her voice cracked.

Maisie set down the porridge. She lifted a plate and a soda farl and buttered the uneven ridges of the doughy bread. Leonard hadn't spoken to his father since his mother had died at the dawn of the war. All she knew was that a girl had been sent up to Broughshane to look after old Leonard and Tam.

"Here, son," said Maisie to Daniel as she entered the kitchen. "Take this wee drap o soda bread and I'll get ye something warm in a minute."

She returned to the scullery and pulled out two stools from the table. "Ye may sit down," she instructed.

"Tam," said Esther. "He took care o me, Mrs Gourley, and there were no weemen in the hoose but me. I only had Tam to tell me what was what and I didnae know any better, Mrs Gourley...honest tae God, I wasnae a bad wean." She sniffed. "Tam went to the army when I was fifteen and I got the hell oot o thon. I took money from the oul fella tae pay for the boardin hoose in Scotland where I had the wean."

"Why did ye no get the wean adopted?" asked Maisie as she tried to register that Tam had a child and that Tam's child was sitting next door in the kitchen. Daniel was Leonard's nephew, but Maisie didn't know if she would ever be able to tell Leonard the truth about his brother. Perhaps it was for the best that Tam was remembered only as a hero.

"I got work in a bar in Ayr. It was right beside the boardin hoose. They let me keep the wean upstairs when I was workin. I towl them the father had died in the war. Heth, I was lyin at the time."

Maisie had taken Esther to be in her late twenties, the same age as her, give or take a year, but it seemed she was only nineteen.

"Why are you here?" asked Maisie.

"The wean needs a hame."

"Ye cannae lea the wean here!"

Esther's eyes clasped Maisie's. "Mrs Gourley," she said softly. "He's cruel."

"Who?"

"Him." She nodded to the door. "He's cruel tae Daniel."

"Your husband? Why in the name o goodness did ye murry him?"

"I didnae know...I didnae know what was goin on."

"What's goin on?"

A blistering silence followed as the woman's shoulders heaved like her son's in the car. Maisie removed a handkerchief from her sleeve and passed it across the table. Esther wiped the blackness away.

"I'm sorry," said Esther, examining the sullied handkerchief. "I've ruined your hanky."

Maisie didn't reply. She focused on the clean eyes of the young woman that were pitiful and red. What was unsaid stifled the air.

Esther coughed and looked up at Maisie. "He's been interferin..." She tailed off and looked away, holding the handkerchief tight to her face.

Maisie pushed the apple tart away, its sweet promise lingering amongst the sourness of the words that had fallen from Esther McCallum's mouth. She stood up slowly and spread a cloth across the food.

"I was eleven when I lost my childhood," said Esther, "and my life's not worth saving, but have pity, Mrs Gourley, for my boy is only four."

The front door banged and Esther jumped from the stool, her body nimble and flighty as she removed something from a small handbag and dabbed her face. She turned away, glossing red across her thin lips with her finger, re-creating the spectre of a woman who had appeared so sure of herself in the light of the Model A Ford.

Maisie walked towards the kitchen and shivered at the sight of him there with her husband, his hand on Leonard's shoulder as the two of them laughed and gyped and carried on. And in their shadows sat a small boy whose green eyes flickered and faded in tune with the dancing flames.

***

The front door remained open and the flames of the fire bowed at the draught that cut through the room. Esther appeared, her nurturing face concealed in white powder and black paint.

"It's about time you did something to help your own," she snapped, her voice mocking up a pantomime that took Maisie by surprise, her eager eyes pleading with Maisie to play along.

"Do you no mind me?" asked Esther, her red lips straining into a smile towards Leonard. "I'm Esther. I stayed with your oul Aunt Libby."

"Esther Gibson," replied Leonard with a tuneful smile. "Is thon wee Esther Gibson all grow'd up?"

"Aye, all grow'd up. I was only a girl when I was sent up til the country tae tend til your da. And Tam, God rest his sowl. I leuked after them, Leonard. I leuked after them like a daughter and a wife. And now I need somebody tae care for my Daniel."

"Ye need the boy minded?"

Leonard turned to Maisie.

"My Maisie's a great han wi the weans. Isn't that right, Maisie? How long are ye away, Esther? Ye got murried t'day, I hear."

"Aye, that's right and we'll be going on honeymoon the night. Wilbur wants til go back to France, ye see."

"France?" repeated Leonard. "What in God's name would take ye tae France?"

Esther looked towards Maisie, her eyes dragging Maisie back onto the stage she had created.

"We could maybe leuk after him a while," ventured Maisie as she turned to Leonard. "Your da would hae wanted it, I'm sure."

Leonard's eyes were dim. His brother's passing had been in God's hands when German guns had razed him down in French waters, but Leonard hadn't been there to help his father when he fell. He hadn't been there when a farmhand had discovered his father's dead body in a sheuch.

"We'll look after the boy," he said eagerly, smiling at Daniel.

"We'll no turn him away," confirmed Maisie.

Leonard removed a harmonica from his top pocket and knelt down by the fire and played 'The Sea Shanty.' Daniel didn't look at him, but Maisie watched the boy's eyes follow the notes of the tune as he stared into the fire.

"Ye'd better be on your way, nu," said Maisie to Esther. "I'm sure ye've a long night ahead."

She avoided the black silhouette of Wilbur McCallum. She looked away when he reached over to Daniel and ruffled his hair with his hand.

Esther knelt down and lifted Daniel's chin. She whispered in his ear, kissed his cheek, stood up and walked to the door.

Maisie closed the front door behind her and tugged Esther's arm. She whispered sharply, "When are ye coming back?"

"I'm murried til him nu," said Esther, calmly. "I cannae come back."

"You're goin tae leave a four year-oul wean wi strangers?"

"Naw, I'm goin tae leave Daniel wi his ain kith and kin. He b'langs here."

"He belongs with his mother."

"I'm the vessel that curried him," said Esther, any warmth that had been on her face in the light of the kitchen gone. "But I was never meant to be a mother, Mrs Gourley, for I never got tae be a wean."

She hesitated and looked away towards the car. "I didnae live in a house with flowers on the walls and apple tart on a clean table. I was sellin herrings in carts at his age and then...I heard about you, ye know." Her head was raised to the ominous sky. "They towl me you wanted a wean o your own."

"And what aboot you? Will ye stay wi thon yin?"

"I will, Mrs Gourley. I'll no part wi him for this is a better life that any I ever know'd." She turned to face Maisie and handed her an envelope. "I did my best for the boy, Mrs Gourley. He hid shoes on his feet and food in his belly, but I cannae give to the wean what I never learnt masel. You'll care for him, Mrs Gourley,

9

for ye've a heart that's plain tae see. Here's all the papers ye'll need. The wean's tae be christened. Can ye get him christened, Mrs Gourley?"

Maisie nodded as she walked Esther to the car. There was too much uncertainty to make promises, yet in the strange, phony light, it was possible to believe that Esther and Wilbur McCallum would never return.

Esther handed a package from the front seat and pulled Maisie aside. "Dinnae let it happen again," she whispered.

Maisie awaited an explanation, but none came.

And then she understood and she shuddered and she turned away.

She pictured the girl in the kitchen with the green eyes when all the blackness had been wiped clean. She could hear her pleading voice: "It started when I was eleven."

Leonard would never harm a child. Leonard's touch was music conjured into the silent air, his half-smile filled with hope and promise far removed from the evil story that lay scattered like unrationed crumbs on Maisie's scullery table.

She needed Esther to leave. She needed the Waterloo Road to be at peace again away from the motor's engine and its yellow, hollow light. She turned as crowds of children ran up the Shore Road after the scent of oil and raucous stream of smoke. She opened the door to number thirty-three and remembered that there was a boy by an inglenook, a boy who was afraid.

Leonard was playing the harmonica. He stopped when Maisie came through the door.

"Daniel's a freen by blood," he said.

Maisie looked at him. Did he know what his brother had done to Esther, getting her into such state so young?

"Esther's a cousin, they say. Reared by my ma's oul aunt Libby. My ma made my da promise to take her in when she was dyin."

Leonard didn't know what his brother had done. Leonard didn't know what his brother had done to his own cousin.

"My da was an oul blirt at times, but he sent for Esther when my ma was laid til rest."

Leonard was still talking, but Maisie couldn't give the story her full attention. Daniel was Leonard's freen. That was enough, a reason to take in a child.

She looked through the window to the black sky and cast two secrets into the night. There would be no mention of Tam Gourley. There would be no mention of Wilbur McCallum.

There would be no mention of demons unearthed on a windy, hallowed night.

***

She awoke the next morning to a treble of soft breathing and the hum of a deep snore. She sat up, her mind hazy in the unfolding layers of darkness. The sweet sweat of childish skin swathed the room as she squinted towards the end of the bed. She tried to assemble the shape of him, but could see nothing of Daniel, the boy who was safe and so far away from home.

It had been a job getting the boy to sleep anywhere at all. Maisie had led him to the back room where Hughie slept, but he had tugged at her skirt, his eyes pleading with her quivering resolve. Ever mindful of her own childhood fears, she allowed him to follow her to her bedroom, where he fell asleep on an old settle at the end of her bed.

She and Jamesina had spent long hours on the same settle at their Granny's farm in Kells. It had been stuffed with straw and stationed right by the fire, and Maisie could still remember the wind battering the chimney breast and the uncertainty of being so far away from home.

Her granny had always said that the world conjured up strange happenings in the night, and none was as strange to Maisie as the ease with which she had taken a boy from his mother, a boy with no more than a bundle of clothes and a memory of dark secrets etched over his timid smile.

She shuffled onto the landing in her slippers and felt her way down the stairs. Leonard had installed electric lights throughout the house, but Maisie was long accustomed to feeling her way through the dark. She used an old oil lamp in the kitchen to guide her as she knelt down at the fire and began to sweep away the ashes from the night before. She lit a newspaper, the first swirl of heat curling the paper and staining her clean fingers black. She took her time to criss-cross the sticks in a grid over the wakening flames, to build up her fire — to rehearse an old routine that served to temper the realisation of a new dawn.

She poured water into the kettle in the scullery and turned to the table where the ghost of Esther Gibson oscillated in the recesses between night and day. She switched on the electric overhead light to remove the unsettling memories and walked back to the stove in the kitchen to boil the kettle. There, on the ledge of the inglenook was Daniel, who had eked out his own place in between the cold bricks and warm fire. He was looking at her through shadowy eyes.

"Och son," gasped Maisie, clutching her dressing gown, "Ye feared the life out of me. What are ye doing up so early?"

"I need a wee wee."

Maisie smiled and took his hand, and she thought back to hallowe'en and all the toing and froing of strangers and lights and realised she was hearing his voice for the first time. "There was a pot beside the bed, son. Come, and we'll take you oot the back."

She repeated the routine of the previous night and returned to the scullery, where she weighed up the contents of the larder, still holding Daniel's hand. There were only half a dozen eggs in a bowl and two slices of bacon wrapped in paper. Leonard needed a hot breakfast before work, but she knew that the scent of bacon would salt the lips and tongues of every person in the house. She led Daniel into the kitchen and pulled down the griddle from above the fire. "Are you going to help me make breakfast?" she asked, pouring hot water into the teapot. Daniel watched with bird-like eyes.

"Here, let me see ye crack the egg," said Maisie. "There's a great boy." She placed the back bacon on the griddle as Daniel's sticky palms spread the uneven yoke beside them. Already the room was heady with a salted remedy for winter's first morning. It wouldn't be long before Leonard and Hughie were awake.

The package that Esther had left was at the foot of Maisie's chair. She untied the strings and found neat, flat lines of clothing — a knitted vest, a nightshirt, trousers, socks, pants and a shirt, all immaculately clean and pressed. Daniel's name was embroidered onto a handmade label on the knitted vest at the top of the pile, and Maisie thought back to the mother who appeared half-demon-half-cherub in her memories of the night. She had taken care of the boy. She had wanted it to appear that way, at least.

A deep tremor stopped Maisie in her tracks. "Oh Danny boy," she heard, as a head rounded the corner and two bright, blue eyes peered out under wispy, fair hair. "The pipes, the pipes are calling."

Leonard's body followed, his clean, white undervest tucked into brown, woollen trousers, his leather braces looped around his pockets. "From glen to glen, and down the mountain side." He was singing, his arms silhouetting circles in the air, his voice rising and falling, glen after undulating glen of fragrant song. "The summer's gone, and all the roses falling." Maisie held out a slice of bacon on a spatula and watched in stunned silence as Leonard knelt down on one knee and spread his arms. "Tis you, tis you, must go, and I must bide." He kissed her hand and snatched the piece of bacon.

His cheeks were brimming with bacon and smiles as he hollered, "Good morning, Maisie. And good morning, young Daniel." The spatula remained in the air and Maisie was sure she saw a spark in her husband's eyes that was reserved for brass instruments and flash motors. What had the Good Lord done with yesterday's Leonard?

"Gie the other bit tae the wean," he said, as he lifted the bacon onto the boy's plate. "There ye go, son. That'll make the hairs grow on your chest!"

Daniel looked up to Maisie with beseeching eyes, his right cheek repressing a dimple of a smile.

"Is the tay on?" asked Leonard, tapping the teapot with his finger and unhooking a cup from above the fire. "Thon's a great cuppa tay, so it is," he went on gleefully as he poured the tea. "Doesn't your aunt Maisie know how tae make a great cuppa tay?"

Leonard handed the cup to Maisie and unhooked two more. "You sit doon, dear," he said, and Maisie sat down awkwardly, conscious that he had never made her a cup of tea in the whole of their married life. The strange happenings of night were spilling over into morning.

The first bell of Brown's Irish Linen factory sounded and Leonard pulled on his jumper and tied up his boots. There was plenty of time to make it to the harbour for half past seven, but he was flighty and unusually happy and apparently eager to be on his way.

"Now Mr Daniel, here's a wee thing for ye," he said before leaving. He removed the harmonica from his breast pocket and handed it to the boy. "Young Hughie has one the same," he explained. Daniel took the instrument with a blank expression.

The ring of the bell on Leonard's bike followed, and Maisie shook her head, confounded by his smile and in wonder of the effusive and inexplicable music.

***

Young Hughie arrived at the door, his hair parted and flattened as though he had slipped into sleep from standing.

"Good morning," chirped Maisie.

"Mornin," replied Hughie, his head tilted to the side as he weighed up Daniel.

"This is Daniel," explained Maisie to her nephew. "He'll be staying with us. Say, 'How do you do?'"

"How do you do?" mimicked Hughie.

Daniel looked back doubtfully. "Say, 'How do you do?'" prompted Maisie. He echoed the words in a whisper.

"How now brown cow!" exclaimed Hughie like an Englishman.

"How now brown cow, indeed," repeated Maisie in an English accent. "There's a boy that's been well educated. Now, I need two strong men to help me stir the porridge. Do the pair o ye know any strong men?"

"I'm as strong as Popeye the sailor man!" blustered Hughie. "I'm goin tae work at the harbour like uncle Leonard when I grow up. He pulls in the boats, ye know!"

Hughie's eyes were alive as he laid claim to his uncle Leonard's dubious working heritage, the harbour job a recent addition to a lengthy list of short-term contracts.

"Do ye know Popeye the sailor man?" asked Hughie in the kind of breathless gasp that heralded the beginnings of a new friendship.

"No," coughed Daniel, his chin dipping again.

"Ye dinnae know Popeye the sailor man! Aunt Maisie, Daniel disnae know Popeye the sailor man! Do they no hae the pictures in his country?"

"Daniel's from Scotland," said Maisie.

"And do they no hae the pictures in Scotland?" he checked, his head cocked perilously to the left.

Daniel shrugged and looked at the floor, his eyes peeking out over his fringe momentarily to seek reassurance from Maisie.

"I'm strong to the finish cos I eats my spinach!" continued Hughie, confidently pulling up his pyjama sleeve to reveal a sturdy arm. "I'm Pop-eye the Sailor man. Toot Toot."

Laughter rattled from Hughie like brandy balls in a cake tin, a cackle that had been inherited from his uncle Leonard despite there being no blood shared between them.

"Can you say, 'It's a braw, bricht moonlicht nicht,' Hughie went on, his words received by a silent Daniel. "Och dinnae worry if ye cannae say it," he said. "for I've a wee song til teach ye the words. Isn't that right, Maisie?"

"Aye, that's right," laughed Maisie, soaking up the brilliant, bright moonlight of her nephew's deep, dark eyes.

***

A voice puffed up the backs of the Waterloo Road. "Mayzeee!" it bellowed, like a band of bagpipers all tuning their instruments at once.

"That'll be my ma," muttered Maisie.

Daniel's green eyes widened in astonishment.

"It's Granny Higgins," explained Hughie for Daniel's benefit. "She huz a voice like a foghorn, and manys a boat's been lost at sea a cause of it."

Maisie flashed a smile to Daniel to address the fear that dripped from his pale cheeks. She then looked up to the heavens to pray for mercy. What in the Lord's name would her mother have to say about her taking in a stray?

"Mornin, Ma," said Maisie.

"Where's Leonard?"

"He's at work"

"Good. I hiddae talk tae ye."

Grace Higgins walked into the scullery and sat on a stool, her legs splayed open in a basin of black, woollen cloth. "Who's this?" she said, wasting not a moment in ascertaining the provenance of the terrified child.

Maisie moved behind Daniel and placed her hands on his shoulders. "This is Leonard's nephew," she said, before she had time to plan her words. It was too late to start talking about cousins now. She held her breath.

"And what's your name?" enquired Grace.

Maisie exhaled, satisfied that no further explanation as to the boy's exact position on the family tree was required.

"He's called Daniel and he'll be staying with us."

Maisie didn't put a time on the notion. She was tempted to add *for a while* to stall the storm, but instead, she walked to the kitchen to fetch the porridge from the stove. "There we are, boys, she said, "and go easy on the treacle for it's to last!"

"There's sodium saccharin in my hoose," said Grace. "Cannae abide by the stuff masel. It aye leaves me feelin starved."

"I've enough of it," said Maisie. "Send it up to Lily."

"I dinnae think our Lily feeds them weans now that the school's started giein' them their tea. There's no a pick on them girls. No like wee Hughie here." She reached over and pinched her grandson's cheeks roughly. "There's a boy wi colour in his jows."

The porridge barely had time to cool before it disappeared from the bowls.

"Now, away and show Daniel how to play that harmonica before we get ye ready for school," said Maisie.

"Is Daniel no goin tae the Pal-ok-yil school?" asked Hughie with a long face.

"Daniel starts the Parochial school next year, son. He'll no be going tae school today."

The boys were barely out of earshot before Grace spoke. "And who's leuking efter the wean til then?"

"I am"

"You are no!"

"I am so."

"How come?"

"His mother isnae able to leuk efter him, so he's for stayin here with me an Leonard." Maisie spoke with confidence, as

17

much to defy her mother as to trample the chances of the boy ever encountering Wilbur McCallum again.

"What in the name of..? Staying h'lang for?"

"As lang as he needs tae stay."

"A week, a month. H'lang?"

"Mibby forever," asserted Maisie.

Saying it aloud was as absurd as the thoughts of it, but now that she had said it one time, she felt closer to the idea of it. Daniel was staying for good and she had only to think of his stepfather's surly face to know that she wanted it. She had only to think of Daniel's fearful expression to know that he needed it.

Feet pattered from the back room upstairs as harmonicas and laughter sounded.

"You could take him to the orphanage," stated Grace.

"Daniel's no an orphan. His ma's alive."

"Ye need your head leuked at! Ye cannae run aroon making a mother o yoursel the way you do wi Lily's weans. Yin day ye'll come hame from your work and the wean'll be away. His ma might no want him nu, but she'll want him. You mark my words."

"You took in enough strays yersel in your time."

"Heth, I know what I'm talking aboot and I can tell ye that she'll be back and your heart'll be broke for as sure as God my ain heart was broke with them weans o yer uncle Harry's. They always come for them in the end. She'll be back when she needs the wean."

"The wean needs somewhere safe to live, Ma." whispered Maisie. "Her man's a bad rip. And anyway, Leonard's da would hae wanted it. He'd hae wanted Leonard to look after his ain. And after the way he went in the end too, God rest his sowl."

"God rest his fut! Oul Leonard Gourley was a bad blirt and you know it! He died alane for he know'd only how to tend til his sheep and not til his ain. And didn't I warn ye that that yin ye married would be just the same? Mair interested in running aboot wi thon band o his. No better than sheep, the lot o them, if ye ask me."

"Naebody asked ye a thing and ye can get along if you're going tae condemn a man in his ain hoose!"

"I'll no be goin anywhere, Missy." Grace looked up at her daughter and winked. "For I heared there was a bit o apple tart."

"Has Jamesina been giein aff aboot me?"

"Aye, she'd a face on her wud hae soured buttermilk. You're for the devil, sez she, but before ye heed south, I'll take a wee bit o the devil's pie masel."

"Well, watch ye dinnae get a penny stuck in them new teeth o yours!" laughed Maisie.

Grace removed her dentures and set them on the table, her cheeks collapsing into the middle of her face.

"Hallowe'en's over, Ma! Put them back in before ye fear the weans. Come on into the kitchen. The tay's brewing. Help yourself tae I get wee Hughie ready for school."

***

The beady eyes of her mother assessed her every move as she poured hot water into a bowl, dipped a face cloth into it and rubbed on some Lifebuoy soap. It was clear that she was in no hurry to leave and that Maisie's only hope of progressing the day was to work around the tut tuts and the tsk tsks that accompanied the morning's proceedings.

"Daniel, you first son," said Maisie, passing the flannel smoothly across his cheeks and around his neck, clocking her mother's exaggerated turn of the neck, tilt of the head and clasp of the lips. Maisie stopped and looked up, conscious that she was not following her mother's script for getting on in the world. "What's up, Ma?" she asked.

"What's up wi me? I'll show ye what's up wi me," brayed Grace, grabbing the tin basin of water and setting it down on the ground between her feet.

19

"Hughie," come here, son," she piped. "Come here til we show young Daniel how Pop-eye gets washed."

Maisie bit her cheeks and scratched her ear as two familiar red, swollen hands ploughed through the water, plucked the cloth and rinsed it before taking Hughie by the back of the head and scrubbing his skin raw. He yelped, "Granny!" but Grace ignored his plight as well as the blotches of purple and white on his face and held up the cloth triumphantly. "See the dirt on thon cloot!" she hollered, heralding her trophy and looking into a middle distance as she addressed not only Maisie, Daniel and Hughie, but seemingly an entire generation. "Youse young yins dinnae know how to wash a wean."

Maisie rolled her eyes and escaped upstairs with a jug of water to get dressed. She slowed down as she looked in the mirror in her bedroom. If her mother was so good at caring for children, then she would take her time and make something of her appearance for a change.

She carefully washed her face and hands and ran some Solibox over her toothbrush. She brushed every tooth individually, as advised by her friend Sally, and checked the reflection of her own smile, all teeth still present and accounted for despite her mother's constant pleas to have them all replaced with dentures. She refused to entertain the idea; her teeth represented the only fortune she had ever known, and she would abide with them and enjoy being the only member of the family who could chew anything more substantial than spam.

She pulled on a tweed skirt and cream twin set, an ensemble hardly warm enough for the cool weather, but it was the only outfit Maisie possessed that looked decent enough to wear down the street. Woollen stockings and the walk up and down the hill would warm her up soon enough.

She untied the rollers and brushed out curls that had been set into an Amami wave. Her sister, Lily, had given her some Brunitex shampoo and she caught the mahogany tints it produced in

20

the morning light on her tamed chestnut hair. 'Moonbeamy Reflections' was what it had said on the label. Moonbeamy, indeed! Folk were going to think that Maisie had been beamed to the moon and back when word spread about Daniel.

She caught the shadow of her body amidst the silver dust of morning. Her tummy appeared rounded on the shadows on the wall. She turned to the mirror and ran her hands down the bones that edged out from her hips, curves that had been rationed between two wars before they ever had time to take shape. She placed a navy woollen jockey cap on her head, pinched her pale cheeks, fixed her wide eyebrows with a brush of her index finger and walked back downstairs, her mind awash with the gift of Daniel, her body incandescent with Leonard and his song.

Clocking In At Home

Maisie was by the Parochial School gates on the Old Glenarm Road, enjoying the medley of sunshine and cool air on the first morning of winter, smiling at the thoughts of Hughie, who had just delivered a playground soliloquy to mark the arrival of Daniel. "He's from Bonnie Scotland! He hasnae the pictures in his country!' I'm teaching him to be Popeye the sailor man! Toot toot!"

The children stood still, awaiting a reaction from the Scotsman. When none came, they wandered off, disenchanted by the silence of the new cousin and eager to play before the bell.

Maisie waved at Sally. She was like a sprig of holly in a long, bottle-green coat with a red beret perched on top of her dark curls. "Good morning, Mrs Andrews," she called cheerfully, covering her own drab trench coat with her shopping basket. "Thon's a powerful handsome overcoat ye've got there."

"Good morning, Mrs Gourley," smiled Sally, "And thon's a powerful handsome boy ye've got there."

"His name is Daniel," explained Maisie, hesitantly. "He's a freen o Leonard's"

"Hello there Daniel," said Sally, touching his chin lightly with her white gloved hand.

Daniel turned away and nestled into Maisie's coat. She lifted him and noted his body fluttering with fear in her arms. "There,

there," she whispered in his ear, forgetting momentarily that he was a four year-old boy and not a baby. "He's a cousin o Leonard's," she whispered as they began to walk side by side. "He'll be staying with us for a while. I'll get my ma to keep an eye on him in the mornings."

Sally dismissed the words with a shake of the head. "A lot of nonsense," she said. "Didn't wee Hughie play at peace when you were working? Bring him with you!"

Sally touched his arm and Maisie felt his elbow stiffen against her own, his face burrowing closer into her shoulder.

"That's wile kind of ye, Sally," said Maisie, "but I dinnnae like tae take advantage."

"Och away! I miss having wee Hughie about the house. It's settled. Say no more about it."

The final bell sounded and Maisie noted the slight acceleration of Sally's pace.

"Thon bell still puts the fear o God in me," she shuddered. "I think back to Frilly Drawers every time I hear it."

"I only hope the good Lord spared the weans of Ulster from her once she left," replied Maisie. "Ye wonder why she made so much effort with her nether regions when she made so little with her face."

"Aye, ye wonder," laughed Sally.

"Was it a sum you got wrong?" asked Maisie, recalling that Sally had passed out on the rough tiles of the girls' lavatories after being lashed to the bone in Sixth Standard.

"Aye, blistered hands and blood gushing down my arms for an incorrect answer. Something about so many rolls o wallpaper costing this, that or the other and how much change would you have from £1. If I could go back in time, I'd tell her that I'd take an extra roll to back the books with and then there'd be no change tae worry about!"

Maisie shook her head thinking about it all. In the absence of a mother, the women of Waterloo Road had tended to Sally's wounds and clucked for an hour about what should be done about Frilly Drawers, and it was agreed that Maisie's mother should be dispatched to the school to deal with Miss Filly in person.

"I'll never forget what yer ma said as long as I live," said Sally, who raised one hand and proclaimed, "Get down on yer knees and pray, Miss Filly! For you'll no get through the pearly gates if your time on earth is spent floggin weans."

Maisie laughed loudly at her friend's uncanny impersonation of her mother.

"Ma hiz a tongue wud clip clouts, but she'd hae backed away if Frilly Drawers hadnae called her cleanliness into question. 'Filthy Woman!' That was the end of the road for Miss Filly!"

"Never cast aspersions on the cleanliness of a Larne woman," said Sally, skipping over a stream of frothy water swirling from a line of terrace houses. "I can just see your her now, marching across the classroom and grabbing the pair o us"

"Miss Filly was jealous of you, Sally."

"Jealous of an eleven year-old girl?" exclaimed Sally. "What did she have to be jealous of? She was a cruel oul targe."

"Aye, she was," agreed Maisie, who remained convinced that Miss Filly had felt threatened by Sally, the girl who could do arithmetic and spellings with her eyes closed, and who was always seated at the front of the class, the first of the top six.

Maisie was in the second row with a clear view not only of the underwear her teacher wore, but also the eyes that scrutinised Sally Ramsey. Maisie had grown up with Sally's dark eyes, graceful carriage and long, brown hair, but it was only when she had started going to the dances in the Plaza that she fully understood the effect of Sally's looks. Men and women would glance at Sally for just a moment before looking the other away. They would look away, disconcerted or embarrassed to be caught staring, and miss the truth of Sally's dark eyes. They would miss the shimmering sadness of the child hidden inside.

"Your ma was aye good to me," said Sally, her face redolent with nostalgia.

"Aye, I suppose she has her uses!" laughed Maisie. "Shure there was none better than your da. He took us on manys an adventure to the shore."

"He was a good man when he wasnae as full as the Baltic," sighed Sally.

"The Ramseys were the greatest men of Little Ballymena, Ma aften said."

"Oh aye," said Sally. "Strong men wi strong backs, who carried the weight of Lambeg drums and the burden of temperance. Da had the lighter load of the flute and the bottle."

Maisie looked at her friend. It was good to hear her talking about life before Mrs Andrews. "You're in good form today," she observed wistfully.

"It's a good day, Maisie. Now tell me, what about this boy here?"

Maisie had almost forgotten about Daniel, whose bony shoulder had slotted so neatly under the crevice of her chin that the tickle of his feathery hair was the only reminder that he was there.

"He needed tae find a good hame, so we're for taking care o him." She winked and left the rest unsaid, aware that Daniel was capable of understanding more than his timidity conceded.

"How long?" whispered Sally.

Daniel had heard the question. He moved his head and adjusted its position. Maisie tried to come up with an answer that was acceptable to the child's ears, but Sally interrupted her thoughts. "I hope it's a long time," she said energetically, "for I could do with a boy to help me with the garden now that Hughie's in school. I wonder if wee Daniel would be good at the garden?"

Daniel's clutch was ever tighter around Maisie's neck.

"I think Daniel likes to sit by the fire," said Maisie, for that was all she knew of him.

"I can maybe read to Daniel by the fire. That would be nice, wouldn't it, Daniel?" It was a question designed to forfeit any reply.

Singing Sadie's house was on the corner of the Old Glenarm Road. She was on a step ladder cleaning the guttering pipe and singing like a lark. "Morning, Mrs Mitchell," Maisie called above the purl of song. Sadie turned around when she saw them approach and reached out for Daniel's hand, "With the toot of the flute, And the twiddle of the fiddle, O Hopping in the middle, like a herrin on the griddle…" Maisie watched Daniel's eyes widen as he looked up and followed the song. Sadie lifted his small hand and circled it in a figure eight through the air. "O Up! down, hands aroun, crossin to the wall. Oh!, hadn't we the gaiety at Phil the fluther's ball." She slapped her thigh and continued with a "Tiddly eye dye dye dye," in place of the next verse as a smile trickled across Daniel's face, his cheeks bunching up tightly around his eyes.

"Good morning, Mrs Andrews. Good morning, Mrs Gourley," chirped Sadie as wedding bells chimed from the chapel.

"Who's gettin married the day?" asked Maisie.

"They say it's a naval officer from Chicago. The wee girl is connected til the oul Reverend Greer from the Church of Ireland, so she must be for turning. Away and enjoy the style!"

"Did your da ever tell you about Sadie's family turning?" said Maisie when Sadie was out of earshot.

"I dinnae think so," said Sally.

"When I got murried, my da towl me that folk were aye prone to followin God tae the nearest soup kitchen. He said that Sadie's family went from the Anglicans to the Covenanters at the time o the Spanish influenza, but what with all their great voices, they were heartbroken to find a church without hymns."

"My father was a man of principal," said Sally. "He towl me himself why he turned away from the Anglicans." She leaned in close to Maisie as they crossed the Victoria Road. "He said that the Reverend Greer gave a temperance sermon in the Olderfleet bar, and my da, being the great man that he was, took the pledge along with all the sailors drinking on the slate after work. His temperance waned within the fortnight, however, and the RIC scooped him up from Quay Street and put him in the Chooky House. The very next Sunday, my da was named and shamed at the front of the church for breaking the pledge."

"God's truth," said Maisie, "They read out his name?"

"Aye, and my ma was terrible ashamed. My da made a great rair about it all and went straight to the Non-subscribing Presbyterians the next week. There, he said, he was allowed his own interpretation of the bible."

"And what was that?"

"That he was only answerable to the Good Lord and not any master, and that he could be filled with the holy spirit as often as he pleased. He was quare and smart, my da!"

"Well, I never!" laughed Maisie. "And yer da was a smart man. Shure he writ music scores that were fine art."

"He could write like a scribe," agreed Sally. "Granny Ramsey towl us that he got his brains from all the hours spent in the company o doctors for he was a terrible sick wean."

A crowd had assembled by the church gates on Chapel Lane. Maisie quickened her pace to catch sight of the bride. "Och leuk," she gasped. The bride was in a gown of powder blue with a bouquet of red carnations, her dark hair assembled on top of her head in a pile of curls crowned with a long, white veil. The bridesmaids wore red, velvet dresses and carried fur muffs, whilst the groom stood tall in his naval uniform with a gleaming smile. Maisie had never seen such style.

"A beautiful bride!" exclaimed Sally.

"Like a queen," agreed Maisie.

She looked at the groom and wondered what life would have been like if she had waited until the war before making her choice. She might have fallen for a rich naval officer from Chicago, like the woman in the powder blue dress.

Her own wedding day had been uneventful, the only hint of romance a fleeting one after the wedding breakfast when Leonard had looked up over his saxophone and caught her eye. She had spent the entire evening alone, and when her husband returned home from the Greasy Pig, he didn't say a single word about his absence. They made love, but Maisie cried the next morning knowing that she would have to live with his silence for a lifetime.

Maybe it was for the best that he was a quiet soul, for there was nothing less harmonic than the hurtful percussion of banged doors and hollering voices that came from a few doors up.

Yet Leonard had sung to her that morning, and Maisie had never before heard his song.

She looked around her at the crowd of well-wishers. "There was none of this style when we were married," observed Maisie.

"We were the same," said Sally. "I didn't even have a wedding gown."

An awkward pause followed. Maisie and Sally were not the same. They had not been the same since the day that Sally had married Dr. Andrews and moved to the other side of the wall. And as far as Maisie could see, the only thing that had ever come between them was the twelve foot wall separating the long skinny gardens of the Waterloo Road from the three large houses occupied by the minister, the doctor and the politician. Each Monday, Wednesday and Thursday, Maisie went to the other side of the wall to play an unconventional game of maid and mistress on the periphery of Sally's life, a game that at times felt nostalgically familiar — a continuation of childhood play, with an abiding sense of incompleteness when the roles were not reversed.

Maisie began to walk away from the church, still holding Daniel who was so light that he could have floated away with the confetti petals that birled lightly over the crisp, orange leaves. She wondered if he had paid attention to the wedding, if it had brought back any memories of his mother's at Gretna Green, but a chill hastened her feet as she imagined him stowed away in the dickey seat of the car throughout the ceremony.

"Watch your back there, dear," said Sally. "You've practically carried him all the way down the street. Here, let me take him off you a minute."

"Light as a sparrow! Isn't that right, wee son?" said Maisie, as she lifted Daniel's chin.

"He's asleep," confirmed Sally. "Tell me what happened."

"They brought him last night," said Maisie. "The man...Oh, you should have seen him all done up like he was no goat's toe. Well, I can tell you, I could see it in him, just the way I could see it in Frilly Drawers for she was good looking too. A bad egg'll always float to the surface, my ma's aye for sayin!"

"So, he was cruel..." Sally raised her head in such a manner that Maisie could have sworn she understood more than what was said. "And they just got up and left him?"

"She heard we wanted a wean," said Maisie, her voice fading in the hurly burly of Larne Main Street as she realised that she and her friend had crossed a path they had never traversed in all their years of role playing up the backs of the Waterloo Road.

Neither of them had ever rehearsed the life of a woman without children.

***

"Catch a whiff o thon," cried Sally in a broad voice as they came closer to the stench of the lough. "It's a good day for picking whelks," she smiled. She looked down Quay Street and turned to Maisie. "Here look, is that no your sister, Lily, and the wean?"

"It couldnae be," said Maisie, assessing the slight figure in the long brown coat gripping the hand of a tiny girl. "Lily's at her work."

She looked again, and was greeted by a wave. Her sister's shoulder-length curls were loose around her neck with no sign of the hairnet she wore in the factory.

"Is this the wee bairn from bonnie Scotland?" smiled Lily as she approached them. "Ma had a thing or two to say aboot this wee lad."

"I'm sure she did too," said Maisie, smiling at young Lily, who gripped her mother's leg. "This is Daniel," she said.

Maisie's sister placed her hand on Daniel's head. "Nice to meet you Daniel. This is my wee Lily. She's the same age as you. Say hello to Daniel, Lily." The children both stared at each other without uttering a word.

"What brings ye down the street?" enquired Maisie.

"Hello there Mrs Andrews," said the elder Lily by way of reply.

"Morning Lily," responded Sally. "You're looking well."

Lily flicked her moonbeam hair, "Aye," she said. "I had a bit mair time on my hands this morning. No rushing out the door at the drone of the factory!"

"And why not?" asked Maisie.

"Did ye no hear? I'm clocking in at home!"

"You're what?"

"I got laid off," said Lily. "Tools down for the ladies as of yesterday at four o'clock."

"You're jokin me!"

"I wish I was for I was the most nimble and quick Tier-in Drawer-in they ever did see. Too many men on the dole. The men are to get their full hours back and we're to get back to where we belong."

"Did ye ever hear the likes of it in your life?" fumed Maisie.

"Och dinnae worry. Uncle Peppy's givin me a wheen o hours in the ice-cream parlour. The early bird catches the worm, so they say."

"That'll hardly cover the bills."

"It'll be nice all the same. A change. This one here needs her mammy." She lifted Lily up and addressed Sally. "The other weans were happy to be passed aboot when I was out working, but not Missy here!" Lily held her daughter tightly and kissed her cheek before setting her down and whispering. "She's four and she still Sinai talkin."

"Och sure, Ma sez ye were the same when ye were a wean and ye hinnae shut up since," said Maisie.

Lily smiled and stroked her daughter's back as she spoke, "Maisie, could wee Hughie maybe move back in?"

"What odds will it make if he stays in my hoose?" choked Maisie. "Aren't ye there nearly every night of the week anyway?" She was reminded that Hughie had first slept there as a result of his mother not knowing when to go home.

"It's just Rab...He wants wee Hughie to be reared wi us."

"Naebody's ever tried to take wee Hughie away from ye," replied Maisie, surprised to find her voice trembling.

Lily looked up at Sally and smiled before continuing. "It's time for Hughie to come hame. It's the way it's meant to be."

"In the name o God!" spluttered Maisie. "We're only two doors up. It's no like he's in Australia."

"I want him hame wi me. You can still mind him when I'm here. I'll be starting in Peppy's tonight. Bring him and Daniel doon for an ice-cream."

Maisie was shaking, her grip on Daniel weakening. Sally reached over and lifted the boy and Lily turned her attention to Sally. "Rab's applied for a parlour hoose up the road tae gie us a bit more room. He got made up, ye know? He's foreman now."

"That's good news," said Sally.

"Wonderful!," said Maisie, swallowing hard and composing herself for the sake of polite company. "When are ye flittin?"

"I'm for Point Street nu tae get the keys."

"Do you need a hand moving?" asked Sally. "I can bring the motor around to help with the furniture."

"Thanks all the same, but for all there is of it, the weans can carry it. They're all up tae hi do!"

"I'm sure they are," said Sally. "Anyway, we had better be getting on. I'm down to treat your sister for morning tea at the McNeill Hotel. Late birthday present."

Maisie looked at her friend in surprise. Sally winked and began to walk on ahead, and Maisie lingered in front of her sister. "Ye might hae waited an towl me at hame!"

"What? An hae ye jumping doon my throat? No thanks." Lily paused and added, "You're aye the lady when you're with the doctor's wife."

"Run on and get the keys to your parlour house," said Maisie. "And ye may sweep the floor more aften for the wean cannae abide by the dust."

Maisie walked on and caught up with Sally, who had stopped in front of a newspaper stall. *I'm clocking in at home* was printed above a Milk of Magnesia advert. Maisie stopped and read aloud with disbelief. "I've said goodbye to that war job and now I'm going to enjoy the simple home life I've been eagerly planning."

"The old world has been restored," asserted Sally.

"The old world?" coughed Maisie. "Can ye ever mind a time when there was a better world than this? All I mind is unemployment and rationing from one war til the next." She thought back to the men standing at the factory corner deliberating workers' rights, whilst women and children scrubbed laundry and sewed for a pittance. "The simple life at home only ever meant raw knuckles, as far as I know'd. And I'll tell ye, mair forbye. Thon girl's in for a quare gunk. She'll need mair than Milk of Magnesia after one day wi her ain weans!"

"I meant what I said about the tea, by the way," smiled Sally.

"My birthday was in March!"

"I hae a wee bit o news."

Maisie looked instantly at her friend's stomach. She reached out her hand when she realised the thick green coat was disguising a slender curve. She awaited Sally's confirmation, and it came with a nod. "Come on. It's on me. There are advantages to being the doctor's wife, ye know?"

"Well, wait til my ma hears I'm drinking tea in a hotel. She'll be telling me I've no notion what side my bread was buttered on." She stopped walking and took Sally's hand. "I'm heart-glad for ye, Sally. I'm heart-glad for ye, dear."

Idle Hands
January 1946

Sally was distracted by her own reflection. She couldn't see beyond it. She couldn't see the old stone wall on this wild January night, but sensed its presence like the comfort of knowing that someone else was at home.

No one else was at home. She was alone in a house filled with cold echoes and marble fireplaces, only a stone's throw from the warm voices and stone grates of the Waterloo Road. There, loneliness had never been her lot. Even on the darkest days, there was always one or another neighbour in the scullery cleaning or fussing over her father. On many occasions Sally had awoken with Jamesina's cold feet next to her face and the fleeting recollection of having been carried next door to number fifteen. "Your da had a bad night, dear," Grace would say in the morning, and she would reach her red, swollen hands out to pet Sally's head before smacking the backside of whichever child was looking the wrong way.

And Sally would sit there, taking it all in.

She would watch Maisie and Lily scratch out each other's eyes with every mutual glance. She would squirm as Jamesina spooned porridge mixed with cod liver oil into her twin brothers' mouths. She would smile as Kenneth Higgins strapped up his braces before taking his piece from his wife. There would be a kiss on the head for each child and a wink for the little girl who would have given anything to have one more smack on the backside and one more spoonful of stinking cod liver oil from the raw hands of her own mother.

Winifred's face had long left her mind. Sally squeezed her eyes shut and tried hard to imagine it, but her only memory was the touch of her hands. Hands that had lifted her onto the scullery table to tend to her cut knees. Hands that had brushed her long, brown hair each morning. Hands that had slapped her bare legs when she had given cheek.

There were no photographs to stock up Sally's memories. There was nothing of Winifred Ramsey left, nothing but the memory of two raw hands that had scrubbed laundry day-in-day-out.

"You set yersel to learnin, Sally," her mother had often said. "You set yourself to learnin and you'll no hae hands like mine by the time your ten."

The water on the windows faltered into a grey haze and Sally's salty eyes mirrored the fall of the rain. She repeated a familiar conversation in her head. "What would you think of all this, Ma? Did you plan this when we walked around Newington Avenue together — me with the white bedsheets set across my arms, you carrying that big basket of pressed shirts? Did you think that I might live here in this house? Did you wish so hard for it to happen that you died? And now when you look down on me, are you glad? My hands are soft. Look, soft as butter, Ma. But if you see me and Maisie here like two weans playing house, you'll know that my hands are soft and you'll know that my hands are idle."

Sally's hands were raised to her mother as the two women stood together, one on the window of Sally's imagination, the other staring at the reflection through two pale hands that bore none of the hallmarks of life on the Waterloo Road.

A scratch on glass brought Sally's hands in close to her chest. She huddled the top of her cardigan and looked outside again, regretting that she hadn't closed the curtains before Alfie had left to call on a sick patient.

A childlike fear skipped along her spine, a fear that she had long ago replaced with the solace of the ghost and guardians of her mind. She walked to the window and stopped. The sound of clawing. It was a cat. That was it. The sound had to be a stray cat. She pulled the weighty curtains along the metal rails, forgetting about the drawstrings that hooked along the top. The screeching halt of the curtain hooks at the corner of the bays forced her hand up to her chest once again. Finally they were closed. She should go to bed. But she wouldn't sleep. She wouldn't sleep knowing that her imagination was let loose in this cursed house with its cursed, cold echoes.

What remained of the young Sally Ramsey was in this one room, the rest of the house a mausoleum to Alfie's grandfather, Captain George Andrews, who, by way of his collections, lived a phantom existence at Dalriada long after his death.

Sally could hear her father on her wedding day telling her that it was right and good that she was here in this house for all men were created equally and there was no reason why his daughter shouldn't have the best of everything, a sentiment that lingered from his days at the factory corner when he stood shoulder-to-shoulder with the other out-of-work socialists. She smiled at the thoughts of her father and his endless speeches and got up and poured herself another glass of port. She held it up to him and welcomed its scorching sweetness as she allowed her shoulders to fall.

She walked to an old dresser, the only piece of furniture she had brought from number seventeen. In one drawer was her father's flute and his tin whistle and in the cupboard the banjo that had ended in the death of a pig. She had never learned to play the banjo, and so it remained in its box with all her father's manuscripts, but she lifted it out from time to time, to take comfort in the memories of its jubilant strings.

She sipped back the velvety fluid and her mother's words rattled through her memories in a sermon thrashed out against a rug suspended from the back wall. "Why I ever married thon good-for-nothing blirt, I'll never know. God's honest truth, ever since I met thon man, I hinnae had two D to rub together. And what for? I'll tell ye what for, Missy! A bloody banjo! That's what for! Did ye ever hear the likes of it in your life?"

Sally pictured the threads of hemp from the old hessian sacks floating into a speckled mist as the pigs stared at one another in confusion.

Poor oul Gruntie, she thought with a smile as she poured another port. She had her heart broken twice on account of that pig — once when she passed out from the shock of seeing Andy Gingles from Mill Street putting rings on Ould Gruntie's nose to keep him from digging up the forecourt of his sty and a second time when Jamesina took her to show her Ould Gruntie's new home. She had squealed all the way home after seeing the carcass strung up in the slaughterhouse along with all the other rent pigs.

And all because Sally's father had bought a banjo with the rent money from a tinker at the Mounthill fair.

A large envelope was filled with music scores and song lyrics in her father's hand. She placed it onto the floor and ran her hands over the banjo and smiled as her mother's voice continued, "Why in God's name did we need another instrument in this god-forsaken hoose? Is it any wonder I never get a night's sleep? Is it any wonder I'm tired morning, noon and night? Is it any wonder my head throbs from the minute I wake?"

Sally pictured her mother's black dress swish tracks along the ground as she poured her heart out to the big wall.

She didn't know then that a brain tumour was the reason for such affliction. She didn't know that she was sick with cancer and so she drummed on like a marching band. "If thon man brings another instrument into this hoose, he may stroke it and strum it six foot under, and I'll tap out a tune on top of his grave for he aye said that a finer dancer was never seen than Winifred Ramsey."

***

Sally drank the last of the port and looked around the room. She felt more at ease now. Alfie would be home soon, and she would tell him about the banjo. He enjoyed stories of her days on the Waterloo Road. He had spent half his childhood peering over the wall and wishing he could play barefoot with the other children. He had watched from his window when Sally came each day with the laundry; so he had told Sally when he courted her and she believed it for there was always a sense that the house was watching her and calling her in. It was a warm feeling then. She had little notion of how cold the house would be on the inside. She had little notion how it would affect her mind.

Nor did Alfie, who was perpetually caught between curiosity and fear as he drove her back and forth from the psychiatrist's study. Hallucinations. Hysteria. Demons particular to a woman's mind.

They were wrong. All of them. It was Dalriada. Sally knew it.

Scratching came from the window again. Sally didn't fret. The port had softened her nerves. She turned off the lights, walked into the hall, placed the chain on the front door and began to pull the curtain across. She stopped, remembering the metallic grating sound in the kitchen and reached for the tassel of the cord.

A clang rang out from the side of the house. She jumped back away from the door.

The bin. It must have been the metal bin blown over in the wind. She walked to the scullery in the dark. The yard light shone upon the concrete path where the binlid swivelled on the ground. The old bath tub that had been hooked to the wall was now sitting near the lavatory in the yard.

But the cats. She thought about the cats scratching at the window and the open bin and pulled back the door. The night air was still. No rain. No howling wind. She lifted the binlid from the ground. It was there again, that feeling of warmth and hope as she stood on the threshold of Dalriada.

A whistle rose like her father's voice and Sally looked up to the sky.

"I was thinking about you both tonight," she whispered. "You were here with me. And I sang 'Let me call you sweetheart' in my head."

The whistle heightened and Sally saw dust and particles of fibre birl through the air. The door slammed, but she felt no fear. She stood still and listened to the sky as the port washed her mind.

"I mind when Da sang for you, Ma, and I heard you humming his song in the garden when you were hanging out Captain Andrews' sheets. You thought it was better over here, didn't you? You had no idea."

The wind rose again and Sally immersed herself in a memory. Or was it a dream? She was never sure which. She could picture a woman reaching into the bath. She could see the bloodied cloth. She could see the skin. Bloodied skin.

She swayed and grabbed the bin to steady herself. A baby. Dead. "Oh my god, Ma." She looked up to the heavens and back to the body as tears tumbled down her cheeks. It all felt real.

"What should I do?"

Was it real? The handles of the bag were open.

"Should I lift the handles, Ma? What should I do?"

Her body rocked as her mind flashed back to December, to the tangle of birth and blood and the baby she had bled for every night since.

"Who would do such a thing?" she cried out in the silence.

She groped around the side of the bag, her eyes closed, her arms outstretched far from her face. She turned her head away and lifted the body, the hot body. It was hot.

Dreams. Memories. The present. Demons particular to a woman's mind.

She placed her little finger between the purple lips. Her finger tingled at the tug. She cleansed the vernix from the face and body with a linen rag, and watched as wrinkled newborn features emerged from the folds of clotted blood. It was a girl communicating life with a dribble of water.

She needed a napkin and she needed water, but she couldn't leave the baby lying there, cold and exposed. She stood up and cried "God Almighty!" in an echo of her mother's voice.

She was in the scullery fetching a napkin, but none of the movements she made belonged to her arms. Was she hallucinating? Was this the hysteria Alfie's doctor friend had prescribed? She stiffened and the baby began to muffle a low, serrated cry against her chest. She lay it across the settle again to quell the tingling sensation of sweat under her arms. But the arms were not her own and the feelings were not real. Yet, the scent of it all was there, lodged in her mind.

She closed her eyes and she could see a figure take both feet between her left index finger and left thumb and place the napkin underneath.

Brown's Irish Linen could dam a river, she had often been told by her father. She lifted the clean baby and held it close to her chest. Its lips touched her neck.

"Good Lord in the Heavens above!"

Her mother's voice again.

The baby needed food and it was softly searching for it on Sally's naked skin. What was she to give a newborn baby?

She hushed and hummed and swayed up and down and back and forth, and as the baby settled, her father's song emitted slowly from her lips. 'Let me call you Sweetheart,' she sang in a soft timbre as her body moved through the house.

She pictured the cover of her father's first record. A woman with a long dark plait running down one shoulder. She had insisted on wearing her hair in the same fashion when her mother had taken her to the pharmaceutical store to have her photograph taken at the age of nine. "Let me hear you whisper that you love me too," she sang. "Keep the love-light glowing in your eyes so true, Let me call you Sweetheart, I'm in love with you."

She turned out the lights in the kitchen and settled into the wooden rocker, the voice of her father filtering her lungs in crystally streams of song as a dim light flickered through the scullery door and a small baby suckled on her finger, tugging dormant vibrations in her womb, tingling ducts along her armpits.

A tug deep within her womb. A face shining between a crystal bell and gold-plated porcelain shoe. A woman rocking a banjo. A woman without a baby in her arms.

***

Alfie was pacing back and forth in the back kitchen, his logic and reality clashing with the soft canopy of song that had encircled the room.

"And the bin lid was on its side? Like the sound of a cat, you said? A baby. Still warm?"

"There's not a woman on the Waterloo Road would abandon a wean on a cowl night," said Sally, as the child slept on her shoulder. "We might have been reared with hard hands, but we only ever knew kind hearts."

She felt the chill of Dalriada.

Alfie knelt beside her and stroked the hand that cupped the baby's back. "Imagine then how beautiful Rebecca would have been then. A child born to a woman with kind hands and a kind heart."

Rebecca. The name they had planned to call the baby. Sally had become attached to it.

Alfie paused and looked at her and she caught the brown eyes of the teenage boy who had peered out the window as the laundry maid walked by.

"Still, she would have spoken the King's English like her father," he added with a smile.

It was true. Rebecca would have spoken like her father. She would have been reared in the ways of the Andrews' family, and rightly so, for Sally had had ambitions for that child. She would have learned French. Or the cello. Or the harp. Yes, that was it. Granny Ramsey would have approved of the harp.

"Where are we to take the baby?" she said finally, over-compensating her clarity to disguise a tongue weakened with drink.

"Take who?" came Alfie's concerned voice.

"The workhouse. Don't take her to the workhouse."

Words filtered in and out of Sally's mind as her vision blurred.

"We need to tell the police," she heard. A familiar voice, not Alfie's voice.

They were in the yard and Alfie was holding her hand and placing the bathtub back onto the hook.

The stars had disappeared. "Goodnight, Ma and Da," she whispered softly. "Thanks for the song for the child."

The car started with a shriek that altered the steady breathing against Sally's chest. Alfie drove by the pitch black of the tennis club where Sally imagined a girl hiding and watching.

No, she thought. The mother would not be out on this cold night with blood streaming from her body.

The lights of the car sprayed their orange dust across the road towards the gate of the Town Parks and the car turned onto The Clonlee. Was the mother there in the park? Was she down on the shore? Sally couldn't bear the thoughts of the woman drowning.

"Maybe she chose us," whispered Sally.

A gear change coughed over the silence.

"Let's get you to the doctor," said Alfie.

Alfie was a doctor. Why was he taking her to the doctor?

"Let's go," he said, only moments later as he parked by the house.

A house. Not the workhouse.

"No, that's alright," said Sally. She'll only cry if I hand her over to you. No need to scare her."

"Sally!" Alfie's tone was hard, his eyes soft.

"What if she's cruel?"

"Who?"

"Exactly. We don't know who? The new mother. What if she's cruel?"

"Sally, you're worrying me. Do you see something? Is it another vision?"

"Keep the baby. She wants us to keep the baby," said Sally, tears warming her face. She could feel Alfie lift her weightless body. Her hands intertwined, empty hands that were not holding a baby. And then there was the doctor and the tapestry chair.

She closed her eyes. She could hear the revellers shout and sing as they returned from the dance at the Victoria Hall. And she could see her mother. She could see hands, the outline of a thin body, auburn hair looped at the nape of the neck, light falling on a freckled face as she smiled.

She could see the face of Winifred Ramsey and she wondered if it would be easier to stand by a twelve foot wall among the pigs and shout and curse and beat two hessian sacks sewn together with wool than to live the life of a stone memorial walking.

"Rest peacefully, Ma," she whispered, her mother blurring out of focus between the crystal and the porcelain shoe. "Your eyes were weak, but your hands were never idle."

"She's delirious," came Alfie's voice. "And she's having the same dream."

"The abandoned baby?" It was the voice of the doctor.

"Yes. The same one she had after the last miscarriage. Five months this time."

"Hold her steady," said the doctor.

Sally felt a sharp pin prick in her arm.

She needed to sleep.

Her eyelids closed and she saw her reflection in the mirror of the China cabinet. She saw the banjo in her arms.

Sleep washed over her. A release from the dream that never ended.

Dusty Bluebells
April 1946

Sally Andrews was a mystery. There she was, all dressed up in a knee-length powder blue dress, staring out the window, a hint of approval sparkling in her enigmatic eyes. Maisie didn't have the heart to tell her that the arm was a delicate thing and that it would be preferable if her friend's hindquarters were positioned on the baize and cherry moquette, but she said nothing. Sally hadn't been herself since Christmas when she had lost the baby. A second, so Alfie had said.

"Ma couldnae see in the end, ye know?" said Sally.

"Och och a nee, I mind it weel," said Grace.

"She used to sit an listen to the weans. I wonder what she would have made o thon swing."

"'Away, and shut thon thing up!' is what she'd hae said," said Grace. "I'm tellin you, one o them wean's is gonna get hurt on thon swing."

"Honest tae God," said Maisie, "Will the folk of the Waterloo Road ever be thankful for anything? If it's not the electric street-lights, it's the tyre swings dangling from them!"

"Humpf," said Grace. "Thon lights is no right for the eyes. "Oh, holy flip!" she said, leaning forward. "Is it the electric lights or is thon Big Melodeon feet himsel I see before me? He hid better no be comin here!"

Maisie rested her duster and watched the minister loiter by the swing.

Hughie jumped off the tyre and ran up the path. "Granny Higgins! Granny Higgins! It's Big Melodeon Feet!"

Maisie held her heart in her hand as she turned to her mother, who emitted a soft te-he.

Hughie, encouraged by his granny's reaction, swayed his hands from side to side as he sang. *Skinny Malink Melodeon legs, big banana feet, went to the pictures and couldnae find a seat. When he found a seat, he fell fast a asleep. Skinny Malink Melodeon legs, big banana...*" Maisie clasped her hand over Hughie's mouth, muffling the last word. Behind the child stood Reverend McCready, the man with the longest legs and the largest feet she had ever seen. She caught the wide eyes of Daniel, who, following behind, was assessing the man's shoes.

"Good morning Reverend McCready," said Grace in her polite, earth-shattering voice.

"Get on and play now boys!" directed Maisie to Daniel and Hughie. "And don't let wee Lily go near thon swing!"

"The young fella said you were here, Mrs Higgins, and I'm happy to find you all together for it's been quite some time since I set eyes on young Maisie. And I take it this is Lily." He continued without further verification as to the identity of the woman on the end of the settee. "It's in matters of education that I call today, Mrs Higgins."

Maisie caught a smirk from the side of Sally's face as she finally settled into the baize and cherry moquette, apparently content with her status of youngest sister. Maisie surrendered her duster and understood that another day was to go by without getting a hand's turn done. "Can I get you some tea, Reverend McCready?"

"Och aye, that would be very good indeed."

"Well sit yoursel down there beside…" Maisie looked towards her friend and concluded it was best to allow her to retain her place in the family. "A wee sandwich, Reverend McCready?"

"Och no, dear, not at all," came his strong voice with its soft Scottish lilt. I'm not to be eating the rations. That wouldn't be right. Just a cup of tea, if it's all the same."

Maisie suspected that Reverend McCready wasn't one for sitting about. There was an urgency in his manner, and it was increasingly clear that he was anxious about the work he was to undertake.

"It's a bit of a sensitive matter, Mrs Higgins. It's about Miss Higgins, your eldest daughter."

"Jamesina?"

"Yes, Jamesina."

"What's she done?" asked Grace.

Sally bounded up and straightened her skirt.

"Stay where ye are, dear," directed Grace. "We're all family here," she added with a wink.

"It's the children at the Sunday school, Miss Higgins. Miss Beatty got a smack from Miss Higgins a few weeks ago for not remembering her verse. The Beatties were most affronted and went straight to the Methodists the following week."

Grace's lips formed a line. Her back straightened.

"We value Jamesina's contribution at the Sunday school, but we think it might be better if she helped with other matters that don't concern the children."

"Reverend McCready, if you don't mind me askin, why in the name of heaven have ye come tae me? Miss Higgins is a grown woman and ye'll find her at the post office."

He placed his hands together and Maisie looked at Sally and prepared herself for prayer, but the minister tipped his chin with his clasped forefingers and spoke carefully. "Mrs Higgins, I've spoken to your daughter several times and she has said to me that God sent her to take care of the children and that there are no two ways about it, she must do the Lord's duty in haste."

Maisie held back the laughter pinching at her cheeks and tried hard not to look anywhere near Sally. Instead, she turned to her mother, who exhaled a yeuch that sent her feet into the air. The minister stared at the ceiling in an appeal to the good Lord himself for sanctity from Grace Higgins' undergarments.

Maisie began to feel sorry for him. She watched the lines on his lips quiver. He placed his large hands on his knees to quell his trembling body and eventually looked down, clasped eyes with Grace and allowed laughter to extend along the long lines of his bony cheeks. Maisie could sense the bottled up laughter within Sally.

"You leave it with me, Reverend," said Grace, composing herself.

The Reverend bounded up from his seat before Maisie had time to pour the tea.

"But you havenae had your tea yet," said Maisie, half-heartedly.

"Not to worry about the tea. I'd better be getting along."

Maisie went out and watched him hurry up by the big wall towards the shore, his body sloped backwards as his long limbs galloped on ahead.

"He's a lang drink o water, thon boy. Did he come doon thon way too?" she checked with Hughie.

"Aye, he did."

"Thon's a quare and strange route to come frae the Victoria Road," she observed.

"Aye," said Sally. "And a gey and smart way of avoiding the post office."

Sally was buttoning her coat and watching the swing creak back and forth as Hughie lay over it on his belly. "You watch yourself, young Hughie," said Sally. "I need two big strong men to clip the hedges on Saturday and you'll be no good to me if you lose your head on thon swing."

Hughie stood up on the pavement and held his arms out to balance himself.

"God's truth," said Maisie, "thon wean's like Rab McNeill on a Friday night. Steady yoursel son!" She reached for him and once he was standing at attention, skelped him on the palm of his hand. "That's one from earlier," she scolded. "No calling the minister Big Melodeon Feet now, d'ye hear?"

Hughie got back onto the swing and Daniel stared at Maisie with reproach, as though he too had felt the force of her hand.

"It's quiet," said Sally as she looked up and down the street.

"Aye, it's a queer sort of day, isn't it?" said Maisie. Them clouds is no for deciding what they're for daein."

Maisie watched Sally give number seventeen a quick glance over her shoulder, as she always did before departing.

"Bye bye, wee Lily!" she said, lifting the child up and spinning her around. "Goodbye, Daniel. Goodbye Hughie."

"Bye bye," replied Hughie. He was lying back on the tyre as it twirled under a cloudy, complacent sky.

Maisie stopped and listened. There was a creak. There was the clip of Sally's court shoes on the footpath. There was the sway of the rope as the silent sky turned black clouds over in its slumber.

***

"Dan Hewitt will never step over the threshold of this house with a hammer and nails," were Maisie's last words to Leonard before he left for work. Now that Dan Hewitt was at the door, she didn't have the heart to turn him away.

Hughie was first to speak. "Can we play in the motor, Dan?" he asked, his eyes wide with excitement.

"Ye can indeed, sir. She's open. Away an take a look."

49

Hughie bounded towards the black Model T, a motor that had been a novelty to each and every man, woman and child on the street since it appeared the previous month in all its ear-piercing glory.

The motorcar was said to have derived from a gambling match up the coast in Glenarm when Dan had made such great winnings that his wife need never have cared for a penny for the rest of her life. Dan had settled for a 1935 Model T in black, and Nancy was never informed of her potential riches. Leonard, meanwhile, spent every spare moment in Dan Hewitt's garage since the motor had been won.

Maisie's nerves were on edge as Dan walked back and forward from his car to her house with the instruments of all his various trades. He had been hired by Leonard to build Maisie a new larder, and having installed a length of wood across the centre of the scullery, much scratching of the head and stammering of inaudible words followed.

Dan assessed the scullery and addressed Maisie, "It's a lang yin, Maisie, can I lay it oot in the kitchen across the settee for it's wet oot thonner in the yard?"

Maisie had a feeling of foreboding as Dan covered the settee with a dust sheet. She couldn't watch. She waited in the scullery.

"Thon's a quare bit o timber, Maisie," called Dan from the front of the house. She joined him in the kitchen.

"It's hard enough getting through it," he continued. The saw slipped free from the strain of cutting, and the end of the wood fell to the ground. Maisie watched as the plank flopped onto the dust sheet.

Dan ruffled his fair hair, his eyebrows creased. "You go on into the scullery away oot o this dust, dear," he said. "I'll get her all cleaned up."

She ignored him and walked to the other side of the settee. The mahogany armrest lay in a pile of sawdust and a piece of white linen poked out from the side of the cushion. She held it up and scrutinised the small tooth marks down the middle.

"God bliss us, Dan," she said. "It wasnae good timber at all. It was Brown's Irish linen that caused ye all the bother."

He had a look of terror in his eyes.

"My ma aye said she would be deed before her linen," said Maisie. She looked Dan in the eye and allowed him her widest smile.

"Boys a dear," said Dan, shaking his head. "I thought ye were for taking the saw tae my heed. I cannae say mair than sorry, Mrs Gourley, but if I have tae sell thon motor o mine, I'll pay for a new settee."

"You'll do no such thing," said Maisie, "but ye may nail thon mahogany handle on as quick as ye can for if Grace Higgins hears about this, ye'll never work again. Get on now." She gathered up her coat and bag. "We're for the pictures."

She called Hughie and Daniel and walked out the door laughing.

"Why do you look so happy, Aunt Maisie?" asked Daniel, who was twirling on the swing. "Oh never mind, son. Just for God's sake get yoursel an education."

***

"Move up! Two deep! Standing room in the back stalls only! Have your tickets at the ready, please!"

Maisie positioned Daniel and Hughie in front of her and stood by her mother as the usher tried to even out the higgledy piggledy line with a chorus of instructions. It was a first outing to the pictures for Daniel and a first outing to hell for her mother, whose fear of every manifestation of modern society had moving pictures at its heart.

Maisie found it hard to believe that Hughie had enticed his granny into the theatre for it had often been decreed that Lucifer was lurking in every corner, all trussed up in gilt and swathed triumphantly in red velvet.

Grace Higgins rarely ventured beyond the Waterloo Road. What use was the Chaine Memorial Park around the corner when she could sit in her own back garden surrounded by wildflowers? Why walk to the shore when she could hear the seagulls from her own scullery? And what purpose did the vast array of stores down the Main Street serve when she had all she needed at the corner?

Maisie despaired of her mother's old ways and wondered why she had ever left the farm in Kells to live in Larne in the first place.

The doors opened up and Grace held up her hand to her chest. Maisie watched her assess the centre of the room, where waterfalls of red velvet flanked each side of a screen flickering with black and white lines. She saw her mother's eyes scan the sweeping staircases as droplets of white light fell on her thick neck.

She tugged her mother's hand and pushed the boys ahead, but Daniel didn't move an inch further than the top step. He stopped, causing a wall of bodies to crash against Maisie's back. Maisie turned to the man behind her and explained, "It's the wean's first time." His glassy eyes were black in the dim light, his lips gently parted.

Hughie was pointing towards the boxes. "Thon's for the hoity-toity folk," he exclaimed. "We're doon in the pits," he added, before leading his charge to his seat.

Maisie took a seat at the end of the row with Daniel and Hughie on her right. Grace was on the other side of the children, already airing huffs and puffs of frustration in the confined space.

'Popeye' was the first short. Daniel's head was tilted heavenward and Maisie could hear the thoughts of wonder tick through his mind as clearly as she could detect Grace's muttering "God's truth" that punctuated the campaign of slapstick seafaring.

Next came 'The Three Stooges.' Maisie kept her eyes fixed on Daniel as the credits rolled. His silence had unsettled everyone within earshot over the last six months. "There's something no right wi thon wean," was Maisie's mother's diagnosis, being at all times a champion of the adage that children should be heard but not seen. Maisie didn't need words from Daniel. She understood every heartbeat and every flicker of his sad eyes, and she found a way to communicate with the silence, something she had failed to achieve with her own tongue-tied husband.

One of the stooges was shot in the behind. Tittering perforated the room in tune with a long series of piercing snores from Grace. Hughie exhaled breaths of amusement at his grandmother and nudged Daniel to alert him to the commotion. Daniel turned to Grace and smiled before resuming his fixation on the picture. The audience followed the three stooges and a bear around the quiet screen as Grace's snores pelted through the picture house. Heads turned in her direction and cries of laughter bounded around the theatre. Maisie sank low in her seat, placed her hand over her face and tried to contain the tide of mortification that streamed through her fingers.

A fanfare of trumpets sounded to mark the end of the short and Maisie took the opportunity to awaken her mother for the main feature.

"Wasn't thon great!" said Grace.

"Granny!" exclaimed Hughie, "Ye didnae see a thing, for ye slept the whole way through it. Ye missed the bear driving the motor and everything, so ye did."

"Och nonsense, son. I didnae miss a single thing. Wasn't Popeye great with thon bear, saving Olive Oyl forbye."

"Granny!" repeated Hughie in a tone of chastisement. "You're on the wrong short. Did ye no see 'The Three Stooges,' Granny?"

"Course I did son. Do ye think I'm a nit wit?"

"No, I think you're a dope," smiled Hughie. "The coyboys and engines is about tae begin."

***

A choir of yellow-legged gulls, their legs dangling prehistorically and uncomfortably close to Maisie's head, welcomed them into the bright natural light after three hours in darkness. Maisie adjusted her eyes and tried not to laugh as her mother beat the air with her hands to stave off the birds and the blinding sun. Hughie's cheeks were stained with the ice-cream that had dripped all over his jumper, whilst Daniel emerged spotless, every last drop of ice-cream licked away.

"If only life were like the pictures," smiled Grace.

"What do you mean?" replied Maisie.

"Two shorts with all the mishaps of the day and a feature length with a happy ending. Wouldn't thon be a quare thing?"

Maisie thought for a moment before responding. The ice-cream had clearly gone to her mother's head. "Aye, Ma," she said finally. "Two shorts and a feature wi a happy ending."

A bell tinkled at a distance behind them as they walked alongside the elegant terrace houses of The Clonlee. It sounded again up close and Maisie was surprised to hear the children call, "Uncle Leonard." It was late for him to be returning home from work. He finished at midday on a Saturday, but there he was in his work clothes at five o'clock. He doffed his cap and pulled up alongside them.

"Where were ye the day?" he asked, smiling.

He had been smiling a lot since the day that Daniel had arrived, and Maisie was bemused by such a change in temperament for there had been nothing but children teeming in and out of their doors since the day they were married.

"We tooked Daniel to the pictures," explained Hughie, breathlessly. "And Granny snored like a pig and everyone laughed, and, sez Aunt Maisie tae me, wouldn't it affront ye to take Granny anywhere!"

Maisie was relieved that her mother's hearing wasn't sharp enough to catch Hughie's round-up of the day.

"Come on up on the saddle and we'll race Granny Higgins home," said Leonard, looking up over his cap at his mother-in-law with an air of uncertainty. Grace delivered a smile that was sweet enough to send Leonard on his way and sour enough to confound Maisie.

"What's up wi ye, Ma?" said Maisie when Leonard had wheeled Hughie and Daniel around Newington Avenue and out of earshot.

"Him," was the response.

"Who, Leonard? What's he done now? He's only gyping aboot wi the weans."

"Aye, he's a gype! Thon's for sure. Him and all them other gypes at the fectory. Maisie, dear, he's no as green as he's cabbage leukin. Mark my words, niver trust a man wi a smile on his face!"

"Oh for God's sake, Ma! Did my da never smile at ye?"

"Aye, he smiled alright. And ye'll heed yer ma when she tells ye never tae trust a man wi a smile."

"Are we all to walk aboot wi faces like Lurgan spades?"

"I didnae say ye couldnae trust a fellow laughin, but a woman pays dear for the smile on a man's face."

Maisie walked beside her mother in silence. The silly old woman! She wouldn't heed a single thing she said. If she had abided by her mother's warnings, she would never have ridden a bike, got into a car, taken a trip to the sea-side or even gone to a dance.

She had just about had enough of her mother's tidings of despair. She was enjoying the new Leonard. Her home was a happy home, and whatever price she had to pay for a smile and a song, she would pay it ten times over.

"I'm going to the bathing boxes tomorrow with Sally," she said to challenge her mother's sense of what was right in the world.

"Ye are no indeed! Ye"ll catch pneumonia."

"The doctor said bathing is good for your health."

"Ye need your heed looked at, Missy! You've a wean tae leuk efter."

"Daniel's coming too."

"Over my deed body. Ye can risk life and limb by getting into cowl water, but there's no a chance ye'll be taking yin o my grandweans wi ye. Did ye ever hear the likes? Sending weans oot tae sea in April. God bliss us all for there's no a single young yin left in Larne that knows how tae leuk efter a wean. Never cast a cloot til the mayflower is oot. Did ye never hear o thon?"

Maisie listened to her mother's sermon to the end, but there was only one word that mattered. *Grandwean*. It had taken six months.

***

"Morning, Mrs Andrews," called Maisie in the mock-subservient chorus she had composed in the early days of her employment with Sally to dispel any awkwardness between mistress and servant.

She held the scullery door half-open with one foot and peered through the uninviting darkness. Damp air shrouded a room that should have been thriving with the scent of hot wheaten bread. She flicked on the light, released the blackout blind and raised the scullery window. She knew Sally's mid-morning routine well. Wheaten on a Monday, soda on a Wednesday, Victoria sponge on a Friday. Where was Sally and why hadn't she begun baking? It had only been a week since she'd been floating around the Waterloo Road posing as Lily for the minister. She'd looked well then.

Perhaps the house was in mourning. Yet, surely news would have reached the Waterloo Road if something had happened to Captain Andrews or his wife.

She continued on into the kitchen where a blue light sidled through the gap in the closed curtains. She opened them and released the latch on the window. How anyone with such a grand house could live in the smallest room at the back, Maisie would never understand. She peered out to the garden, where the grass was mossy gold in the morning light. She could see her old bedroom over the wall. She could see Sally's old house over the wall. And for the first time in many years, she felt sad, the kind of sadness that a child suffers alone when no one is watching.

And no one was watching Maisie after Winifred Ramsey died. No one saw the tears she cried into her pillow for her friend's mother.

Winifred was the only mother on the street who played with the children, the only mother without a newborn baby to tend to. Maisie remembered the long rope tied up to the washing line at one end of the garden, Winifred standing at the other circling, singing and rhyming. She could hear the song in her head. *On a mountain, stands a lady, who she is I do not know.*

The air was sweet in the kitchen, and Maisie understood why when she saw a crystal glass beside an open book. She lifted the glass and inhaled the sticky residue of port. She walked into the hall and called out, but there was no response.

The front parlour was dim, the blinds a quarter open, the red, velvet curtains tied back on brass hooks by their tassel cords, allowing the sun to branch across the floor and cast leaves of gold and bronze light onto the dark carpet. Maisie released the blind and took a deep breath as the sunlight flooded the room. There was a bracing air to the space despite the unwieldy antiquities of Captain Andrews' past; she imagined it stripped back to the bone, its white mouldings naked against burly yellow walls.

She walked to the cupboard under the hall and fetched a long feather duster. She began to move it around the ceiling rose with its sculpted leaves, harps and shamrocks. She continued along a wall of shelves packed tight with books, across paintings and portraits hooked to picture rails and around the eerie glass bell domes filled with fossils, insects and butterflies. She looked up again, away from the fracas of a life lived and enjoyed the beginnings of the wide open space, of the elegant windows and haughty ceilings.

Why on earth didn't Sally use the room overlooking the beautiful garden she tended to day-in day-out?

Perhaps she was afraid of what Captain Andews might say if she removed the artefacts of his father's past.

She recalled the words of Mrs Andrews at the Larne Musical Festival the previous month when Hughie had won the cup for singing under her adjudication. *Jesus bids us shine with a pure clear light, like a little candle burning in the night.* It was a simple hymn that had stolen the breath of the audience in the Victoria Hall, and Mrs Andrews, all done up in furs like a creature from a glass bell dome, had stood up on the stage in the Victoria Hall and said. "The winner knows how to find joy in sadness and sadness in joy."

Maisie stopped by the door of the main bedroom and watched as particles of hazy sunshine danced across the made up bed. It was an elegant room of dark wood and white linen that framed the distant turquoise sea. Sally took care of it herself, as she did the back kitchen and the scullery. Maisie knew well that her friend had been trained to scrub from the time she could crawl, and she continued to exercise her hands where she could, leaving Maisie the task of cleaning rooms that were never used.

She finished the upstairs quickly and made her way to the ground floor, a daunting inclination that she should no longer be there quickening her pace. She walked to the back door and hesitated, the warmth of spring sunlight beckoning her feet to an entrance radiant with sunshine. She stopped in the garden to admire the golden heads of Sally's daffodils, their heads dipped, living — just.

She exhaled, casting off the scent of disinfectant and the dust of a house that now seemed draughty with fossils of the past and in exile from the sights and sounds of modern life. She walked out the front door and continued on past the tennis courts. She reached Newington Avenue and drifted around each room again in her imagination, trying to see what she had missed in the fragments of dust floating through her mind. She paused when she reached the corner of the Waterloo Road. There a group of girls danced in a ring, their cropped hair choppy in the wind as they threaded the needle and rhymed.

In and out go dusty bluebells
In and out go dusty bluebells
In and out go dusty bluebells
I'll be your master

Tippa rippa rapper on my shoulder
Tippa rippa rapper on my shoulder
Tippa rippa rapper on my shoulder
I'll be your master

Maisie pictured Sally's long, thick hair meandering down her back as she tippa rippa rappered on the shoulder of the girl in front, and she recalled singing and dancing and playing at the corner for hours on end between factory bells, school bells and dusty bluebells. She recaptured that time for just one moment and prayed.

One child was all she would ever pray for. A plea with God. A bargain. One child. Her own flesh. Her own blood. Her own immemorial reflection.

The Kelp Hut
September 1946

Sally pictured a woman in a shack of mud and stone at the shore. There were no chairs in her dwelling, no table upon which to serve tea. She lived off the rocks, scuttling over limpets, dipping her hands into rock pools, drying ribbons of kelp on the low stone wall as tourists in long skirts watched from on high. Sally looked up. One man sat alone on the ridge of the cliff, watching.

She hung her beret and coat up on the railing and walked through the shingle. She reached the railing of the bathing box and walked barefoot down the slipway. Her toes gripped the wet algae. Her eyes flitted back to the old kelp hut with its stained green walls and chimney-stack void of smoke. She stepped into the grey-blue sea, the chill of the water lacerating her pale feet, its icy embrace halting her breath as she immersed her body and swam towards a pink horizon of sea and sky. She swam, rising and falling over the rolling September tide, drifting through the water, basking in its dangerous, dusky light.

And she remembered the baby, the baby she had imagined.

Alfie had put it down to hysteria, a fantasy played out in his wife's mind. But it was real, and no amount of searching through medical journals to find the cause of her affliction could convince Sally that she had lost her mind.

She had lost two babies within two years. She didn't need the talking, the hypnosis, the endless analysis. She didn't want to be an experiment for Alfiie's bemused doctor friends. She wanted to gulder hard at a twelve foot wall and beat out her frustrations with a broom against a rug, to be wild and free like the woman of her mother's bedtime tales, the one who lived on the shore. But if she let go, it would be a confirmation of hysteria — a validation of the ails that women possess.

She swam and immersed herself in the dream again and she was there in her kitchen begging her husband to keep the baby.

And then there was Sally's mother-in-law, Margaret, on her knees scrubbing the floor in a Christmas party frock. She too despised the fossils in the jars. She had said so in the midst of screams as honey-warm blood seeped from Sally's legs. A soul gifted. A life lost.

It was Margaret who had proposed the extended stay in France. She was suspicious of the medical interventions of Alfie's doctor friends. "No more, Alfie, son. Let nature heal Sally."

Sally swam backwards against the tide to the shore and emerged from the water, her feet twisting around the rocks as she walked to the kelp hut. She looked inside. It was empty. No metal cups strung to the wall. No shawl hanging by the door. Mary Beth was gone. The kelp hut was long gone. In its place was a changing hut. Four idle walls to protect the dignity of pleasure seekers bathing at the shore.

***

"Where have you been? Look at you! You'll catch your death!"

She walked across the kitchen and huddled near the fire.

Alfie placed a woollen blanket around her shoulders. "What are you doing out at this time of the night?" he said.

He stared at his wife and Sally could feel the intensity of his worry burn through her skin. He lifted a strand of hair. "You're drenched! Why are you so wet? There's only a light mizzle."

His words fell flat on her temples as sincerity charged through his brown eyes. The light had only just gone down. It couldn't have been later than eight o'clock.

"I saw the kelp hut," she said, "where Mary Beth lived."

"Mary Beth? Mary Beth who?"

"Mary Beth Clarke from the shore."

She looked over her husband's shoulder to the fire as a flame of the present stoked her mind. What was she saying? What had she done? She looked down at her clothes and out the window.

Alfie walked to her chair and lifted the small glass on the table beside it. It was empty. "This needs to stop," he pleaded.

"But the baby?"

"The baby. I know you lost a baby. I know you lost two babies. We lost two babies in two years. But we need to carry on. We need to find a way." He paused and stepped back again. "You're soaking," he said. He lifted a strand of hair and inhaled. "You've been in the sea. You've been bathing."

Alfie was holding her shoulders and she could see the pain in his eyes. She felt small and she felt tired. She wanted to fall into his arms but stood tall. She wasn't drunk. She wasn't mad. She wiped away the hair that was clinging to her cheek. What was she doing in the water? Why was she thinking of Mary Beth Clarke?

"I want to sit a while," she said, dropping to the floor by the fire. Alfie fixed the blanket around her shoulders and sat beside her, holding her, staring into the grate.

"You need to see a doctor, Sally."

"You are a doctor. I spend my life with doctors. I don't want another doctor poking and prodding at my mind. I just feel tired. I must have slept after drinking the port and I got up and went to the sea like I did in France with your mother. I haven't lost my mind. The sea helps me feel awake. I don't need a shot of Valium. I don't need to see your friend with his light hypnosis. You don't need to worry."

"But the talk of Mary Beth Clarke?"

"My mother used to talk about her. She said she bought dulse from her, that she spent time with her down at the shore. It must have been on my mind."

"Were you thinking of your mother?"

"I don't remember. Maybe. Sometimes, I sit here and look out the window and I can see her. I can hear her voice."

"Your mother's voice?"

"Yes. I'm not hearing voices, Alfie. You needn't worry about that, but I talk to her. I talk to her in my head. It's like a daydream. I'm not mad if I daydream. If I sit in that chair and I'm alone, I can think of her. I can't find her anywhere else, but here in the kitchen of Dalriada. She used to talk to me for hours. She talked about Mary Beth Clarke."

Alfie looked at Sally in the way that he had looked at her on the promenade, the night that they were engaged. He had kissed her in the middle of the conversation about her mother and had told her that he would look after her until the day she died. Sally had smiled and they had continued walking and talking. There had been no bended knee and no response — just an intense kiss and a perplexed look in his eyes.

Sally cupped his face in her hands. Alfie kissed her fiercely. Each kiss was a first kiss; she the girl with the laundry in her arms, he the rich boy ready to take her in — to rescue her like the maidens were rescued in books he had read in a gigantic attic in a lopsided folly.

And each time he kissed her, Sally wondered if he would have hungered for her still if his love had been shared among the babies he had delivered, unbreathing, with his own busy hands.

***

The pillowcase was still wet in the morning, the scent of sea lingering on the bedlinen and in her hair. She reached over to hold him again, but he was gone. She hadn't heard the telephone. Hadn't dreamed a single thing. Alfie had lifted her onto the bed

63

and all her incoherent wanderings had been consumed by his body in a safe and even tide.

A distant grandfather clock chimed ten times. She had slept for more than twelve hours. She stood up and walked to the end of the bed where wet clothes and a blanket lay crumpled on the floor. She held them against her face and turned towards her full naked body in the mirror. Alfie had loved her intensely. He had touched the face that appeared bronze in the morning light. He had touched the dark, loose hair that stopped by the crevice of her back. He had touched her toilsome, quick beauty.

She covered herself up and stowed all the skin away; it had only ever served her well in Alfie's eyes. And how fortunate she was to have a man love her when she could give him so little in return.

The back door rattled and a voice came from below. "Good morning, Mrs Andrews."

She smiled. She ran a hairbrush through her hair, curled it into a bun at the nape of her neck and tempered the wildness of her flesh with her gardening dress and an old cardigan. The water in the jug was cold but she poured it into the basin and splashed it across her face.

"I'll be there in a minute!" she called out as she set to work stripping the bed. She paused and held the sheets close to her face, the sweat of passion like sweetened wine against her lips. She pulled up the largest window, assembled the sheets and ran down to the scullery, her steps as light as a breeze.

"Morning, Mrs Gourley," she sang as she skipped past Maisie with the sheets. She laid them on the mangle of the Swift washing machine and lifted the detergent from the window sill.

"Did you get the cheque?" she called.

"Yes, I did get the cheque and I got the letter." Maisie was standing by the door. "You're a queer one, Sally Andrews, running off to France like thon! I never heard of anyone going away without saying goodbye!"

"Sorry. I wasnae weel."

Sally hesitated and poured the bedclothes into the machine, aware that Maisie was looking at her stomach. "The house is spotless. Never mind cleaning and come and hae a wee drap o tay wi an oul freen."

She had been in the company of wealthy English people for almost five months. It was a relief to drop the airs and graces that had come so naturally to her in their society.

"When did you get back?"

"Yesterday. We came the Free State road. Long oul drive. The boat from Rosscoff was rough! I was still sick last night at eight o'clock."

She paused and thought back to her swim and wondered if she could divulge something of her day to Maisie.

"Come round to my ma's hoose and we'll get a drap o broth," offered Maisie. "It'll settle your stomach."

"I cannae think of anything better after a week o hobnobbing wi Margaret Andrews," she smiled. "I'll take a look over the garden and then come round."

Maisie began to walk away with her duster and Ewbank when Sally called her back. "Maisie," she said. "Did ye ever hear tell o Mary Beth Clarke? She lived on the rocks."

"Mary Beth Clarke? Oh aye!" said Maisie, resting on the settee. "The weans at the corner used tae talk about her. Said she was a mermaid."

Sally smiled. "Tell me this, did she live by the promenade?"

"I couldnae tell ye, dear. My ma would could tell ye better. Did they no used tae say that she lived in the wee kelp hut?"

"And didn't she sell dulse to the tourists?"

"That's right," confirmed Maisie. "She had the kelp drying the length of the promenade. Before our time, mind."

Maisie looked awkward perched on the edge of the settee, and Sally wished she could relax a little more when she came to see her. If she wasn't cleaning, she liked to give the impression that she was, always armed with some implement when her hands were loose by her sides. Perhaps she worried that Alfie would come through the door and catch her doing nothing — catch them both being equals.

"Was there no a yarn aboot the wean too?" said Maisie.

"What wean?"

"Mary Beth Clarke's wean. They said she birthed it from her body and flung it back into the sea when she saw that it had the tail o a fish."

Sally twitched and Maisie bowed her head.

"Sorry, love," said Maisie. "I wasnae thinking." She stood up and began to move the duster over the photographs. "What made you think of her?" asked Maisie. "What made you think of Mary Beth Clarke?"

"Oh, that. I dinnae know. She came into my heed. Never mind. Let's go and get some of thon broth from yer ma. There's nothing more tae clean here."

"I gave the fossils a good spring clean when you were away."

"Did ye now?"

"I was tempted to box them all up and put them in the loft. I was up there one day. I was sure I heared a wee mouse scratchin so I got Leonard to lay a few traps. I hope ye dinnae mind."

"No, don't be daft! Did you catch anything?"

"It's all sorted now. Ye'll no be bothered with any mair mice this autumn! Leonard took care of it. Daniel was with us. He was amazed by the size o thon loft It's a quare space for a wean's imagination."

"Alfie said he had every toy a boy could wish for up there, but all he ever wanted was to run barefoot wi the weans on the Waterloo Road."

"Mrs Andrews wouldnae hae been too happy wi thon!" Maisie raised her eyebrows.

"Mrs Andrews ran aboot barefoot hersel," said Sally, who was surprised by what she learned of her mother-in-law in France.

"She said she took her shoes off and ran wi the other weans to the national school so that she would fit in."

"I cannae imagine Mrs Andrews without her furs!"

"She has the look of one that was born in them, doesn't she!" Sally agreed. "Maisie, let's do it!"

"Let's do what?"

Sally took Maisie by the hand and led her into the parlour. The rain was pouring outside from a black sky, but the room was bright and airy. "Let's make this a room for the new Mr and Mrs Andrews. We'll be married eight years this December. It's about time. What do you think?"

"I think ye could protect them there fossils from ruinous sunrays by turning thon loft o yours into a museum."

"That's a fine idea. Will you help me once we get some of your ma's broth? Bring wee Hughie and Daniel after school. Shure, wouldn't they love to be let loose with Alfie's toys?"

***

Sally assessed the thirteen boxes and rubbed her hands together to remove the dust. They had each done six runs up and down the stairs to the attic, the boys managing only one before getting distracted by the toys. A wooden rocking horse from the 1920s was deemed the best ride east of the Appalachians as the boys sped off to the wild west and left the women to carry the rest of the captain's belongings up the stairs.

The loft was immense with large maps marked out with pins, books crammed into oak shelves and old oil lamps suspended from the rafters. It was a tidy space. Sally could see that Margaret had afforded her son a blank page for his imagination.

"No wonder he ended up a doctor with all them there books!" exclaimed Maisie.

"It's a wile shame not to use them anymore. Take some for the weans, will ye?"

"No, I will not indeed," said Maisie. "Alfie might want to keep them. We'll not take a single one of them."

"Nonsense. Take this, the pair of you and start reading it." Sally swiped dust from Treasure Island and handed it to an eager-eyed Daniel.

"Just one each, do ye hear?" warned Maisie. "Just one book. That'll be all. Say thank you to Mrs Andrews."

The boys rhymed their gratitude as Sally's hands fell on a box packed with postcards from around the world, each of them arranged and sorted by country in alphabetical order.

Hughie sifted through the catalogue of the captain's global travels and rested his hands on *I*.

"It's Ireland," laughed Maisie. "Boys a dear, ye could hae picked anywhere and ye picked Ireland."

Hughie showed Sally the first card. It was a postcard of Henry McNeill's tours, an image of an old jaunting car filled with tourists going through the Black Arch.

"It's the promenade!" exclaimed Daniel, holding a second postcard.

"God's truth, thon wean," laughed Maisie. "Ye wud think he had just discovered Paris. Here now, let me take a leuk." Maisie held the card close. "Sally," she said, excitedly, "come here and take a leuk at this. It's a postcard frae 1914."

"That's thirty-two years old," said Daniel quietly.

"And you not yet six," smiled Sally. "A quare and smart boy!"

'Powerful!" said Maisie.

Sally looked at the photograph. To the left were women in long dresses and wide-brimmed Edwardian hats; to the right a young woman crouched low on a stone wall in front of the old kelp hut that was still fresh in Sally's mind.

Sally looked at the face, but could see nothing but a vague blur of features imprinted with a wild and solitary expression. She turned to the back of the postcard. There were no lines for an address, no message from a wandering traveller — merely an inscription in slanted writing. *Mary Beth Clarke, 1914.*

Birdsong
August 1947

Leonard was not on his side of the bed and Maisie knew it without turning around. She got up and looked out the narrow window towards the magpies assembled in groups like semi-quavers on the telegraph lines, their mantles glossy white, their feathers sleek and intensely black.

She walked to the landing and stopped by the door to the back room where Hughie lay at the tip of the bed — all swarthy skin and long lashes against white linen. Daniel slept nearest to the door, his peach face camouflaged by the pale blanket. Maisie left the door ajar, knowing that the chorus of birdsong would travel to them and stir them from their exquisite rest.

Hughie had never fully moved into the new parlour house as had been planned nearly two years before. On the third night of his relocation, he had fallen fast asleep on Maisie's woollen mat by the fire whilst awaiting his mother's departure. Lily had lifted him upstairs with her own hands and Maisie had said nothing more about it.

Maisie had grown fond of Lily's company in the evenings for Leonard had been present in neither song nor sound. Dan Hewitt had his uses, after all, securing Leonard a job at the new power station at Ballylumford. Leonard got up each day at the crack of dawn, cycled to the harbour and travelled by ferry across the short slip of water between Larne and Islandmagee. In the beginning, he returned home at five o'clock each afternoon, only to wash, eat and walk straight out the door at six o'clock, his new jazz band having signed up for the entire season at the Plaza. And Maisie had more than once wondered if she should stalk the loanen after midnight to search for him. Would she find him there with a season ticket holder, a Lancashire lass impressed with his command of the saxophone, or a Glaswegian girl keen for a birl up the alleys after a square or two of old-time dances?

She couldn't see it. She couldn't imagine Leonard spending energy doing anything that did not concern his newly acquired motor or his newly assembled band. She had been indifferent to his music, but when it had stopped conversing through the walls of her home, she understood what it was that she missed about Leonard.

Hope was what she clung to as she removed any thoughts of her husband's nocturnal pastimes from her mind. She ate some toast and marmalade and laid out two bowls of hot porridge on the table for the boys.

"Wakey wakey!" she called up the stairs. There was a flutter of bare feet on the floorboards and a tinkle of water against the tin pot before they appeared at the top of the stairs. She tussled each head of hair on her way by them.

"Morning, Aunt Maisie!" they both chimed.

"Morning Daniel, Morning Hughie," she smiled. "Wash your hands! Your breakfast is on the table."

She paused by the fire to look at a photograph from the 1920s. Jamesina, the tallest of her siblings, stood at the centre of five children. They all towered over her eventually — first Maisie, then Lily and finally Ken and Roy — yet what Jamesina had lost in height, she had gained in knowledge.

Maisie fixed her hair and grabbed her handbag. Why hadn't she thought of it? Her sister may have practiced moderation in matters of slander and gossip, but it was a fortuitous consequence of her trade to be able to locate the whereabouts of every sinner in town.

***

Jamesina was perched behind the bars of the post office counter like a contented cage-bird. Her brown hair was pinned to the back of her head, half spectacles sitting on the end of a nose long enough and fine enough to sniff out the sins of a saint. Her voice echoed the ring of the metal bell on the door in a sharp and punctual chime. "Yes, Mrs Greer, how can I help you?" she smiled, addressing an old school friend.

Maisie joined the queue and waited with bated breath, knowing that Jamesina would be sure to straighten out her tongue or her clothes or her life with some passive insult that would leave her seething for the rest of the day. Minutes dragged, the post office filled and by the time Maisie reached the front of the queue, there was no way back. She had to procure something of her sister's services.

"Good morning, Mrs Gourley," said Jamesina by way of greeting.

Maisie rolled her eyes. "Good morning, Miss Higgins."

"And how can I help you this fine day?"

Maisie tried to repress a smile and carry on with the spectacle that was played out for the women behind her. "I'd like to post these letters, if you will."

"Set them on the scales," ordered Jamesina, adding "if you will" with a wink. "And how is Mr Gourley this morning?"

"Mr Gourley must be working hard at the moment, Miss Higgins. I've barely seen him." Maisie lowered her voice. "What about you?"

"Me? I'm well, Mrs Gourley," said Jamesina, continuing to play the childish sibling game.

"No, what about you, have you seen him?" she whispered. "He hasnae come hame."

Jamesina had a look of panic in her face, her professional veneer threatened by a sister who might at that moment cause her some embarrassment on account of an errant husband, or worse, an errant vowel.

"They cannae hear ye," Maisie smiled.

Jamesina paused and wrote something down on a piece of paper. "Your stamps will be tuppence, and here's the address you were enquiring about for your electricity. Have a good day, Mrs Gourley. Next customer, please!"

***

Maisie clasped the piece of paper in her hand and walked home, weightlessly. She had no need for any information about electricity, and she had no friends in the village of Glenoe. She had been a fool to fall for a man who talked through his fiddle, but she was not fool enough to search for hope in the name and address scribed in her sister's neat handwriting: *Ellen McDowell, Horse-Shoe Cottage, Glenoe.*

Maisie rushed through the yard and scullery and into the kitchen. She knelt on the floor and pulled out a box from underneath the sofa. She examined the brown court shoes, her Sunday shoes bought in Hamilton's at the end of the war. They were simple and suede, clean but worn. She felt ashamed of her feet as her mind assembled a picture of what she was about to do.

Glenoe, uphill all the way from the Glynn village. Six miles from the Waterloo Road, at least.

They had passed Glenoe on an outing to Carrickfergus one day. Maisie had wanted to stop and look around at one of the few bastions of the past, a village that had not yet seen the advent of electricity, but now, as she recalled, Leonard had been distracted and anxious, hurrying her away from the waterfall when she said she wanted to stop and swim.

She examined the contents of the larder. A soda remained from yesterday. It would be stale, but she didn't have time to dally over a griddle. She packed it along with some cheese and an apple. That would be enough.

She filled her thermos flask with tea and poured some milk into an old medicine bottle. A string messages bag with long handles was hooked over the backdoor. It looked tatty, but it would be easy to carry and light on the road home.

She placed the flask in the bottom of the bag, the court shoes wrapped in tissue paper in the middle and the food on top. She weighed it on one shoulder and then the other. It was light enough.

Her trench-coat, at least, was new and much less unsightly than the woollen coat she wore each winter. She tied her scarf around her head carefully and paused to check that her handbag contained a comb and compact mirror; there was little point in fixing her hair into place with clouds brewing a tantrum against the will of the sun.

She called on the children and gave them their instructions. "You're to be good boys and look after Granny and Granda Higgins."

Hughie nodded and Daniel listened with care. "You're to stay outside, away from the fire. Mind what I towl ye aboot the wee boy who was scalded with the kettle?"

"Yes, Aunt Maisie," they both rhymed.

"Hughie, you're to take Daniel to your ma's for luncheon. Take this tin of spam with you. And don't forget to take last week's books back to Mrs Andrews."

The children had made their way through dozens of books since their first visit to Sally's attic last year, and although there was no real urgency to return anything, Maisie knew that Sally would be pleased to see them. She kissed them each on the head, stood back and assessed the two sets of eyes — so innocent, so eager for a summer's day. They would have liked the waterfall, but there was no time to think about that. She needed to go before she lost her nerve.

***

The Main Street was packed with buses and trams destined for the Coast Road. Tourists mingled under striped canopies shading a medley of yellow man, dulse, postcards and linen handkerchiefs in emerald, satin ribbons.

She felt self-conscious about her appearance in the midst of the English ladies in all their furs and finery, but passing through Point Street, the colours of tourists faded, the streets narrowed and her position in the world mattered less. There were no hotels near the grime and dust of Howdens' Coal Merchants. She kept to the right of the road, close to the old whitewashed cottages that rimmed the steep, mossy hill overlooking the lough.

The moan of a motor truck alerted her to move to the side of the wall. It came trundling by, casting dirt from the asphalt road into the air. Maisie coughed into her handkerchief and turned her face away from the dust.

The lough peered through the trees, its green water dark and rising as the Glynn village came into sight. Her eyes climbed to the summit — to Glenoe, and she willed the sun to burn through those clouds for at least another hour. She needed to remain dry until she reached her destination.

The sloping, white cottages of the Glynn marked a rest stop on the journey. She ate her piece on a bench by a chestnut tree in the village green. Beside her, the schoolhouse with its bell tower was quiet, but children were dotted around the village enjoying the freedom of summer. In front, a tall house stood out among the low thatched roofs, its proportions stronger, its tiles as telling as the furs on the English tourists in Larne.

An elderly woman dressed in black was seated in front of a thatched cottage on a stool. She watched over the village, ancient and tribal-like, and from a distance, Maisie could see that the lines on her skin were carved as deep as those on the chestnut tree. She ran her hands along the bark and nodded towards the woman.

"Looks like a storm," the old lady called across the road. "I would take shelter if I were you, my dear," she said.

Maisie smiled. Stopping meant thinking and thinking would lead her back to the Waterloo Road. "Thank you," she said. "I need a good walk."

Each step up the Glenburn Road was in rhythm with the thud of her heart. What if someone saw her? What if someone stopped to give her a lift? It was best to keep her head held high, to appear purposeful despite the self-awareness that could so easily have swept her back down the hill.

She continued steadily to the top. The air was pure, the scent of foliage dense — a contrast to the smoke-filled fumes of the Waterloo Road.

A look over her shoulder revealed the bounty of her climb. The Glynn was hidden below the ridge, the lough swollen, ever closer to a dark sky. A shaft of light shone on the red bricks of the new power station in Islandmagee; Leonard would be there, working for the best pay packet he had ever earned. She turned and proceeded on the narrow road ahead, the sign for Glenoe indicating one mile to go.

An old stone wall beckoned her to rest and prepare. She balanced the small mirror inside the top of her handbag and assessed the impact of the first five miles — a face blossoming with colour, hair sticky against her head. She tipped her head forward and shook out her curls from the net that kept them in place. That'll do, she thought, tempering the most savage lock to the side with a clasp. She changed her shoes and walked.

It was a long mile, the road sweeping around endless yellow fields of hay. Her eyes itched. She blinked furiously to contain the aggravation, finally passing a wooden sign for the waterfall by Crooked Row.

She inhaled the sharp air and walked on, passing a message boy on his bicycle and a little girl playing with a doll. In front of her was a row of cottages, hooked up around the village. She smiled as she caught the outline of an old woman crouched beside her cottage door, her black dress spread so wide it was unclear if there was any stool holding up the effigy of the past at all.

Her mother still wore the long, black skirts of her generation, but this material was of a different age, a thick black wool, decorated at the neck with an ornate lace collar that was as pristinely white as the cottage. If the woman was not cut from the same cloth as her counterpart at the Glynn, then her dress certainly was.

Two ancient women perched on their stools like magpies. Were they to be separate harbingers of sorrow or a collective harbinger of joy?

"Good morning," said Maisie, before realising that it was more likely to be midday. The woman held onto a stick and nodded. If she cared that Maisie was the only stranger in the village, she didn't let on. She merely looked into the distance with a face that said she had seen it all before.

Maisie walked around the horseshoe bend to meet a perpendicular incline. There were no electricity cables in the village. Each tiny cottage conducted life through the clink of metal, the scent of simmering broth and turf smoke swirling from chimneys — all against the percussive echo of water falling. There was also the sound of children playing, a glockenspiel of screams rising and falling from the direction of the waterfall.

It was warm enough to strip off, despite the threat of rain, and Maisie imagined herself immersed under the cool, thudding water, away from this acute climb. She pictured Leonard standing by the stones of the waterfall as he had that spring, distracted and restless, anxiously awaiting his wife.

The road rose sharply and Maisie's heels pinched her feet. She had to be close now. How much higher could she possibly climb? A church crowned the top of the hill, and below it, to the right, was a detached, white cottage with a new slate roof. The air was clear, the hay fields at a distance, yet Maisie's breathing became erratic. She left her picnic bag on a wall and took deep breaths before walking the few yards to the cottage. She noted the freshly painted green of the square windows and rapped at the green door.

A woman appeared with chestnut curls as wild as Maisie's. She was smiling, her face glowing with rouge and cherry lipstick, her body relaxed and easy. Maisie had expected someone younger, but everything about Ellen, from her slight build to her long features, was a mirror image of her own person.

Maisie clung to her handbag, her feet clamped together, her body erect. "I'm Mrs Gourley," she said.

Ellen didn't respond. She raised her eyebrows and smiled an uncertain smile.

Maisie glanced at the horseshoe on the door. "Would your husband be available?" she said, a serene confidence rising. The expression on Ellen's face changed.

"My husband?" she checked.

"Yes, I would like to speak to your husband."

"I have no husband." Ellen removed her hand from her hip. "Who are you?"

"I'm Mrs Leonard Gourley."

Ellen had one arm across her body, the other fluttering apprehensively towards her head, settling finally on her neck. There was a voice and there was a song, and Maisie was not prepared for the voice and the song. She was not prepared for the clear voice, the deep and resonant voice, the singing voice that emerged from the scullery as audibly as the waterfall that reverberated around the village. She was not prepared for Leonard's voice singing 'Danny Boy' as he serenaded his lover in the hallway of her cottage at the top of a glen.

***

Maisie was running. She collected the string bag from the wall as she passed it and descended into the village once again. She didn't pause to observe who was present, but kept her head low and skipped as fast as her Sunday court shoes could carry her. She stopped at the corner, the line of cottages a white blur to her right. The road ahead was mercilessly open.

She recalled what her mother had said after her first visit to the pictures. *Never trust a man wi a smile on his face.*

How long had Leonard been smiling? He had been due to go to Glenoe that Hallowe'en night almost two years ago when Esther had brought Daniel into their home. Had he been gallivanting to Glenoe all this time?

She followed the pitter patter of the waterfall into the dark forest on the left, where the dirt path was wet and uneven, where stones and rocks were wedged into the muck. She wanted to change her shoes, but pride guided her swift movements onto the slippery terrain. Children were running towards her, screaming, holding out their hands. The rain was falling hard and the waterfall roared its tenor song.

She kicked off her shoes on a large, flat, basalt rock, dropped her bags and her coat and slipped into the stream, gulping as the cold water smacked her legs. Her mind was already below the thundering waterfall but her feet held her back as they grappled the brutal stones in the shallow water.

She could hear her name. She blocked out the pathetic warble and steadied herself with her arms out to the side as her feet found a path of shallow shingle. The water was up to her thighs. She moved closer to the white froth of the fall.

There was only the sound of the waterfall. No birds chirping. No children playing. No Leonard calling her name.

The waterfall pounded her head, heavy and unyielding, sending her backwards into the icy pool. She stood up swiftly, startled from the weight of it, and tried again, raising her hands above her head as an orchestra of strumming called her under. She moved through the fall, gripping her head tightly with her arms, the water bruising her skin with its heavy, violent rain.

She was floating in a deep, still pond and above her and beyond her was nothing but lush foliage set beneath a deluge of silvery shards falling. She inhaled the purity of it through every pore, sucking in the mist and the sap of the trees, swimming through the music of the waterfall, sinking every thought, every pleading look, every sorry tale that had given her hope.

Hope was now a wall of water thundering in front of her and she was safe from it, separate from the world, swimming in circles, rolling in bliss.

***

The bliss didn't last. The fool had got into the water and was wading towards her, his trousers rolled up to the knee. He had a look of fear on his face, the kind of fear that Maisie had never seen in the eyes of a man. It was a greedy fear, one that needed to settle something quickly. She stood opposite her husband in the water and promised herself that his greed would not be answered with any sorry words.

She stripped off her dress on the rocks, mopped up the water from her face with her scarf and wrung out the wet clothes purposefully.

All the while, Leonard stood stooge-like on the rock below, his braces hoisted tightly over his shirt. He had looked happy and carefree when they had been dangling by his side in Ellen's kitchen, his light chest hair exposed by the clean vest that Maisie had scrubbed with her own busy hands.

He wasn't clever enough to think of something to say. At least there was that. It would have been worse if she had married someone clever enough to think of something to say.

She was conscious of her body, exposed and cold, purple smudges of breast prominent through the wet petticoat. She removed the petticoat that clung to her skin and pulled it over her head.

There they were, husband and wife, alone in a forest, secluded behind jutting rocks, Maisie's body thriving and breathless, Leonard looking up at the sculpture of it, awakened perhaps, seeing for the first time.

She placed her coat over her shoulders and buttoned it up tightly. She left her stockings behind on the rock, crumpled and soggy — like a discarded skin. She tied the belt tightly around her waist, ran her fingers through her hair and walked.

Leonard followed her, at first closely, and then at a distance for they were about to emerge into the village and it wouldn't do for him to be caught with his wife.

***

The motor rumbled slowly by her side. She didn't look right, not once, but kept her head held high as a buoyant wind propelled her to the top of the Glenburn Road. Water dribbled from her soaking underwear, patches of water emerging through her brassière and onto her mac.

She saw the school bell first and then the war memorial from halfway down the hill and still Leonard stayed by her side, his motor choking and spluttering among the trees like one loud, flat voice in a harmonious choir. With any luck, it would conk out.

She stopped by the chestnut tree and looked out for the old lady, who was in the doorway of her cottage, as mystical as a rainbow after a storm. Maisie walked towards her and saw her eyes glance at Leonard's car.

One for sorrow. Two for joy.

It was sorrow, after all, sorrow that had soared into bliss and carved a crevice in Maisie's smile.

The woman touched Maisie's hand and Maisie tried to smile as disillusion and hope battled in her mind.

The car was close to her. "Get in, Maisie," pleaded Leonard. She ignored him and looked into the old lady's blue eyes.

"The birds follow the wind through the storm," said the woman, holding Maisie's hand in a firm, consoling grasp, "but they aye find their way back. Come back when the storm has passed."

Maisie nodded, turned from the woman and walked another half-mile. Her ankles bled. Her body trembled. She approached the bend before Howdens and felt cold, her underwear stinging her skin, her body shrivelling and shrinking. She broke down, every last morsel of strength departing her limbs as hot tears streamed down her face.

Leonard got out and took Maisie by the hand. He opened the door and she looked at him for the first time since she had emerged from the waterfall. He ran his right hand through her hair and placed it on her shoulder.

He drove in silence. He drove amidst a birl of colour, fur coats, motor cars, horses and traps. He drove through the narrow dirt paths caked in clabber and wide streets gleaming with the blue tint of tarmacadam.

Maisie closed her eyes as they passed Brown's Irish Linen Factory, with its machines and its shuttles and its looms heaving back and forth, its yarn yanking up and down, its threads and lint and dust floating through her memory to the tune of loud, pulsating drones.

She was relieved to be home. She stopped by the mirror in the kitchen and moved her hand across all the lines on her face that were not yet there, but that already had claimed their place. Leonard was behind her and she was too tired to argue with him.

She spoke to his reflection in the mirror. "I never want to hear you sing again."

The Resurrection
April 1948

Sally was drawn to the fire, to the orange flames, to the benevolent warmth conversing from the static grate of McNeill's Hotel. It was the same room in which she had once told Maisie her good news. All Saints Day. Two and a half years ago. She still remembered.

Running her hand across the chair she had occupied as two souls, she surrendered once again to visions of a baby swaddled in cream, of droplets falling from a minister's fingers onto a downy head, of long plaits swishing across a grey school pinafore, of gutties tip-toeing at the corner of Waterloo Road — never ending visions that circled her mind like a skipping rope beating in tune to an old rhyme.

On a mountain stands a lady,
Who she is I do not know.
All she wants is gold and silver,
All she wants is a fine young man.
Lady, lady, turn around,
Lady, lady, touch the ground,
Lady, lady, show your shoe,

Lady, lady, run right through.

Sally sang the words aloud and immersed herself in a dream-scape she knew well. The abandoned baby. The lady she did not know.

Movement flickered in the mirror above the fireplace. She turned, half-expecting a doctor to be there to sedate the wife with the broken mind. Two men stood behind her: a concierge hovering; a well-dressed gentlemen watching, then turning away. She had been caught singing to herself in a hotel lobby. She straightened up and reached out her hand to the adjudicator as the concierge walked away.

"Mrs Sally Andrews," she said, assessing the high cheekbones and direct, blue eyes. "I don't usually talk to the furniture."

"Jeffrey O'Reilly," he replied, shaking Sally's hand. "At least you weren't talking to the dead."

She blushed and forced a smile.

"According to the porter," he went on, "there has been some-thing of a resurrection in Larne this morning."

"A resurrection, indeed?"

"I need to practice the accent before I tell you it with any ac-curacy."

"You'll be fluent by the end of the Main Street," smiled Sally. "You happen to be in the company of an expert in Larne lan-guage."

"A useful trade indeed, Mrs Andrews. You'll travel far."

Sally led Jeffrey along the corridor past reception.

"Thanks for coming to greet me," he said. "There was no need, of course, for I know Larne well enough by now."

"Mrs Tweed wouldnae hae it any other way," she replied, play-fully. "Besides, it gets me out of the hall and into the fresh air. We've been setting up since seven."

The pavement was busy with a democracy of silver metal frames hoisting black, nylon umbrellas. The heavier and more weighty glints of the past were missing from the scene, and Sally had never quite adjusted to their absence. Every ornate balcony, lamppost, gate and fence had been stripped away for the war effort, the Post Office depot opposite the hotel now forlorn and barren without its metal.

Sally put up her umbrella and crossed the road. She stopped and watched as Jeffrey looked back at the hotel. A row of motor coaches blocked the view of the central portico, but the balcony emerged on the second floor, square and resplendent. Above it, a large, electric sign climbed up the centre like an escaped intruder clasping a thick, black cable for support and reaching up towards a Union flag that was puckered in wet folds.

The beauty of the hotel had never been lost on Sally, despite the addition of the intruder. While her own home rose up relentlessly tall and out of sync with the sky, McNeill's Hotel was safe in its symmetry, emerging serenely from the lough behind it. Jeffrey was no doubt accustomed to more stately buildings in Belfast, but he seemed enamoured with the hotel as he took it in.

"My father used to play at the hotel saloon with his band during summer season," she said, pointing to the bar on the left.

"What did he play?"

"Everything and anything. He could make a musical instrument from a brown paper bag. I mind him playing the banjo and the flute for the tourists."

"A man after my mother's heart. She teaches music."

"Da picked it up at the kitchen dances and in the pubs. I used to go with him and sit outside on the summer seats and listen. There was also an amusement park out the back of the hotel. A magical place for a child."

She checked his face again and, as he smiled, she understood where she had seen it. "Have I met you before?"

"I was going to say the same thing. You have a familiar face."

Are you related to Mr Peter O'Reilly?" she asked as they began to walk along the Main Street.

"Peter is my father."

"You're the image of him. I knew him when I was a girl. He taught a class down at the Gardenmore Hall. It must have been twenty years ago now."

"I came with him from time to time, so I met you then perhaps. Do you still dance?"

"No, That was a good while ago."

"You should have stuck at it."

"The legs were too long and the arms wouldnae settle." Sally demonstrated by placing her hands akimbo, stretching out her umbrella and skipping over a puddle by the door of Alexanders' store. "My ma taught me tae dance in the country way."

"Tut tut. We can't have that at all, Mrs Andrews." Jeffrey swiftly placed the umbrella back over Sally's head. "Straight arms, relaxed by the side, my father always said."

"My dancing ambitions were limited to getting a day off school for the Larne Musical Festival. Verse speaking, singing, the recorder, Irish folk dancing and the flute. Five days guaranteed."

"I'm surprised you became so proficient in Larne language with all those days off school," he observed brightly.

Sally pointed to the Gardenmore Hall when they reached the Town Hall. "Nearly there," she said, "but before we go in, you owe me a story about a resurrection, and in Larne language too."

"I'll try my best," he said, clearing his throat. "I'm at the door of the hotel this morning when this fella stops to yarn to the porter. Sez he to the porter, 'Boys-a-dear, I jist had a quare yarn wi a fella that was deed.'"

Sally smiled at the transformation from an educated Belfast brogue.

"'The porter,' sez he, 'deed, son? Ye spoke tae a man that was deed?' 'Aye, deed,' the fella went on. 'And I'll tell ye more forbeye, I towl half the toon he was deed.'"

Sally interrupted to praise Jeffrey's accent. "No bad," she said. "No bad, at all."

"Why, thank you Mrs Andrews." He removed his cap and held it out with grave expression. "'Sez I til masel, I was certain thon buddy was deed, but naw, it must hae been some other buddy. When ye think on it, son, it might o been the same buddy resurrected. It wouldnae be the first resurrection after a fall.'"

***

"Did you hear who's back?"

So much tittle-tattle was floating around the scullery that the small room was opaque with steam. Sally paused to listen to the conversation and then walked on by, squeezing her way through the men standing at the back of the hall.

The promise of the senior dancers had brought in the crowds and throngs of soaking, wet spectators assembled in a queue that began on the steps of Gardenmore Hall and hooked one hundred odd yards up to Thorndale Avenue.

Women, breathless in conversation, occupied rows upon rows of wooden chairs inside the hall, as stale smoke permeated an atmosphere dense with perfume, setting lotion and damp clothing. Men, meanwhile, stood along the back and sides, coughing, spluttering and mumbling in the thickening din.

The first few rows had been cordoned off as a fire escape, or more likely to keep the rabble away from the dignitaries in their furs and three-piece suits, not least Alfie's parents, Captain Andrews and Mrs Andrews, who were seated in the front row.

Sally was in the perfect location to survey the multitude of wet caps and demi-waves. She held up her wooden placard and waited for five hundred people to ignore the words, *Silence in the hall.*

Mr O'Reilly occupied the centre of the room and was raised on a platform like a god, a secretary from the festival committee by his side. To the front of the stage, a wide banner read *Larne Musical Festival,* and below it an array of silver cups glistened on a table clothed in green velvet.

The first group of solo dancers lined up on the stage, their skirts voluminous on skinny frames; and among the deep reds, rich purples, emerald greens and navy blues, was the odd drab-look- ing shade of army green.

The musicians began to play, heralding a shift in atmosphere as the audience became a patchwork quilt of colour, feet tapping and hands clapping.

Sally's eyes were drawn to the far side of the room as the dancers commenced their steps. The captain had got up and was making his way past the cordon and through the crowd. Sally's eyes roved back to Margaret, whose head was bowed, a hand covering her face.

Mr O'Reilly's bell brought the dancing to a stop, allowing the attention of the entire room to turn to the carfuffle at the back of the hall.

"She was too good for a soldier," a voice emerged.

Mr O'Reilly's bell rang once again, a cue for the dancers to bow and walk down the steps. They remained unmoving on the stage.

Sally's eyes flicked to the back of the hall. An old man with erratic, woolly hair had climbed up the first few frames of the gym bars. He held aloft a newspaper.

"She was my mermaid!" he cried. There was no further expla- nation as to what he meant before two burly men in caps removed him from the hall.

***

Sally didn't know where to go during the break. Should she ap- proach Margaret? She was more at ease in her company now than in the early years of her marriage, but she still lacked the confidence to speak to her when older society ladies were present.

She crossed the long queue for tea and made her way into the scullery, where the steam rising from whispers competed with that of the giant kettle. "He was long thought deed," came the voice of one customer. "A triangle of love and heartache," said another.

"Mrs Andrews!" It was young Hughie. He was at the door and he was alone.

Sally walked towards him. "What is it Hughie? I didn't know you were coming. Is Maisie here?"

Hughie took her by the hand and led her outside. "It's Aunt Maisie. Come quickly! We need Dr. Andrews."

"Where is she? And what's happened?"

"It's the baby, I think." said Hughie, fear flashing in his dark eyes.

"What baby?" Sally had been preoccupied with the festival, something to take her mind off her own endless headaches, but she hadn't missed a rounded tummy, surely.

"Hae ye got the motor?" asked Hughie, his cheeks beaming with life despite the cold.

"No, I don't. Is Maisie sick?" asked Sally.

"She had a sore back," he replied breathlessly. "I heared her say to uncle Leonard that there was a babbie. I wasnae meant tae know. Uncle Leonard was yappin at Aunt Maisie aboot cleaning and I never heared him yappin at Aunt Maisie before."

Oh God, thought Sally. Maisie had been doing a spring clean at Dalriada. She had been climbing up ladders, cleaning windows and dusting spider webs in the cornicing.

"Why didn't she tell me?"

"It's no your fault, Mrs Andrews," replied Hughie. "We all need tae earn wer keep."

Sally couldn't help but smile in the face of the eight year-old's wisdom.

"Don't you worry, Master Hughie," she said. "Your aunt Maisie will have a search party out looking for you on a night like this!"

***

Jamesina seized Hughie by the hood of his coat. "Where in God's name did you get to?"

"He was with me," said Sally.

Jamesina had terror in her eyes and a newspaper in her hand. She folded the newspaper and flung it into the fire. "The boy gave us a terrible fright, Sally. Out at this time of the night. He's lucky not to feel the back of my hand."

"Where's Maisie?" said Sally, unsettled by Jamesina's violent eyes.

She softened and breathed deeply. "Maisie is fine, m'dear. There was some blood, but she's fine."

"How far on is she?"

"Four months. Four months and she was cutting back hedges and all sorts. Never seen the likes of it." "Sit down and take this," she said, offering Sally a towel. "Dry yoursel or ye'll catch your death."

Jamesina ran a towel over Hughie's head. "Get out of them there wet clothes, son, and get yourself into bed. Up you go. And quiet now for wee Daniel's asleep."

Hughie kissed Jamesina on the cheek. "Night night, Aunt Jamesina. Sorry for fearin ye. I thought Doctor Andrews might help Aunt Maisie."

"I know you did, son. Now, there's a good boy. Say night night to Mrs Andrews."

Hughie walked towards Sally with eyes so dark that she could have delved into them. "Night night, Mrs Andrews. I'm heartsore and sorry for making ye miss the festival."

"Not to worry, wee son." Sally kissed him on the head. "Your heart was in the right place. Mr Andrews would've been here straight away if he'd known Maisie needed help."

Hughie walked out of the room, his shoulders sloped like a row of old cottages and Sally's heart sank as she followed him. "The poor wee critter," she said, turning to Jamesina. "I'm sorry about Maisie and the spring cleaning. I didn't know. She didn't tell me."

"Well, it's no secret now, m'dear, for Leonard has half the factory towl. Running about like a peacock, he is. Hmmf."

Jamesina took a deep breath and looked into the fire. "I'll tell you the honest God's truth, Sally, for you're one of our own, thon man is one good-for-nothing blirt. If I could get my hands on him for all he's done, I'd take him plume by plume and I'd fry him for I believe in the Word of the Lord and I fear that the iniquity of the father shall be visited upon his children."

Sally was confounded, as much by the loosening of Jamesina's tongue as by the attack on Leonard. What sins had Leonard committed? He was an affable sort, always welcoming and helpful. A man of few words, it was certain, but not a useless critter as far as Sally could tell.

"All things are become new," said Sally, a response that was consumed among the crackles from the fire.

The silence that followed was easy, and Sally was warmed by the fire and comforted by the company of Jamesina.

It was the Jamesina of her childhood, the older sister who had taken care of all the children in the street. It wouldn't last, this moment; it would be gone soon enough and everyone would return to the grown up roles they had been assigned — Jamesina, the post mistress, Sally, the doctor's wife, Maisie, the maid.

They both stared at the fire as large, bold letters from the newspaper swirled into black flames. *HE WAS CRUEL.*

Sally thought about what she would be doing at home at that moment, with Alfie out doing the rounds. There would be a book by her side. There would be a glass of something at her lips.

Jamesina was the first to break the silence and she did so by way of a deep breath. "I suppose I had better be going home now masel," she said. "I'll walk you round the corner."

"You'll do no such thing," replied Sally. "I can walk by myself."

"You need to watch on a Saturday night, dear. There's a rough lot about at this time comin frae the Pavillion."

"Dinnae worry," laughed Sally, "I'll be alright."

"You need to take care."

"Around here? Sure it's as safe as it's home."

The silence lingered on, but Jamesina spoke again, her voice emerging from the fissle of fire.

"It happened to me." She glanced at the burning newspaper as though it were responsible for her sorrow.

Jamesina was not one to talk of personal things. Sally averted her face and concentrated on the black flames of the newspaper.

"I was sixteen and I was good," she went on, her violent eyes flashing towards Sally. "Do ye understand me?"

"I think so," croaked Sally with uncertainty. Jamesina was unpredictable and she knew that the intimacy between them could be snatched away by the same hand that had grabbed young Hughie's hood.

"Rain, hail nor shine, I never missed a trip to Ballymena on a Sunday. Manys a time I had to walk the twenty miles home."

Sally knew Jamesina's routine well, and had often been taken to Ballymena in the company of the Higgins children to see the little girl who had been raised by Jamesina's maternal aunt. The child was called Grace, and Sally often wondered if Grace Higgins had insisted upon the name as part of the bargain that was struck. It was perhaps Grace Higgins' way of claiming her first granddaughter.

Young Grace was an only child. She was pretty, with an exuberant smile that was not inherited from Jamesina. Sally had once witnessed a reel that Grace had demonstrated to her cousins when she had first taken Irish dance lessons at the Protestant Hall in Ballymena. On a subsequent visit, Sally had given Grace one of her own musical festival medals — she could still remember the warmth of the smile she was awarded for the gesture.

"Is Grace not down for the senior championships tonight?" asked Sally. " Didn't she do well in it before?"

"Aye, she did, dear. But she's too oul tae be dancing now. She's a grown woman with a job."

"She must be twenty-two. I remember her fifth birthday party when she danced her reel for us."

Jamesina looked at Sally with a face so passive that Sally was sure she was going to cry.

"I never could figure out if the devil was in the man or the devil was in the drink," she said. "I could study his face today and still not know."

Was she referring to the face of the man who had wronged her?

"Yes, him," concurred Jamesina, agreeing with the thoughts in Sally's head.

"The man," said Sally. "He's here?"

"Of course, he's here, dear. Where do ye think he is? Do ye think he felt shame enough to leave the country? No, he married and had a wean at the time that Grace was born. God bless her and keep her for I'm sure she asked for it no more than I."

"What are ye saying, Jamesina?"

"I never towl a sowl but my da, though I never telled his name." She stared into the fire. "I always said I would take it with me til the grave, and God only knows why I'm telling ye this. It was a dark night on Pauper's Loanen and I was feared. I was just a girl walking home from a message, and he was a middle aged man and he was drunk. I've never seen someone so intoxicated. And Sally dear, let me tell you, he was a handsome man. God forgive me, but I looked at him and I smiled at him, and for many years, I believed that I had done wrong for smiling at him. Not anymore. I'm not ashamed anymore."

Sally was perturbed by the pain in Jamesina's eyes.

"I was fortunate enough, Sally. Take no pity on me. The tears tripped down my da's face when I towl him that the figure had set upon me like a crow. He placed his hand on mine and said that I was never to want for a penny and that the baby was never to want for love. He paid for it all. The elocution lessons. The typing lessons. He took me on a train to Belfast to do the post office exams and he took me on a train to Ballymena to my aunt Isobel's home when I started to show. The other girl learned that a man is to own his wife, and I can tell you, Sally, I never wanted to be owned by any man."

"Lord Almighty," sighed Sally, unable to contain her reaction.

"I pray for her every day of my life. I even pray for him and the drink that controls him. And I pray for every young girl out on a night alone among the devil and the drink. Don't take pity on me, Sally. I'm free, dear. I'm free for I trusted in the Lord."

Sally had always thought of Jamesina as the one who was trapped, a spinster serving her incarceration behind the bars of the post office; it had never occurred to her that solitude was Jamesina's freedom.

"There's no need for me to rush home," said Sally. "We can wait here until Leonard comes. Leonard will walk us home."

"Alright, love. It would be a shame to waste a good fire. Ma is going to crack at the seams one o these days. Jack Frost himself couldn't convince the same woman to burn a bit of coal! It's no wonder my da spends his days in the pigeon shed. He likely gets mair warmth from the birds."

Blue Blood
August 1948

"Quit them birds yapping," hollered Grace Higgins as she stomped towards the window.

"No, wait," protested Maisie, "I like the breeze."

Her mother tilted her head towards the midwife. "She's no thinkin straight, Mrs Ross. Ye cannae open the window, for half the street will hear ye when ye start tae sing. And believe me, dear, ye'll be singin soon enough!"

"Mrs Higgins," said Mrs Ross. "I dinnae want tae cause ye any injury, but I'm here nu to take care of Maisie and it would be powerful good if ye could get yersel along to the scullery and make a drap o ginger ale for your daughter."

Maisie watched as her mother puffed her cheeks before finally lowering her head and moving towards the door.

She turned, clutched the door handle and looked back at Maisie. "You're in safe hands," she said, "for I've know'd Mrs Ross all ma puff and she's delivered every wean safe on the Waterloo Road."

Grace left the room as another pain cramped Maisie's abdomen. She doubled over onto her side and yelped pathetically. She had been careful since the first scare in March. She needed to deliver this baby safely. Another plea with God. Another bargain.

"They'll be closer t'gether nu," said Mrs Ross as she immersed her hands into the hot water.

Maisie watched her work mechanically, providing a narrative that mismatched the turn of her hands. "Ye'll be needin tae get into your nightgown," she said tunefully as she assisted Maisie with the removal of her drawers. "I hear wee Daniel's learning the pipes" was her reflection as she sought the space between Maisie's legs.

It was like seeing a talkie for the first time, the lips not quite aligning to the script. Maisie tried to respond, but her words broke up and remained suspended in mid-air.

Mrs Ross poked diligently and swiftly, and Maisie clenched every muscle in her body, her mind tuning into the whistle of the birds.

The birds. She remembered looking at them a year ago all hooked up like a music score that she had somehow been able to read and understand. She shuddered at the thoughts of the walk from Glenoe. All the coldness. All the sadness. And now this, her painful reward.

The midwife was already scrubbing her hands. "Yer no quite ready yet, dear," she said. "See if ye can get a wee bit o rest. Turn til your side and take another keek at them there birds thonner."

Maisie did as she was bid and settled into a pattern of pain and relief until darkness began to pervade her thoughts. In the throes of pain, death seemed like a peaceful alternative to the weighty burden of life. The pain would then subside and she would become aware of the other heartbeat and the other soul and she would pray hard to live long enough to deliver her baby into the world.

Hours tiptoed by before the gushing, hot water freed itself from her body. A loud whimper ripped from her mouth in jagged disharmony and she became infant-like again, reverting to indulgent tears and unrelenting fears.

"It's time tae push, Missy. A deep breath nu. Let it all oot."

Maisie exhaled a strangled whimper, and knew from the smile creeping across the midwife's lips that a more fortified effort was required.

"Push through the pain!" hollered Mrs Ross.

Maisie tried to do as she was bid, but she was tired and needed to retreat from the world. She needed to sleep. "I can't do this anymore," she said faintly, lying back.

"None of thon nonsense now, d'ye hear?" said Mrs Ross, who was like a great threshing machine in toil. "There's the heed," she said before lifting Maisie's feet onto her shoulders and placing her heels neatly into the space below her collarbone.

"Deep breaths nu, Missy. Deep breaths!"

Maisie sucked frantically, but lost momentum when her body dissolved into uncontrollable shivers. "I don't want…" she began

"Deep breaths now, d'ya hear me! In and oot. That a girl. In and out now. That's it."

She followed the pattern of Mrs Ross's breath, in and out through the cursed pain as a guttural sound emerged that was foreign to her own ears.

"Push frae the back!"

Maisie didn't know her front from her back or her left from her right. She was lost in tears and sweat and panting, aware that Mrs Ross's instructions had started to synchronise with her actions, but unable to break down what she was saying.

"Let oot what you're howlin in," said Mrs Ross. "Heth! Let it oot girl! Come on now."

What the hell did she mean? Let what out? Let the baby out? The baby from the back? Was the baby coming from the back? Maisie broke down into a sorry, weeping howl.

"Great sweet mercy," came Mrs Ross's voice. "It'll no keep til morning. Push frae the back!"

The back. She pushed and puffed and heaved and choked, but there was nothing. It wasn't working. There was no baby coming and she needed to sleep.

"The heed's doon, dear. Ye"ll have tae keep pushin."

"I am bloody pushing," yelled Maisie and felt nothing when Mrs Ross slapped her thigh like the flank of a horse.

"That a way!" Mrs Ross's voice echoed, a smile bringing her peach cheeks to life as Maisie rose into growling teeth and claws in white linen.

"I can't do this anymore," she yelled. She lay back and admitted herself into the arms of Jesus. "Come and take me," she said in a whimper. "I can't go on."

All was quiet. Maisie was drifting. In the waterfall. At the top of a glen. Surrounded by scented, green foliage. Floating in bliss.

"Yer no deed yet, love," came the gruff voice of Mrs Ross. "Now pull yersel together for there's a bonnie wee bairn stuck in a tight tube between them thighs o yers and it's no for goin back up."

Maisie tried to look away, to pay no attention, to search for that restful, blissful place again, but it was gone and she was awakened by an almighty clap. Resurrected onto her elbows, she let go of the covers, scraiched a cacophonous wail, and pushed. She had found the back and the baby's head tore through her skin, scorching and scalding — metal nails clawing through Brown's Irish linen.

A lump slithered from her body and Maisie lay back and closed her eyes. "I can't do this anymore," she murmured.

She looked up at the window where the birds had been hooked to their stave. Mrs Ross was there, a treble clef holding a mass of skin, mucus and blood. "A bonnie lassie, Mrs Gourley."

Maisie smiled, her eyelids closing and opening in the dim light. She jolted herself to attention and looked again as a soft cry emitted through the air. The baby was laid upon her chest, and she looked down and saw the soft edge of a fist, a hairy head, two slits of eyes and a rounded nose.

She had a baby. She had given birth to a baby and she had felt the painful hand of joy. "Thank you, God," she whispered as a draught wafted across her body.

She looked down and saw that she was naked. She was naked in front of Mrs Ross from Factory Row. Where had her night-gown gone?

Mrs Ross must have read her thoughts for she returned from the settle with a thick, soft blanket, which she laid across Maisie and the baby. "You'll need tae take a sip o this before you start pushing again, said Mrs Ross, holding a glass of water. "There's a bit mair work to be done."

Maisie nodded and remembered what her mother had said about the pictures. Two shorts and a long feature with a happy ending.

Mrs Ross lifted the baby's head onto Maisie's naked breast and Maisie watched it clasp its lips around a long, blackened nipple. She laughed inwardly at the thoughts of herself, laid out on the bed like a great naked, dairy cow, and wondered if she would ever be able to look Mrs Ross in the eye at the corner shop again.

The laughter didn't last, for Mrs Ross had her pushing once again and she understood that she couldn't depend on the mid-wife to deliver her to that place of infancy, to carry her as before. She was a mother. She was feeding a child and she could only cry on the inside as the pain of the afterbirth slipped away with easy, blistering pain.

***

Ye've a wean nu. Is this what ye wanted?" asked Maisie, her eyes averting Leonard's. "Will it make ye happy?"

It was a cruel note that her mouth played without her mind's licence, but Maisie had kept her thoughts to herself since the day of the walk to Glenoe. She had accepted Leonard, and learned to love a new version of him all over again.

A year had passed since she had found Leonard at Horseshoe Cottage and she had grown accustomed to a new routine and a husband who was absent in a more useful way. He had taken to the garden — sowing and reaping and saving Maisie at least one chore — and he had taken to being a father to two boys who were not his own.

There was no more gallivanting at night, no more shifting through the shadows of life without words. He played in the band, and then came home and communicated a new kind of love — sowing and reaping, so it seemed to Maisie, as she listened to her baby's snuffling noises.

They had never spoken about Ellen or Horeshoe Cottage. Their bodies had learned to communicate where words had failed them.

Leonard lifted Maisie's chin. "You've aye been a mother," he said.

Maisie stroked the baby's back to avoid his gaze. "Is this why you did it?"

He placed his hand on Maisie's. "No," he said. "It was the way things were, dear, and I'm brave an sorry for all I done."

Leonard caressed his daughter gently, placed her into the wooden cot, and climbed into bed. He kissed Maisie on the forehead and spoke nervously, "I wasnae good enough to marry a girl like you, Maisie. An that's the truth o the matter."

"Thon's daft talk," said Maisie. "We were all reared the same."

"No, Maisie. I'd a heartless critter for a da, a far cry from Kenneth Higgins. We werenae raised the same for you were reared wi the blue blood o a prince runnin through your veins."

Leonard lay on his back and looked up to the ceiling. "You were meant tae be on the other side of thon wall along wi Sally."

"Nonsense," said Maisie, sitting up on her elbow to look at him. "What in the name o goodness would make ye say such a thing?"

"I watched ye comin hame frae the fectory wi yer eyes swelled up from lint an I heared ye wheezin, and I was sick, sore an sorry for ye, Maisie. My ain mother niver had tae work in a fectory. My da niver gien her much, but he gien her thon."

"He gien her a black eye or two forbye," said Maisie. "I'd sooner want for butter than accept the heavy hand o a man like yer da."

"An ye did want for it. Ye saved all the bacon an eggs for me an I felt shame that I couldnae gie the woman I married what she needed. And I ran away."

"From the time of the first war to the last, I only ever know'd rations," said Maisie, leading Leonard away from the whys and wherefores of what he had done. "I mind my da bringing home a great shank o lamb for the broth, but not one o us weans could stomach the smell. My da took each bowl and poured it into his ain. My ma did a great rair aboot the ungrateful weans she had brought into the world. We were sent tae bed wi nuthin, and we were glad for our stomachs were only ever hungry for bread."

Leonard took Maisie's hands.

"Ye changed the day they sent ye hame frae the doctor," she said.

She thought back to that time, when she was still working at the factory and wheezing and coughing through the night, when Leonard had failed his medical for the army. That's when he had changed.

"My da aye said I'd come tae nuthin," he said.

"You didnae walk through French waters wi a gun over yer head, but ye gave manys a Yankee soldier in the Legion a tune tae take on their way."

"I didnae lay doon my life like Tam. He had courage, Tam."

"No, he just got tae spend what he had. A whole army of brave sinners got to spent what courage they had. Do ye miss Tam?"

"I do. When he was a wean, he towl me he would either be a drum major or a soldier, for he was a great hand at leading the bands. When I play a marching tune, I think on him twirling thon stick, but it makes me quare and sad tae think o him as a soldier."

***

Never in all her years had Maisie dreamt of owning something so luxurious as a navy Silver Cross perambulator. Her mother, who was making her way up the road towards number thirty-three, would certainly have something to say about it all.

"Well I niver!" she exhaled upon arrival. "God bliss us and keep us for thon is the most handsome perambulator I ever did see!"

Maisie laughed and stood back and watched her mother move around the perambulator with her hands on her hips, paying no attention whatsoever to the baby on Maisie's shoulder.

"If Winifred Ramsey could see us today!" exclaimed Grace. "Thon poor critter wheeled Sally aroon the fectory in an oul wooden cart!"

Maisie set the baby upon the white satin blanket and read the note aloud to her mother.

Dear Maisie

Sorry I can't be there to see the baby. I'm at the hospital getting my head examined. Maybe they'll find the pea I stuck in my ear when I was wee. I wish you and the baby well. I've asked Alfie to pick you something nice, so apologies if it's not what you needed. I'm knitting her a wee cardigan too. Please hurry and pick a name!

Yours Sincerely,

"Not what ye needed, indeed! Tell them there doctors that Grace Higgins knows what's wrong with Mrs Andrews' heed. Too much bathing in cowl water. That's what!"

"Och Ma, you're like a broken record! What could be keepin her four nights? She hasnae even seen the wean yet. And why would they need to take her to Belfast?"

"Nuthin but the best for the doctor's wife, Maisie. Dinnae you be worrying yer heed for Sally's a strong girl. She'll be alright."

Maisie followed her mother's clear blue eyes along the row of terrace houses down to number seventeen.

She looked at the note. She had told Sally that she needed her head examined on many occasions, almost always on account of an over-generous gift like the one that was sparkling in the August sun.

"She aye brings up the yarn aboot the pea in the ear," laughed Maisie. "We were picking peas from the pod when Winifred caught us sticking them into wer ears. Some days I can still hear Winifred's words rolling doon the backs o the Waterloo Road. It's a quare tragedy that she was taken so young."

"Death is never tragic," said Grace, flatly, as though she had been dead and born again herself enough times to know it for a fact.

"Was it no tragic for Sally to loss her ma?" asked Maisie.

"Death brings peace and peace brings joy," asserted Grace, turning to look up the street towards the parlour houses. Here's our Lily coming. She must o heared aboot the perambulator. Oh, the eyes'll be green with envy."

"Morning Missy-No-Name!" she said, lifting the baby into her arms. "What kind o mother doesnae gie her wean a name?"

"I towl ye, I'm waiting til it comes to me — like inspiration."

"Your heed's a marley. Ye've been spendin too much time wi the doctor's wife! My wean's were all named within the hour. Iris, Rose and young Lily were picked like flowers in bloom."

"And what aboot Hughie, thonner?" said Maisie, pointing to Lily's third child.

"He was Petunia for a day, but we thought better of it and named him after a Scotsman Rab met on the boat."

"I can hear everything you're saying, Ma!" hollered Hughie from the front yard.

"Who's thon coming up the road?" asked Lily, who hadn't so much as glanced at the gigantic perambulator.

"God bliss us and save us," said Grace, "if it's no a ghost."

Maisie studied the figure, an old tramp by the looks of things — ragged, yet handsome in the even symmetry of his long face.

"He looks like he's doon and oot," whispered Grace.

"Good morning," said the man, gently removing his cap to address Lily. "A bonnie baby, you have there."

"Oh she's not mine, sir, but if her mother doesnae mind, I'm going to take her for a wee scoot up the Waterloo Road in this fine perambulator. Is that alright, Maisie?"

"Yes, dear," said Maisie. "Take the weans forbye. She's due a feed, so dinnae be long."

She waved Lily and the children off and turned to see her mother's eyes fixed on the man. Maisie tried hard not to stare, but noted a golden pocket watch and chain that clashed with his shabby attire.

"Martin Andrews, is that you?" said Grace.

"I'm sorry, my memory fails me, Mrs—?"

"Grace Higgins. McKay til my own name. Remember? From Drumalis. I worked there just before I married and I met ye when ye came and went by the Smileys. Honest God's truth, I thought ye'd passed."

He laughed, "No, Mrs Higgins. I'm still standing. If I'd stuck with the temperance lodge, I might well be standing straight."

"Terrible affliction, the drink," observed Grace. "Are ye stayin wi the captain in Carnlough?"

"No, I'm afraid my brother and I haven't seen much of each other these thirty-odd years, Mrs Higgins."

"I'm sorry to hear that," said Grace, and Maisie watched on bemused, not only by her mother's glow, but by the gentleman's voice whistling from the bristly face. Sally had never mentioned the captain's brother.

"The price of youth, Mrs Higgins. This young woman would never believe what a dashing character I cut back then."

"Och och a nee. If ye don't mind me saying so, I mind ye well for ye were the greatest dancer," said Grace, a smile streaming from her pale face.

Maisie stared at her mother in disbelief.

"I maybe stayed out a little too late dancing on occasion," said Martin. "But you're a young girl yourself, Mrs Higgins. You wouldn't remember an old fella like me."

"Oh I mind ye alright, and you're still in your prime, Mr Andrews, for we're both the same age. I mind ye at the Smiley's servant's ball when I was a maid. A fine waltzer ye were, Mr Andrews."

"These bandy legs of mine footed it to one too many waltzes, I should think." He hesitated and bowed his head and then spoke in a low voice. "Mrs Higgins, do you mind Mary Beth Clarke?"

"I worked under Mary Beth Clarke," confirmed Grace. "She was the housekeeper at Drumalis before she went tae Dalriada." She looked intently at Martin, and after a moment raised her hand to her chin. "Mary Beth Clarke," she said in a whisper. Her hand dropped to her side as she straightened up. Martin looked at the ground and Maisie contemplated walking away to leave them both to it, but knew that one foot advancing or retiring in any direction would break the spell that had been cast.

Martin raised his head. "If God spares me and keeps me, I'd like to find her."

"But Mr Andrews, Mary Beth fell on hard times before the Great War and went to live by the shore. She ended up in the workhouse. My Jamesina was gey and fond of her. Mary Beth gave the wean dulse. Honest God's truth, I could never fathom why a woman with such knowing was a housekeeper, let alone a pauper."

"I asked a man in a public house if he had ever heard tell of Mary Beth Clarke, and he said that she was a mermaid, no less." Martin laughed forlornly and Maisie watched a smile emerge mechanically across the white bristles of his unshaven face. "A mermaid, who tore her own baby from her body before returning to sea."

Grace sighed. "The things folk say! I'm heart-sore and sorry to hear Mary Beth spoke o like thon. She was a quare woman and a smart yin."

Martin stood still a moment, his head drooping. "I should go," he said. "Thank you Mrs Higgins. You've been kind to talk to a man like me."

He walked away, his head slightly more elevated than before.

"Wait," called Grace. "Where will we find ye?"

"Corran cottage. My brother owns it."

"It'll be harsh there in the winter," said Grace. "See that ye keep yerself safe and warm."

"Think of me as a mad man keeping an eye out for mermaids by the sea," he said, a smile revealing yellowing teeth that were as straight as a row of kitchen houses.

"I will," smiled Grace.

His figure moved on up the street, and Maisie thought back to the picture of Mary Beth Clarke in the attic of Dalriada, her face featureless, wild and solitary.

"Tragedy's what ye see among the livin," said Grace with glassy, distant eyes.

"Maybe you're right."

"He could hae been mine," sighed Grace.

"What in the name of—?"

"Martin Andrews once asked me tae dance at the servants' ball."

"He did not!" laughed Maisie.

"Aye, he did, but I know'd my place. Martin had looks to kill and an education forbye, but your da had a trade and wheen o pigeons, and your granny aye said I should find a man wi a trade."

"Thanks be tae God," said Maisie. "Are you sayin I could hae been living on the other side o thon wall?"

"I doubt it very much, dear, for thon fella's a romantic and a romantic he'll die."

"What's wrong with being a romantic?" protested Maisie.

"Romance is all right if ye marry a thatcher, ma dear, for a romantic will squander his worth, seek alms frae his brother and end up in a thatched cottage by the shore. But here, dear, he must have been the man that wronged Mary Beth Clarke, and I'd niver hae guessed it in all my days."

A Doll Called Sally-Anne
August 1948

Sally kept her eyes on the grand houses prospering like garden cities only minutes from the chimney stacks and back-to-backs of urban Belfast. She couldn't look at Alfie, suffer the trembling of his red lips, listen to a voice that was raw with tears over a coffin he could not shoulder.

Alfie had seen death up close, but he didn't understand what it looked like beyond an etched marble headstone and mid-morning service of ashes to ashes and dust to dust. He didn't understand what it looked like even as it occupied the space between them on the return journey from the hospital.

Sally knew death and the spirits it awakened. She could feel their inexorable and inexplicable presence. Her mother. Her father. Her unborn children. The exiled faces that invaded her daylight dreams.

Losing her mother so young had bestowed her with courage — to set herself to learning, to leave the comfort of poverty behind, to move from one world to the next — so that when the doctor had diagnosed cancer, she had felt a sense of oneness with her mother that had comforted her and made death a promise and not a curse.

An ounce of wormwood in a quart of boiling water. It was a voice, not Alfie's, and it was not the first time she had heard those witch-like words. She closed her eyes and spoke. "A woman told my mother to take a cure. I can hear the voice, but I can't picture a face."

"Your mind is playing tricks on you. You're tired. You need to rest."

"Words from the deed," she laughed.

Alfie's hand tapped the steering wheel. "Don't talk of death."

"I wasn't talking of dying. I was saying that the voice is maybe coming from—"

"Please don't talk of such things."

The motor slowed.

"I have memories and I don't understand them. I see a baby. Another baby. Not our babies."

She sat back and closed her eyes. She would sleep. Alfie was right. She needed to rest.

She drifted and she slept, words tuning in and out of her mind as the motor moved from asphalt to gravel.

"The tumour is in the occipital lobe, Mrs Andrews."

A consultant's circumspect voice, pre-empting a marble head-stone and mid-morning service.

Or, perhaps it was another doctor preparing the way for a stone slab to be etched with the words *Winifred Anne Ramsey, 1883-1926.*

But that wasn't possible. Winifred wouldn't have been to the Nervous Diseases Hospital. Winifred wouldn't have had an electroencephalograph. She wouldn't have been wired up to the giant machine — one of only a dozen in the UK, so they said.

How did they know it was a brain tumour? Sally recalled her father holding up a hen's egg to demonstrate the size of it.

She could have asked Doctor Andrews how Winifred would have been diagnosed, but she couldn't acknowledge the connection between herself and her mother in front of him. She couldn't acknowledge it because Alfie was not merely a doctor of medicine, he was also a healer and a man of hope, and it was his hope that propelled the car at speed.

She would ask the consultant at the hospital next time. He was old enough to have treated someone in the 1920s. She would tell him that it was a brain tumour, and that she had never asked her father how they knew.

Alfie's hope was deafening, louder than the drone of the engine, and Sally wanted to respond to him, to tell him that she wanted to live life in Dalriada, her own garden city set behind the chimney stacks and back-to-backs of the Brown's Irish Linen Factory, a disproportional destiny with a turret and mismatching windows.

What did other people do when they found out they were dying? It seemed like a reasonable enough thought for Sally to express in the internal chambers of her asymmetrical mind. Maybe now was the time to find some purpose, a purpose other than that which was wrenched from her body. Twice.

She would be like Alfie's mother. She would behave as a Mrs Andrews ought to behave. Join committees, run variety shows and organise fairs with tombolas and raffle tickets. A real Mrs Andrews would sell raffle tickets.

And she would find God. Yes, that was a priority. *Seek, serve and follow Christ.*

She had tried that, but she hadn't found God, at least not in the way that the evangelical minister on the wireless had found God. He had been born again, his sins washed away. Sally was a part-time believer and couldn't think of a sin she had ever committed, except the sin of wishing that she were dead so that she could see her children again.

But she didn't need to see them again. Not flesh and blood. She had their spirits in the garden, giving life to the white heads of the water hawthorn and the yellow tips of golden club. She smiled. She couldn't help it. "Alfie, can we build a little sculpture?"

"What kind of little sculpture?"

"You know, one of those sculptures you see in gardens. I saw them in France. All across the Garden of Versailles. They were very grand, but I'd like a little one. The pond was filled with colour this summer. A white sculpture by the pond. Something small and tasteful."

He smiled and reached over to squeeze her hand. His voice was steady. "Yes, we'll build a sculpture for our children in the garden and I promise that I'll take care of it until the day I die."

He understood, Sally realised. He understood death beyond the grave. And she loved him. She loved her husband serenely, and she knew that he loved her in return.

She asked herself who he was in love with. She was the daughter of a sick man one day, an orphan the next. She was a mother-in-waiting, a mother-in-mourning. Twice. She was a gentleman's wife and a friend of the maid.

Perhaps the look she had seen so often in Alfie's lost eyes was not that of a boy perpetually falling in love with the laundry girl, but that of a man perpetually falling in love with a stranger. And now that she was dying, there was a whole new person to love.

***

How easy it had been to accept death on the route home from the hospital, to think that it was possible to drift into it without a response, without a fight.

Sally had lain in bed for twenty-four hours, awaking to drink water and then falling into a sound sleep again with no thoughts of death, no thoughts of the hospital.

She awoke and washed and had breakfast, a slow breakfast of kippers and toasted soda with a glass of ginger ale to awaken her senses. She had enjoyed that meal, a first after days of not wanting to eat a bite.

She glanced at the newspaper. Nothing but advertisements and notices the length of the front page, the largest of all of them 'The Herbal stores,' 57B Main Street. Herbal remedies for coughs, colds, catarrh, asthma, bronchitis, stomach and liver troubles, kidney and bladder complaints, rheumatism, sciatica, nervous conditions, boils, pimples, eczema, piles and constipation. No mention of brain tumours.

She rarely read the paper, but now she read it through the eyes of someone who had no permanence, and she felt connected.

She had been disconnected, content in her garden, her kitchen or by the sea. What did people think of her walking around Larne in such dresses and coats, her white gloves pristine, her smile and small-talk perfection?

A photograph of Miss Larne 1948 caught her attention. Two rows of beautiful women. How young they all looked. Young and so full of the future.

She would walk. Alfie was at work after days away from his patients. She would walk alone, and she would wear the red cardigan that Grace had knitted her. She had always been afraid to damage it, to tarnish its sentimental worth. Today was the day to wear it.

She skipped the first half mile, energy fizzing through her body like carbonated ginger ale. Her senses were keen, the air salty on her lips and tongue.

It was a calm sea with rippling cones of water, stretching beyond the twin islands of The Maidens to the lowland hills in Scotland.

The dark outline of the Black Arch appeared close at first, but as she walked on, it stepped away from her, out of reach. She stopped and caught her breath. The black basalt rock of the ancient cave blurred to grey, a silent moving picture from the past.

It was happening again. She was not to be permitted this short walk. She would not reach the dark rocks. She would not run her hands across their ancient, silken edges. She would not stare into the Devil's Churn, hear the water glugging and slurping against the cavern of rock.

She pleaded silently with God to allow her to reach her destination, but she knew her prayers of desperation were futile and that they would go unheeded. She turned around and grasped the railing with her glove, trailing her fingers across the rusty bumps and sharp edges of paint.

She dared not look left to the sea, to a horizon that would become faint. She would not see Scotland because the same symptoms that had propelled Alfie towards the hospital in Belfast were once again shaking her confidence. Her vision dimmed. She felt heart-sure there would be nothing but light in her eyes and darkness in her heart by the time she reached home.

Tears soaked her face. She had acquiesced with the diagnosis, willed herself to enjoy the present, but the present kept changing like an evolving, bewitching wife.

Why could death not be a straight line, a symmetrical horizon she could cross without this unerring pain and torment?

She walked and she paused at the sloping brae on her right, one that ran from the top of Waterloo Road down to the shore. She had forgotten that Maisie was coming to visit with the baby at eleven o'clock. She needed to get home.

She rested at a shelter at the top of the Chaine Memorial Park. She had sat there so often with Alfie that even now, with her eyes closed, she could see the rugged rivulets of grass shimmying down to the sea. A gull broke the stillness, its piercing cry a metallophone of sound against her temples. She tried to tune it to her mind, to welcome its natural call, but she could not abide its discordant echo. She needed to go home.

Disappointed by her failure to walk a mile, she made her way across the road, running her hand across the walls, testing her ability to be blind — a milestone that would mark the life she still had and the death that awaited her.

She reached the front door of Dalriada and walked into the parlour, a room she had never used, even when all its fossils were removed. She admired it now for its tall windows and ceilings and its yellow, curing light. She lay on her side on the sofa below the bay window and wrapped herself in a blanket. She squinted towards the clock. Half past ten. She could rest her eyes for half an hour.

***

She awoke to the scent of fresh bread on the griddle and the sound of a baby crying. She sat up and took in the warm colours of the garden, noting the seamless space of burnished red and yellow, questioning why she had wasted so much time hiding in the small corners of Dalriada when its open arms were there to embrace.

"Is that you up, dear?"

Sally looked at the clock on the mantelpiece. She had slept for more than an hour.

"Maisie?" she called, her head clearer than it had been on the walk, yet foggy from the nap. "I'm in here."

"Oh I know where you are," replied Maisie, who stood on the threshold of the door, her face a halo of freckles shining over a bundle of white linen.

Sally was stunned by the earthy beauty of Maisie — the smile that overflowed with life, the chestnut hair that danced in uncultivated curls. She felt tears stir in her eyes, and then she was holding a baby and emotion streamed from the depths of her womb, tears christening the small head of soft, dark hair.

She looked up to Maisie and back to the baby. The baby's cheeks were red and shining, her eyes opening for just long enough to tease Sally with two dark blue flashes. Maisie wore an indistinct outfit of a bottle green skirt and a cream cardigan that hung loosely over her rounded tummy, but her body pulsed with the riches of nature. She knelt onto the carpet by Sally's knees,

115

her hand gently clasping the baby's, and all the energy that passed from mother to child coursed through Sally's bloodstream. She had never felt so present and alive.

"Don't cry," whispered Maisie.

"She's beautiful," said Sally.

The baby was beautiful. There was nothing more exulting at the gates of death than the touch of a new life.

"Sit back and give her a wee nurse on your knee. I'll get us some tea. I made some slims on the griddle while you were asleep."

Sally felt an ache in her stomach, but it was not a pain for the babies she had lost or for anything that had gone before her. It was the pain of feeling someone else's joy so intensely. Daniel, Lily, Hughie, Rose and Iris had all brought laughter and smiles to Dalriada, but she had met Grace's other grandchildren when life seemed interminable.

Teach us to number our days. The words on the old lychgate. Sally had read them often enough, but she had never dreamed she would live them so soon.

She recalled a doll that Maisie had, a topsy-turvy rag doll called Sally-Anne. There was a black American mammy at one end and a white girl at the other. The children had been mesmerised by the doll, and they took it in turns to play with it for months until it disappeared. They found it eventually, torn into pieces by a neighbouring dog. Sally had buried it in the back garden with a stick inscribed, "RIP Sally-Anne." She thought of the devotion they had both given to that doll as she held Maisie's baby in her arms.

Maisie re-appeared at the door with a tray, resuming the role of the maid for the lady.

"What's her name?" asked Sally.

"Little Miss-No-Name," said Maisie, setting the tray on the table. "I'm still thinking about it."

"Five days later? And what does Grace Higgins have to say about that?"

"She's not as concerned as the Reverend. He called with us this morning and said he'd be back tomorrow evening to baptise her. Ma said she never heared tell o a wean being christened without a name. I was hoping you might be able to help me."

"Let me think on it," said Sally. "Is there a name you liked as a wean? A doll maybe?"

"A doll," said Maisie, pausing to think. "You're a geg, Mrs Andrews, for you know well my ragdoll was called Sally-Anne."

"Ye would do worse than to name a wean Sally-Anne. The Anne gies it a bit of gravitas."

"Gravitas," Maisie repeated with a smile, "Is that right?"

"I'm only keepin goin. Honest God's truth, the wean looks more like a Lily than a Sally. Would ye not name her after your sister?"

"I'm not sure what Jamesina would think of that."

"Jamesina," said Sally softly as she looked at the baby. Her eyes flicked back to Maisie's. Her lips trembled with laughter.

"What in the name o goodness was Ma thinking?" laughed Maisie. "Jamesina. Did ye ever?"

"What about Clara? I like the name Clara. Reach that wee picture down from the mantelpiece."

"This one?" said Maisie, lifting a tiny oval, brass frame.

Sally looked at the faded portrait of a small girl in ringlets.

"Who is it? I've dusted that frame a hundred times and never thought to ask."

"I don't know. It says Clara on the back. She must be a freen of Aflie's. It was here among all the other photographs when I moved in. I always liked it. It sort of gave me hope, I suppose — something to look forward to."

Maisie bowed her head. "I'm sorry for you. You know that I'm plain sorry for all your trouble."

"Och, not having weans was one thing, Maisie, but it never occurred to me to number my days."

"No," said Maisie. She had her head down and searched for a handkerchief around the cuff of her slieve.

"Did Alfie tell you everything?"

"I think so." She ran her fingers over the frame, a tear escaping down her cheek. "He told me about what happened at the hospital." She sniffed, cleaned her nose with a handkerchief and looked into Sally's eyes. "I'm heart-sorry," she said. "Heart-sad."

"Tell me this, Maisie, did ye hear about the mystery uncle?"

"Martin Andrews? I did, and I met him the other day. I think Ma took a shine tae him." Maisie smiled through her tears.

"I haven't seen him yet, but Alfie was introduced to him for the first time before I went into hospital."

"He didn't know him before?"

"Not as an adult, although he has vague memories of spending a day with him as a boy. His uncle came home in March and caused a great ruckus at the Larne Musical Festival. Then he disappeared. I knew that the captain had a brother, but was warned by Alfie when we were courting that the brother was best not to be mentioned in front of his father."

"Does your Alfie know about Mary Beth?"

"Mary Beth?"

Sally's vision flickered again.

"The woman," said Maisie. "Did Martin no fall oot wi his father over Mary Beth Clarke?"

"All I know is that Martin took to the wrong side of the blanket with the maid."

"It was Mary Beth Clarke," said Maisie. "Mind, ye show'd me her picture in the attic?"

"But it couldn't have been. Mary Beth was a pauper."

"Mary Beth wasnae always a pauper," said Maisie. "She was the housekeeper at Drumalis when my ma worked there."

Sally thought back to the picture in the attic and a chill washed over her.

"There was said to be a baby," Maisie added tentatively. "You know the rumour as well as me."

A long silence followed as Sally tried to piece the information together, but the discordant jumble of thoughts and memories made her tired. Her arms began to loosen around the baby. "Maisie," she said softly. "I think I need to lie down. The tiredness, it comes and it goes."

"Of course, said Maisie, lifting the baby from her arms. "Would you like me to pull the curtains?"

"A wee bit, thanks. You get on home now. Daniel will be back from school soon. And Hughie. Give them my love."

"I will," said Maisie, as she pulled the curtain cord.

Sally lay her head on the cushion and watched as Maisie moved around the room with her baby. She added more coal to the fire and placed the photograph back onto the mantelpiece. She fixed the blanket over Sally's shoulders.

"Goodbye, Sally," she whispered, the door closing softly behind her.

An Ounce Of Wormwood
October 1948

A vision of an old lady with skin like the bark of a chestnut tree
came to Maisie in the early hours of the morning when she had
awakened to settle Clara. The child had taken to arching her back
and screaming in such a manner that not a single member of
Maisie's family could entice her into the handsome carriage, not
even her mother with her vast wisdom on how to rear a wean.

Grace had, on one occasion, rocked her grandchild up and
down so much that she had accidentally ventured beyond the
margins of her own self-confinement, walking as far as the
shore, and Maisie had willed her mother to demonstrate the defi-
ciencies of a younger generation in matters of child-rearing to
allow Clara some relief from the pain; she was only ever at peace
wrapped in a shawl, tight to Maisie's chest, and she was snug
there when the lorries of Howdens hissed past them.

A misty, indistinct road revealed itself one yard at a time from
the motor coach. Maisie followed the lead of two passengers and
got off in the centre of the village, close to the bare chestnut
tree that now seemed shrunken and bereft of all its significance.
To her right, heads of children were visible through small, square
panes in the schoolhouse, and by the roadside, the light from an
old street lamp swayed back and forth like a long skipping rope.

Maisie turned and walked towards the smallest cottage, not entirely sure why she was there or what she was going to say. She knocked the red door and ran her hand across the musty whitewashed walls.

"Come in!" called the voice from inside. Maisie hesitated before pushing the door ajar.

"Come in out of the damp, dear," said the woman, as though she had known Maisie all of her days.

"I came back," said Maisie. "I met you one day, the summer before last.."

"I mind ye weel," came the cheerful reply. "I'm Cathleen. Cathleen Carmichael."

"Maisie Gourley. Nice tae to meet ye."

Maisie took in the ingredients of the past: an old dresser, a settle, two low stools, a wide inglenook fireplace, an ale plant on the windowsill. The room was spacious and clean in its simplicity, the line of brass bells and buckles on leather straps down the side of the fireplace the only adornments.

"I see you've been blessed," said Cathleen. "Reach me the child while you sit and warm yersel. I would get up, but the pains afflict me when it's neither one season nor t'other, and no amount of thyme nor clove can ease the rattling of oul bones like mine."

"Clara will go tae naebody but me, but I could lay her on her side in the settle if that's alright by you. She slept all the way. We came frae the Waterloo Road."

"Here, hang up your coat to warm it, dear," said Cathleen, pointing to a line hooked across the fireplace, where Maisie hung her coat and the baby's shawl. She pulled up a stool and sat by the fire.

"The tay is fresh. Help yoursel." Cathleen pointed to the kettle and then to the dresser. Maisie got up and lifted two tin cups. As she poured milk into each of them, she noted the small line of medicine bottles on the top shelf of the dresser.

"Do ye live here all alone?" asked Maisie, a question that needed no answer for the room was made up for one.

"I sent my man off tae war a long time ago," replied Cathleen. "He never did come back."

"The Great War?"

"Oh no, dear," Cathleen laughed through well-worn teeth. "No, it was Africa. I couldnae heal my ain husband, Mrs Gourley. I dinnae offer that kind of healin, you see."

Maisie bowed her head, not quite comprehending what Cathleen was saying.

"That's why for ye came, isn't it?" said Cathleen.

Maisie shook her head in confusion and sat down on the low stool opposite Cathleen.

"They know me tae be a healer, Mrs Gourley, but I see them downcast eyes and I can promise ye there's no witchery here. Just a wheen o potions and an oul pair o hands."

Maisie looked up and was comforted by Cathleen's smile.

"The young yins dinnae comprehend the healin," she went on. "They would as soon put an oul woman like me in the madhouse. Healing is either a burden or a gift, Mrs Gourley, and I take it to be a gift."

The echoes of bible school teachings niggled Maisie as the old lady spoke, but she looked at the bundle of Clara on the settle and felt sure that she had not been dealt the hand of the devil.

"It's no somethin ye talk aboot," she went on, apparently clocking the wanderings of Maisie's mind. "It's kept quate," she confirmed with a nod.

"I've never met a healer," ventured Maisie, "I never did learn about such things."

"I had goose bumps up my arms and around my neck when I seen ye pass by," said Cathleen.

Maisie stared. What was this woman? She didn't look like a fortune teller at the circus or at the Hiring Fair.

"A storm came in that day," continued Cathleen, "and I watched for ye coming back. You were away a quare while."

"I walked to Glenoe," said Maisie.

"And ye found him there."

"As happy as a lark."

"When ye passed me on the road hame, it was a different sowl walkin."

Maisie hugged her tea with both hands, confused that someone should know her more than she knew herself.

"You had shed an oul skin. I reached oot and held your hand."

As far as Maisie could see, the only skin she had shed in Glenoe was her naivety. She heard the echo of Esther Gibson's voice. "I was eleven when I lost my childhood." Maisie had lost hers at thirty-two, the day she realised that Leonard's song was not for her.

"I know'd not a thing about the healin," said Maisie, adding, hesitantly, "I wasnae leukin tae be healed."

"Ye know'd not a thing aboot the healin, Mrs Gourley, but as sure as God, you were leukin tae be healed."

Maisie was curious, her reticence subsiding. "How did you know?"

Cathleen smiled knowingly. "Healers are as thatchers, my dear. Folk nae langer knock on my door, but they come. They stap and they tell me what I already know."

Their eyes met and Maisie knew there was something between them.

"What did you heal?" she enquired. "A broken marriage? A broken man?"

Cathleen cradled the tin cup in her lap and reached out her hands. "I follow the winds on my skin, voices in my head, pictures of times in front of me, memories of times I never had. I know'd that you would howl a wean twixt these two hands. You were feared of it. You were feared of birthing a child."

Cathleen held Maisie's hands tight and then let go, a shock of air passing where the warmth had been. Maisie jolted. She stood up and saw that she had spilled tea on her dress. It was true. She had been afraid, yet she hadn't known it until now. She pulled a handkerchief from her pocket and turned towards the medicine bottles as she cleaned away the stain.

"I've a friend," said Maisie. "She's no weel."

"What's the matter?"

"A brain tumor. They say she cannae be healed."

"Your friend may be short on time, Mrs Gourley, but she can be healed from pain. An ounce of wormwood in a quart of boiling water three times a day." Cathleen pointed to the dresser. "Top shelf, third bottle frae the left."

Maisie walked towards the dresser and paused before lifting the bottle. "Her husband's a doctor," she said, thinking of how Alfie might react. She had always gone out of her way to impress him, to ensure that he never thought ill of the factory folk.

"He'll be troubled so," said Cathleen, "for he's a healer wi learnin forbye. He'll no understand why."

"None o us understand why."

"Does your friend understand it?"

Maisie thought for a moment. She lifted the bottle and sat back down.

Sally had never deliberated the whys or wherefores of her illness with Maisie. She had a fighting spirit when she was up and walking and visiting Clara, but when she was lying down in Dalriada, she looked pale and gaunt and ready to die.

"I think aboot her dyin withoot lea'in anything behind."

"Because she has no kin?"

"Her ma died when she was only ten. Her da died at the start o the second war. Her uncles are in America and her mother's family was small. She has no brothers or sisters. And she suffered two misses."

"Maisie dear, she bore two weans and their spirits are amongst us."

Maisie smiled as she followed Cathleen's eyes to the heavens.

"What do they call your friend?"

"Sally. She married a doctor and moved to Dalriada at the other side of the wall. She was born in the kitchen hoose next tae mine."

"Dalriada?"

"Aye, it's the name o a hoose, a sort of castle even. Tall wi a turret on the right side."

"I met a maid from Dalriada yince."

"Was it Winifred, Sally's ma?"

"No dear, I dinnae mind the name Winifred. I aye forget names, but the face I'll niver forget. Terrible tortured she was." Cathleen's expression turned cold. "Mary Beth," she said, shaking her head. "God's truth, I mind the look o terror in her eyes."

"Did you heal her?" asked Maisie.

"No, dear, I didnae heal her, for the kind of healin she was leukin for is no the kind o healin I provide."

***

"An ounce of wormwood! Maisie, folk'll be thinking you're away with the fairies."

"Try it all the same for she said it'll help."

"A healer, you say?"

"A healer, and dinnae be tellin my ma!"

"I wouldnae dare. So, what do you think she was sayin?"

"They say she had a wean, didn't they? I wondered if she mibby wanted tae get rid o it," said Maisie, forlornly. She looked up to see the thin silhouette of Margaret Andrews at the parlour door. "Sorry," said Margaret. "I didn't mean to surprise you." "Come in," said Sally. "Maisie was telling me about a healer she met at the Glynn."

Maisie straightened up.

"It's alright, Maisie, Margaret won't be for telling your ma any of this."

"No," Margaret confirmed. "I wouldn't do such a thing. And how lovely to hear your news, Mrs Gourley. How old is the baby now?"

"Eleven weeks. Hae a wee nurse if ye like."

"That would be a pleasure."

Margaret took Clara and sat down beside Sally on the large settee.

"And how is the boy with the voice of an angel?"

"Wee Hughie?" said Maisie.

Margaret looked up towards the ceiling rose. "Every time I hear that hymn, tears come to my eyes." She sang into Clara's ear in a whisper. *"You in your small corner and I in mine."*

"A wean on loan from heaven, thon yin," said Sally.

"He can be a quare gype when he's showing aff," said Maisie, "and he's aye showing aff."

"Sit down and tell me all about this healer, Mrs Gourley," directed Margaret. "Was it Oul Cathleen Carmichael?"

"It was," said Maisie, intrigued that Mrs Andrews should know someone like Cathleen.

"Och don't look so surprised," she smiled with teeth as rounded as the pearls that adorned her neck. "Do you think I lived in a folly like this my whole life? Mrs Gourley, I'm from the Glynn myself and I've known Cathleen all my days. She's a harmless critter. I went to her when I was carrying Alfie. I didn't tell Alfred Senior anything about it, mind, for he would have thought it the height of nonsense. She prescribed a potion of mint and nettle for the sickness, and I shared it with Winifred, for she was expecting Sally around the same time. I overheard you mention the name Mary Beth before I came in. She worked here."

"Mary Beth worked here?" repeated Sally, looking around.

"Yes, she left the big house over at Drumalis and she came here. She cared for my mother-in-law when she was dying."

"How long did she stay for?" asked Sally.

"Several years. When I first met my in-laws, Dalriada welcomed all the great folk of Ulster. There was a to-do about Gaelic culture, you see, and Mary Beth was a novelty because she spoke Gaelic. Later on, the Unionists brought in guns to defend the union and when the Great War came, it all went quiet at Dalriada."

"And what about Mary Beth?" said Sally.

"She had some kind of dalliance with my husband's brother, Martin. Then there was a row between Martin and his father after Old Mrs Andrews died. Mary Beth was sacked. I tell you, there was something odd about the whole thing for anyone with half a wit could see that she was too educated to have been a maid, and I mean no injury to you when I say those words, Maisie."

"Don't mind me, Mrs Andrews," said Maisie, her back rising unexpectedly as she recalled Mrs Frilly Drawers telling her mother she would do well to be anything more than a maid. "I know you mean no harm."

"She conversed in Irish with the great scholars of the time. Had an encyclopaedic mind for literature and poetry. She claimed to have been the last resident of a ghost village in the Glens."

"Was the problem that she was a maid?" asked Sally.

"All I know is that Mary Beth left Dalriada and got more attention than ever posing as a pauper down by the shore," said Margaret. "Martin went to Liverpool and it seems he didn't have the wit to get on in the world and get over it all. Meanwhile, my husband kept a candle burning for his brother and went back and forward to England every couple of years to find him, sober him up and give him more money to wash down."

Maisie's mind drifted back to Margaret's observation about maids, and it occurred to her that the boy who had sat beside her in the second row at school was now a medical consultant in a hospital in Belfast. Perhaps she too could have been successful, given half a chance. "When did you move into Dalriada, Mrs Andrews?" she asked, curious as to how Margaret had acquired the ways of a lady.

"George gave us Dalriada in 1914, after his wife died."

"A generous gift," said Maisie, looking up and around the stucco ceiling, wondering if she should have tried a little harder to escape the Waterloo Road.

"A gift that takes more than it gives, at times, and I'm sure Sally would agree with me. It's not the kind of house that runs well when there are fuel rations. The winter of 1915 was harsh and I had a baby to keep warm. With a husband at sea and half the men in the area at war, I moved out, back to the farmhouse at the Glynn."

"I didn't know that," said Sally.

"Yes, Sally, dear. I stayed with my mother right up until the end of the war. Your mother and father kept an eye on the house for us. Most of the men were in France, but your father couldn't go because of his diabetes. There was no insulin in those days."

"But Da was a drunk and in and out of jail."

"Your da was a great man and he was no drunk. He was told to drink alcohol to help with the diabetes. An old wives tale indeed!"

"And so they stayed here?" Sally looked around the room.

"Yes, they stayed here, but knowing your mother, she would have stayed in the kitchen. Now, this beauty in my arms, what's her name?"

"Clara," replied Maisie, thinking back to the little girl with ringlets on the mantelpiece.

"It's a beautiful name."

"It's from one of the Andrews' cousins," said Sally.

"Which cousin?" asked Margaret.

"The little girl on the mantelpiece."

Maisie walked to the mantelpiece and reached for the photograph.

Margaret shook her head. "I don't recognise her. Did Alfie say she was a relation?"

"I maybe got confused," said Sally. "It's been there since we married. I thought it was yours. Check the back for me, Maisie."

Maisie unclipped the back of the frame. "There's a *Belfast News-Letter* stamp and it says 'Clara, 1919.'"

"I don't know where it came from," said Margaret. "I don't know any little girls called Clara, except this one, and I'll have to hand her back to you if I'm to get the messages. Maisie, can you stay with Sally for a while?"

"Of course," said Maisie.

Margaret stopped by the mantelpiece as she was leaving and looked at the frame once again. "Clara," she said, holding it to her chest. "I can't think of any Clara."

***

Maisie came downstairs after feeding Clara to find the fire roaring, the wireless blaring and the windows steamed up with the breath of the entire Higgins family, all assembled to read the monthly letters from Roy and Ken.

"It's as thrang as three in a bed an a fourth yin wantin in," said Grace, who was seated comfortably in Maisie's chair by the fire. Hughie, Daniel and young Lily were on their hunkers by the fire, Iris and Rose in the chair by the window and Lily on the settee between Rab and Leonard. Jamesina, meanwhile, stood at the door between the kitchen and the scullery with a haughty look of importance on her face. The heads of Maisie's father and uncles were discernible at the scullery table behind her.

As ever, there was no seat for Maisie. It mattered little that she still suffered pains from giving birth for not a single person in the room got up to offer her a seat.

"Are we all quite comfortable?" she grumbled as she hop-scotched over a line of feet towards the scullery, dodging the apples dangling from the electric light cable. It was clear that no one noted the irony in her voice when they collectively replied, "Oh aye."

Maisie's father pulled out a metal stool from the table in the scullery and handed it to her. "Thanks, Da," she said, lifting it and making her way back through the kitchen.

"Mind your feet now," she said cheerfully to Rab, whose giant legs took up half the room. "Looking cosy, ladies!" she added as she passed the nieces who sat like two china dolls on the most comfortable chair in the house, her attempt at irony lost for a second time when they smiled sweetly back at her.

Maisie was still the sister without children in matters of sitting up at night, and God forbid that anyone should sully Lily's spacious parlour house with their feet. "It's too cowl in that hoose o mine," was the excuse that Lily often proffered in order to avoid having to clean up any mess.

"Dear Ma," trumpeted Jamesina's voice, and they all came to attention against the noise of the wireless.

"Wait, wait," said Grace. "Turn thon wireless aff, wud ye?"

Hughie jumped up and turned the knob.

Jamesina began to speak again, "We were in Blackpool when they told us we were to pack."

"Howl on!" hollered Grace, red in the face. "Tell us who it's from. Is it Roy or Ken?"

Jamesina turned the page and looked up over her spectacles. "Roy," she confirmed with an unrestrained smile, and Maisie was transported back to the scullery of her childhood at number fifteen. There was Jamesina carrying around her little brothers like real-life dolls, one on each hip, her smile easy — not yet overshadowed by a lofty scowl. And there was Grace cooking and cleaning and delighting in the timidity of Roy and Ken, who did not fuss or scraich or scream or challenge her way of getting on in the world.

Grace had a look saved for sons and sweet apple pie, and Maisie smiled when dimples formed at the corner of her mother's lips.

Jamesina continued to read the letter.

"We were surprised when word came through that we were to go to the north of Germany."

"The north of Germany!" puffed Grace, holding her chest. "What in the name o goodness!"

"Ma!" complained Lily, "would ye keep quate and let Jamesina read the letter?"

"The airlift," said Rab, with the same child-like look of self-assurance that Hughie often had when proclaiming his intelligence. "Ken and Roy must be delivering food tae West Berlin."

"Terrible thing," interjected Leonard. "They say the weans is starvin."

Jamesina peered sternly over her glasses at her audience. "Would someone else like to read, or will I continue?"

"Och, keep your knickers on!" said Grace.

"We didn't know what was happening," continued Jamesina.

"Did they keep them tigether?" interrupted Grace, her hands ever tighter on her chest. "Did they keep our Ken and Roy tigether? For they were the best weans when they were tigether."

"Ma!" guldered Maisie and Lily together in a chorus.

"Well!" she protested. "It's no right to set twins apart. My boys niver asked for mair than the company o yin another. And I'll tell ye more forbye, there was niver a jealous streak between them. What yin was gien was aye offered tae his brother."

"A plane goes up every three minutes from our base," resumed Jamesina. "The roar of it is something else altogether. I'm on the coal planes and have been back and forward to Berlin every other day for three months. When I first went, I couldn't believe my eyes for the buildings were in tatters, the children half starved. They begged us for food, but all we had for them was the chocolate from our rations."

"God bliss us and keep us for isn't thon a sin, even if they are German!" exclaimed Lily. "And these girls o mine willnae eat a bite between them. Didn't I tell ye the weans is starvin in Germany!" she said, looking at Lily, the thinnest of the three.

"The city is in ruins," read Jamesina, loudly, drowning out Lily's voice. "And it looks no better though I've been fifty times. The children call out 'Tommy Tommy Shokolade' when they see us coming."

Jamesina paused and added, "that's German for chocolate."

"I cannae read and even I knew thon!" said Grace.

"I towl ye I can teach ye tae read," said Hughie.

"Son, I dinnae need tae read for my granweans are the best educated weans in Ulster. Dinnae you worry your heed aboot me!"

Jamesina coughed and took up the letter again. "Our Ken saw a child being held at gunpoint by the Russians up against a wire fence, and I think it touched him for the child could have been no older than our Hughie."

A deafening silence tore through the room as every head turned towards Hughie. Maisie glanced at her father in the scullery and saw red blotches appear around his eyes.

Jamesina waved the page and kept reading. "Ken's a driver for the Padre. He's away with him this weekend to Norway to deliver him to a weekend retreat with the other priests. They've become very good friends. The padre prayed for him before he went to Berlin and his prayers were answered for Ken came back in one piece."

"Well thank the Good Lord for the Catholic priest and his prayers," said Grace. "Imagine the weans starvin! Why?"

"Ma, do you no listen to the wireless at all?" asked Jamesina. "Your sons are on active duty, so it would serve you well to pay some attention to the news. The Soviets won't let food and fuel pass through to West Berlin by land. Ken and Roy are helping deliver the coal in the RAF airlift."

"God's truth, I'm no daft altogether, but last time I got a letter was in July and so I took it that Ken and Roy were still in England," hollered Grace, injured by her daughter's rebuke. "I hae been heart-broke these last three months waiting on word from them. What kept them writing to me?"

"There's little recreation time," read Jamesina. "Ken's enjoying the driving all the same, but Germany is like a country under a shroud. It'll be good to get back to England. I've told Ken to write to his mother, so you'll get a letter from him soon. Say to Hughie that his letter was the best I've ever read and that I'll take him to the pictures next time I'm home. Congratulations to Maisie and Leonard on the birth of the baby. With love, your son, Roy."

"With love, your son, Roy," repeated Grace with a coy smile. "Is that it? Is there nuthin aboot courtin? Our Roy aye tells a yarn about the courtin!"

"No, Ma," said Lily, forlornly, "Shure, didn't he say Germany is under a shroud? He'll no be chasin weeman if they're all depressed." "Did ye ever imagine we would be sending claiths and toys to the Jerries?" she continued with a dreamy look about her. "It's funny the way things work out. One minute we're at war with them, the next we're saving them."

"That's what the good Lord teaches us to do," said Jamesina in an authoritative tone.

"Well thank the Lord in the heaven's above that my boys are safe," said Grace, her hands clasped in prayer. "And may He bliss us and keep us for I had a father and two uncles at the Boer, three brothers at the Somme and now my only sons are in Germany." "Good Lord," she went on, her eyes raised to the ceiling, "if ye could get them bloody Soviets the hell oot o this, I wud be most thankful, for I've had it up tae here with foreign wars, I tell ye, Lord, up tae here!" Her clasped hands were now above her head.

"Amen to that," said Leonard.

A long silence followed before the attention of the room was drawn to a to a faint conversation on the floor.

"Why do we hae Hallowe'en?" whispered Lily to Hughie, who was lying on the floor hugging the bucket of apples.

Hughie sat up straight and replied with an air of brotherly importance. "It's for when your sowl leaves this world and flits til the next. Like when we flitted til number fifty-one. Wer bodies went up the road, but wer sowls stayed doon this end. Isn't thon the way it was, Aunt Maisie?"

"That's right, son," said Maisie, laughing, and trying to keep the conversation out of earshot from Jamesina, but it was too late for her sister was glaring across at them with a scowl.

"What nonsense are you teaching the weans?" she said.

"It's a holy night," Maisie persisted, aware that everyone was now listening. "I was towl it at school by the Reverend Greer."

"It's a Pagan tradition, young Hughie," explained Jamesina in clipped tones. "And you'll do well to remember that the Pagans hadn't heard about Jesus. Now, I've read the letter and I'll be on my way for it's a Sunday and a holy night indeed. I'll leave you all to the devil's party."

"Sorry, Aunt Jamesina," rhymed Hughie as she went to get her coat.

"Now girls," she directed. "Let's get along with you. I don't want my best Girl Guides to learn that drinking on a Sunday night is the way to the Lord. We'll go to number fifteen, light a good fire and have a game of Snakes and Ladders. You can sleep in the return room on top of Uncle Bertie's lambeg drum and that way I know you're home safe."

Iris and Rose got up and followed their aunt with their heads down.

"Here, take a bottle o Braid brown lemonade and some boiled sweets with ye," said Maisie, noting that young Lily was hiding behind Hughie and Daniel.

"I already did," smiled Jamesina, holding out the bag and unwrapping a sugary smile. "I was sweet for a bit o Butter Scotch masel."

The front door closed and a breathless whisper came from Hughie's lips. "Will I go and get the beer bottles for ye now, Leonard, for the wee shillin?" He winked at his uncle.

"Son, ye may get your da one too," said Rab.

"And what aboot me?" said Lily. "I'll take a wee sherry."

"A wee deoch an' doris for me," declared Grace, and Maisie awaited the inevitable eruption of song.

Hughie took to the floor. Placing his thumbs in the sides of his woollen vest, he got into position on the hearth.

Thon wean's been here before.

Maisie recalled what Sally Andrews had said, and Hughie must have met Harry Lauder in that life because he adopted the Scottish singer's comical swagger as all eyes turned towards him.

"Just a wee deoch an' doris, just a wee drop, that's all,'" he sang, "Just a wee deoch an' doris afore ye gang awa.' He hiccuped and stepped forward to lift his mother's hand. "There's a wee wifie waitin' in a wee but an ben. If ye can say, 'It's a braw, bricht moonlicht nicht,' Then yer a'richt, ye ken."

Lily was as giddy as a schoolgirl as her son sang, and Maisie caught a look of pride in Rab's bright eyes.

The song ended in a wall of applause, but Maisie's attention was drawn to the scullery and to an indistinct noise. Amongst all the commotion, she could hear it. *Tap Tap Tap.*

The milk in her breasts dropped painfully, Clara's cries came from upstairs and voices amplified in Maisie's head like a child-like rhyme. *Tippa Rippa Rapper on your shoulder.*

She called for Lily to comfort Clara and walked into the scullery, only to see her own reflection in the glass of the win-

135

dow pane. Her father was on his feet and at the door, and Maisie looked back into the kitchen towards Daniel. Goosebumps clawed at her back — a reminder of what had passed before, a premonition of what was to come.

"Hello, I'm looking for Mrs Gourley," came the voice of a woman when Maisie's father unlatched the door." A Holy Eve, thought Maisie, when souls move from one world to the next. She stood and faced her master.

***

"I towl ye she'd come back," whispered Grace, who had followed Maisie into the scullery.

At first there had been silence from the kitchen as eager ears awaited the revelation of the woman's identity, but Hughie had earned his shilling, and while drink flowed in the kitchen, Maisie knew that none of them would be too concerned about the goings on in the scullery.

"I see ye've him well fed," came the voice that Maisie had hoped never to hear again.

She had always been conscious that Esther might return. She had looked for her on street corners, jumped when yellow light intruded quiet nights by the fire and shivered each time she detected a sparrow-like frame with charcoal eyes at the market.

"I didnae come back for Daniel," stated Esther, whose face was clean of paint. "He belangs here. I came tae say goodbye to him for I'm bound for Canada."

"Where's Mr McCallum?" asked Maisie.

"Mr McCallum left lang ago."

"Where hae ye been all this time?"

"Here and there. And in the boarding hoose in Ayr. Word came that my aunt Libby had passed and so I came hame for the funeral."

She spoke slowly, the bluster and theatrics of her last visit stripped away. "I never towl Libby aboot marrying Wilbur," she began, "and I never towl her aboot Daniel." She expelled a dry smile and looked up. "The crafty beggar had worked up a small fortune selling kippers from thon oul cart." She paused and reached into her bag. "I've got this for Daniel." She passed a brown envelope across the table.

"We'll no take your money," said Maisie, pushing it back. She felt her mother's knee nudge her under the table.

"It's no charity, Mrs Gourley. It's no much, but it'll buy him school books and uniforms, and maybe an instrument forbye. Daniel was aye a smart wean. He could go on til secondary after elementary, or technical even. There's a new exam for the weans that are smart. Time won't be long in passin til he's eleven."

Daniel appeared at the door. He sat down beside his mother and spoke. "Do what she says, Aunt Maisie. Take it."

Esther smiled and placed her hand gently on Daniel's. "I picked the best ma I could find for ye, Daniel, and that's all ye need tae know aboot me." She stood up. "Ye can be heart-sure that naebody will take you away from the Waterloo Road. You're safe here." She kissed his head and turned to Maisie. "I'll go back oot the way I came, if it's alright."

Daniel surprised Maisie a second time. "It's a braw, bricht moonlicht nicht," he said, repeating the words in Hughie's song. "Can ye say it?"

"It's a braw, bricht moonlicht nicht," said Esther, softly.

"You'll be all right then, ye know. That's what the song says. 'Then yer a'richt, ye ken.'"

Esther kissed Daniel a second time and smiled a smile so dark it could have eclipsed the brightest moonlight.

Maisie stood up. "Daniel, you're missing the deuking for apples. Away ye go. Ma, take more sherry in to Lily." She walked to the back door and opened it and watched Esther's skinny shoulders cross the yard. In the narrow alleyway at the backs of the Waterloo Road, she could barely see her face. There was only a voice and the glint of two eyes.

"My aunt got in touch wi me three years ago, before I came here. She writ tae tell me something, Mrs Gourley, and I've asked masel if Tam found out and drowned himself in France knowing it."

"What are you trying to say?" asked Maisie, the premonition of bad news blackening her mind.

"I need ye tae know that I lied to you, and that I'm here now wi the truth."

"Go on," said Maisie.

"Wilbur McCallum never laid a finger on Daniel. And Tam Gourley never did the things I said he did. Them lies was better than the truth."

"And how can I trust you?"

"When ye look in the wean's eyes, does he seem troubled?"

"No," said Maisie. Daniel was a shy boy, but not troubled.

"For as long as ye live, Mrs Gourley, ye may never worry aboot Daniel for he had good beginnings and he was never harmed."

"What is the truth?" asked Maisie. Something else was brewing and it was hard to believe it was worse than the first lies that had been uttered.

"I was fifteen and Tam was twenty and he didnae force me."

Esther's voice was flat and easy as though she had been rehearsing the speech every day since her last visit.

"Leonard Senior, he found oot the night before Tam went away, and he said not a thing til the next day. I think the oul bugger was fond o me in his ain way for I could see he was shakin when he asked me to leave. He gien me money for travel and towl me never to come back. I had enough that I didnae have to work at first. And then it was hard to keep the wean and tae work forbye."

"Why did he tell ye tae leave?"

"I took it tae be for what I done. For carrying on under his roof wi his son."

Maisie stared into the alleyway where blackness moved, silence swayed and two watery eyes rippled like buoys. She was looking at Esther, standing in a small corner of darkness, and she was reminded of a boy stowed away in the dickey seat of a car.

"I foun oot who my ma was in that letter from my aunt Libby, the one she sent the day before I murried Wilbur."

There was a pause. Maisie folded her arms around her chest, rocking her own body in a steady rhythm as Esther spoke. Her breasts were inflamed. Her head was splitting.

"Jane Gourley left her husband for another man."

Jane Gourley. Leonard rarely spoke of his dead mother.

"Your Leonard was nine and Tam was four," Esther went on. "After a year, she went back til her husband. Her aunt Libby reared the bastard wean."

Maisie was silent in her thoughts. *Leonard Senior.* So long the villain. Here he was emerging as a cuckolded man.

"Oul Leonard knew aboot it," said Esther. "Oul Leonard knew aboot me. He gien Libby money tae rear me and then he sent for me when his wife died."

Maisie looked up to the sky. The air was tranquil. The sky was black. No theatre of noise and voices. No 'Sea Shanty' playing by the open fire.

The song of incest was silence.

"I'm a half-sister to your Leonard," said Esther in a whisper. "A half-sister to Tam. And I cannae forgive masel, Mrs Gourley. I can't forgive masel.

Her feet turned on the gravel and Maisie listened to the crunch of each step until she was gone. She looked up. Tears trickled freely down her cheeks and she cast another secret into the night.

She looked into the black sky and prayed for forgiveness. She had been blessed with Daniel while Esther had served a sentence for Tam Gourley's crime. Or was it Jane Gourley's crime? Or Old Leonard Gourley's crime? The lines in all the badness were blurred and it was not clear if anyone knew they were committing a crime at all. Perhaps there were no crimes — only sin and want and sorrow.

Maisie thought back to Ellen, with her glowing face and cherry lips. She would have to go to Glenoe once again. She needed to see if there was a Silver Cross perambulator sitting outside Horseshoe Cottage. She needed to make sure that the past would not repeat itself.

She stepped back from the alleyway and closed the door to the bitter lies and bitter truths unearthed on a still and hallowed night.

The Reflection
November 1948

"We can tell him to come back another time," said Alfie. "Lie down if you're tired."

"I can lie down later," said Sally. "I sleep sitting up most of the time anyway. I want to meet your uncle."

Sally was intrigued by this uncle of Alfie's, who had disappeared after the Musical festival more than six months ago, only to be found in a public house in Carnlough when she was in hospital. She was curious about the member of the family who was not quite as polished as the Dalriada silver.

Alfie opened the front door and Sally was surprised to find a well-groomed version of the man who had climbed up the gym bars of the Gardenmore Hall. His hair was as soft as candy floss, a gold pocket watch glistening against a smart Scotch tweed waistcoat and matching jacket.

"I thought I might get myself something new," he said by way of greeting as he removed his hat. "My nephew shamed me when he came to see me in his smart attire."

"And you look well for it too," replied Alfie, who had been helping his uncle back to sobriety. "Martin, this is my wife, Sarah."

"A pleasure to meet you, Mrs Andrews," said Martin, bowing theatrically and lifting her right hand to his lips. "Every bit as beautiful as Alfie said you would be."

"Call me Sally. And welcome back to Dalriada!"

Martin's eyes roved around the entrance hall, up beyond the portrait of his father, Old Captain Andrews, towards the electric candelabra.

"Would you like to look around, Mr Andrews?" offered Sally, assuming he would wish to be acquainted once again with his childhood home.

"No, no," he said too quickly. "No, dear. I'll see it some other time. It's been thirty-odd years. I can wait a while longer."

She directed him into the parlour, where the fire was high, but he stalled by the door. "I would prefer, that's if you don't mind...would it be alright to go to the kitchen?" She laughed and held out a hand to lead him to the room where the fire was all but dead. He sat down beside it and turned his ear to it, as though to hear its receding whispers.

"How long have you been away?" she enquired as Alfie poured the tea.

"I got work in Liverpool at the dawn of The Great War, and I never found a good time to come back. Or, should I say I was having too good a time to come back? I'm sure I was long gone before you were born."

"I was born in 1915," said Sally. "I mind the end of the war — the soldiers coming home and the thunder of their feet. I thought there was an earthquake."

"But you couldn't have," said Alfie. "You were only three or four."

"Nothing," stated Martin, "is more perfect than memories of early childhood." He paused to clear his throat. "Memories are the blessings of a solitary soul. I should know. If you're long enough alone, you'll know memories from the womb."

Yellow light blazed across the window and the sound of an engine saved Sally and Alfie from responding to Martin's observation.

"Who could it be at this time of night?" said Alfie. "I'm not working."

Sally knew instinctively who it was. The only people in possession of a motor who ever came to Dalriada were Alfie's parents. Martin too seemed to understand for Sally saw him shift uneasily in his seat.

The front door bell rang, despite the car being parked adjacent to the scullery. Alfie answered the door and Sally could hear her mother-in-law. "Is Sally well enough for a visit? We were passing on our way back from Belfast."

"Yes," said Alfie. "Come on through."

Alfie hadn't forewarned his parents of Martin's presence, and it only took four strides across the hall to the back kitchen for the captain to appear by the door.

"I should go," said Martin, standing up. "You have visitors."

"Sit down," said Alfie. "You're my guest. The past is settled."

"And the prodigal son has returned," said Captain Andrews, folding his hands in a mock blessing. "So long as you don't dart out the door to the nearest saloon, brother, we'll all get along just fine." He squeezed Sally's hand on the way to the settee.

"You've finally made the acquaintance of my daughter-in-law," he remarked to his brother once he was seated. "Did she tell you she's a great hand at the music, just like her father — Jimmy Ramsey."

"There's a name from the past," smiled Martin. "The Ramsey brothers used to play here."

"Our father was quite the entertainer," explained Captain Andrews, and Sally became conscious that she was the conduit in a conversation between two brothers who had not yet made eye contact.

"There was always a Ramsey with an instrument at hand," the captain went on, directing his words towards Sally. "Dalriada hosted all the greats. Francis Joseph Bigger, Benmore, Alice Milligan. They all came at the time of the first feis in the Glens when I was still a scholar at Larne Grammar School. When was it, 1904?"

"That's right," said Martin, he too addressing Sally. "When we needed music, we only had to walk around the corner to find it. There was scarcely a fella who couldn't play the melodeon or the fiddle."

"Ah, but the Ramseys were of a different ilk," said Captain Andrews, who had never been so expressive towards Sally when her life had held more longevity. "They say four of them survived the Boer War and returned home from Africa without so much as sea sickness. Sally, can you still play?"

Sally wasn't accustomed to the captain's face. She had only ever conversed with him when he was hidden behind a newspaper. She stopped for a moment to compare him with Alfie, who had the strength of the Andrews' build and the softness of the Andrews' expression. Only the faithful brown eyes of his mother separated Alfie from the Andrews brothers.

Captain Andrews walked to Sally's old cabinet and took her father's flute from the drawer. "I don't know if I'm able," she said. "I was never much good and it's been a long while."

"Father, please," intervened Alfie. "Sally isn't well enough for this. Put the flute away."

"Wait," she called. "I'm no in ma grave yit."

They laughed.

"Reach it over. I'll think of something."

She ran her hands across the cold instrument and placed it to her lips. A familiar touch — an uncertain kiss.

She stood up and positioned her fingers on the keys, her father's eyes clear to her, blue eyes that had roamed heavenwards when he played. Her body swayed and her fingers found their own way through the notes of 'The Raggle Taggle Gypsy' as the small audience stamped its feet in time to the music. Her mind drifted back to the first musical festival she had attended; the tune had coursed through her body as her mother clapped. Then, she was with her father at a party celebrating her engagement, the same tune rising and falling from his lips in their kitchen on the Waterloo Road. And now she was in the present with two brothers looking over their own invisible flutes, getting to know each other one furtive glance at a time.

The tune came to an end and she cried on the inside knowing that it might be the last.

Martin clapped heartily, placed his hand on his chest and got up to sing. He paused and raised up his brother by the elbow. Sally sat back and watched two siblings with parallel pasts communicate safely in song, their haunting, rasping voices heralding 'Glory Glory Hallelujah,' and as sleep fell heavily on her eyelids, their voices marched on to that solitary place where infant memories are reawakened from their slumber.

***

Sally awoke to an easy silence, broken by a confession.

"The child may have been mine."

It could have been Captain Andrews for the two men had become indistinguishable by voice, but Sally understood that it was Martin. She continued to rest her eyes and listen.

"God bliss us and keep us," said Margaret, soberly.

"I knew she was with child when I left to go to England," he continued, "and it was sadly prophetic for she believed that she could live freely. She was like the gypsy in the song, with no liking for the riches that marriage might bring. I pleaded with her to marry me, but Mary Beth had no interest in the goose feather beds of Dalriada."

Sally opened her eyes.

Martin was smiling. "Alfie explained what became of Mary Beth to me today."

"Alfie?" said Margaret, turning to her son. "What do you know?"

"I found something." He stood up and walked away.

Eyes stormed about the room.

"I still don't understand," said Captain Andrews, turning to his brother. "What caused a row between you and Father that meant you couldn't see fit to come home for thirty-odd years?"

"I barely recall the details myself," confessed Martin, who looked at his hands as he spoke. "I was the disobedient son who was recklessly spending his father's money on joy making. He was in mourning and ill-humoured and we couldn't be in the same room without pitiful words piercing the air."

Alfie had returned with something in his hand, but the captain was eager to speak. "You had a brother," he choked.

Thirty-four years of separation lingered on like an unwanted guest.

Alfie held out a photograph and Sally had to blink long and hard to adjust her focus to the features within the familiar oval frame.

"This is Clara," said Alfie. "The stamp on the back of the photograph is from the *Belfast News-Letter*, so someone ordered the print from the newspaper. Clara is Mary Beth's child."

"I did think the child was vaguely familiar," said Margaret. "Perhaps she looks like her mother. Let me take a closer look."

"How do you know it's Mary Beth's child?" asked Sally, her senses awakened. The girl in the photograph had so long been her secret friend that it was disconcerting for everyone else to share an interest in her too.

"I found this newspaper clipping in the attic. It's from 20 March 1919." Alfie lifted the cutting from an envelope as he spoke. He read aloud, '*Miss Rosa Devlin held her annual assembly at the Ulster Hall last night when a large audience had the pleasure of wit-*

nessing a clever and picturesque display by pupils attending her classes. The youngest performer, Miss Clara Clarke, stole the limelight with a sprightly jig whilst her mother, Mary Beth, performed an old Irish step dance called 'The Blackbird' and accompanied Dance Master Peter O'Reilly in a two-hand reel.'"

"Mary Beth taught me a two-hand reel," smiled Martin, who was animated by the story. "And so it seems I may have a daughter called Clara."

Sally looked at Martin. Something about the response felt as incomplete as his physical transformation from tramp to gentleman.

Captain Andrews coughed and reddened. "I recall Mr O'Reilly at one of father's Gaelic parties a few years before the war," he said. "He had won some Ulster title or other for his dancing. Mary Beth was working at Drumalis House over the road at the time. When I think back on it, I'm sure that she had arranged for him to come. She was a friend of his."

"Maybe she was from Belfast," said Margaret, nervously. "I was never convinced of the way she spoke Gaelic. Her folk ways were a little too refined. She didn't have the country ways of the Glens about her."

"And nor do you my dear!" smiled Captain Andrews. "And you're from the Glynn."

"And nor do I pretend to," she retorted.

"Mary Beth liked to have an audience," Margaret went on, "and that newspaper article tells me that she didn't change. Performing in the Ulster Hall and dancing 'The Blackbird' in her thirties!"

"Och, now, Margaret," laughed Martin. "I can still do the rising step with these bandy legs and I'm near sixty."

"There's more to the story," interjected Alfie. "And we've Maisie's nephew, wee Hughie, to thank. He spent a whole afternoon last week sorting through the postcards that Grandpa sent to Grandmother when he was at sea. He noticed that most of them were addressed to my grandmother, but some were addressed to a woman who worked here."

"Mary Beth?" asked Sally, inexplicably hopeful.

"No," said Alfie. "The mysterious Mary Beth went to Canada. Look here. It's a postcard of the Rideau Canal. It was once under R in my collection, but wee Hughie was quite adamant that it should be under C in his reformed system. You will want to read the message on this one. It's from May 1919."

"*Dear Winifred,*" read Sally as her hand drifted up to her cheek. *"I'm settled with Clara now and we have a comfortable home, much warmer than the house on the Antrim Road in Belfast. The canal was frozen over last month like it is in this postcard, but we are inside and we are safe and warm. I will soon have enough piano scholars to live comfortably. I have enclosed a cutting from the newspaper I bought on 'The Olympic.' The night in the Ulster hall was one of great sadness and happiness to me and I feel blessed that you were able to come. Yours Sincerely, Mary Elizabeth.*"

Sally looked up at her husband. She couldn't imagine her mother going as far as Belfast for a night's entertainment. "I didn't know they were such great friends," she said.

"They worked together for a couple of years when my mother was dying," offered Captain Andrews. "It was natural for them to be friends."

"There are nine of these postcards," said Alfie. "I wonder if Winifred left them here by accident."

Sally doubted it. Her mother owned too little to be careless. Photographs were stored up high in a tin box and were only to be touched around the edges.

She looked at each postcard in turn. "This one's from 1925," she said. "It says that Clara did her first recital and she's pleased to hear the results of the Larne Musical Festival." She paused. "That was the year I came home with four cups."

"I remember it well," said Margaret with a look of pride. "I adjudicated the recorder section."

"Clara must be my age," said Sally, and it was strange to think that she had based all her dreams of a child on a picture of an adult who was thirty-three years old. And the more she looked at the photograph, the more she understood that it had been with her all along. "Our mothers would have been expecting us at the same time."

"It would seem so," said Margaret. "I remember your mother when she was expecting. She had a difficult time of it."

"I must have met Clara on several occasions," said Sally. "Look at this one. It says, '*Thank you for the photograph of Sally. How she has grown! It seems a life-time since we trailed four short legs around Belfast on the day after Armistice.*'"

Sally sat back and closed her eyes again. She could see her mother's tin on top of the wardrobe. Her mother was placing it carefully onto the bed. She was pointing to the picture of Clara. The one in the frame.

She could see the missing piece of the newspaper. She could see Mary Beth in a two-hand hold with the dance master in the kilt, her long hair flowing down her back, a cape hanging from her shoulder, her features clearer than those of the woman selling dulse.

Mary Beth was the woman who appeared in daylight dreams in a garden far from home, a garden beyond the chimney stacks and back-to-backs of Larne.

It was Mary Beth from the postcard. Mary Beth who had once sold dulse by the shore. She lived in a red-bricked house at the foot of a mountain. Sally was walking away from it. She was walking down the Antrim Road in Belfast. She was walking under the archway of a station with columns and pediments and robust stone.

Stone faces walking. Long dresses tripping. A bright tunnel. Garlands of flowers falling from wrought iron arms. A myriad of times on different clock faces. Five O'clock. Time to go home. "Say goodbye to Clara." "Say goodbye to Mary Beth."

The hiss of steam. The scent of burning. The thunder of feet on the platform. Soldiers in uniform. An earthquake through her body. A glance out the window. A wave to Mary Beth.

A glance out the window. A wave to her own reflection.

Sally stood up and looked through the window of the kitchen of Dalriada. She held out her hand and touched the woman in the glass.

A sister. A twin sister. She went back to her seat and looked at the photograph in the oval frame. "I have to lie down," she said, and she glanced casually at the four of them in turn, smiling politely.

"Don't run after me, Alfie," she said. "See to your family and don't mind me."

She walked slowly into the hall, the low rumble of their well wishes following her until the door closed behind her. She clung to the bannister and took each step, one at a time.

She was weak from her illness, but strengthened in her mind. She would not fall. She did not need Alfie or Captain Andrews or Martin Andrews to hold her up.

She had a sister and the only explanation was that Mary Beth had given birth to twins. The only explanation was that Mary Beth had given one of her twins to Winifred.

Winifred had been expecting. Margaret had seen her. Sally paused by the window of her bedroom and looked beyond her own reflection to the sea. It wasn't inconceivable for a woman to lose a child.

Then there was Martin and his talk of being a father, the dubious pride on his face as he made public his claim to Mary Beth's body.

He couldn't see what Sally could see. He couldn't see that his claim meant he was also the father of Sally. He couldn't see that his claim meant an illicit marriage between Sally and Alfie. Cousins.

But they weren't cousins because Martin Andrews was deluded. He was not the father of Mary Beth's child. The girl in the window of the train was not his image. The girl in Sally's reflection was not his image.

She closed her eyes and immersed herself in memories. She saw a skipping rope turn. One end was tied to a tree. One end was held by Winifred. And at the centre was Mary Beth, teaching two little girls to skip in time to her rhyme. *On a Mountain Stands a Lady.* And then they were all in line, and Sally was tapping Clara's shoulder. *In and out go dusty bluebells...I'll be your master.*

***

Sally was alone. She could no longer suffer Alfie's concern, rely on his pleading brown eyes to bring her home. She needed to feel the sea.

The water appeared opaque from a distance, but she could remember its transparent stillness. She could remember how clear it was when the waves came to a shivering halt and the sky rested its fierce breath. She wanted to step into it, to consume its healing salts, but Alfie had begged her to stay on land.

Her sanity, at least, was no longer in question. The visions and dreams were put down to cancer encroaching on the mind. Sally had once played along with Alfie's game of doctor and patient, half-looking for a cure, but now she understood the truth.

Winifred and James Ramsey were her parents in every way but one. She didn't carry their blood, but she carried their love and she would give it as freely as they had done until she drew her last breath.

Her mother had lifted the old tin box from the top of the wardrobe, showing Sally the pictures of Clara and Mary Beth. Sally felt sure she had planned to tell her the truth one day, but didn't understand why her father had not explained all of it once her mother was gone.

She heard a stick trail along a stone wall. It was a man. She could tell from the crunch of his confident stride. He turned the corner from Bankheads Loanen. "Good morning," said Sally.

"Good morning," he replied.

She moved over to the left, sensing the summer seat was his destination. "There's room for two," she said, indicating the space beside her. She stared at the long profile. He was familiar in the appointment of his commanding physique.

"You mustn't know me," he said, removing his felt hat and sitting down.

"I don't think I do," she replied.

"You wouldn't invite me to sit with you if you knew me." His accent was a blend of Ulster and English.

"You remind me of someone from years ago," she said.

"They say I'm the mirror image of my uncle, Reverend Greer. He died some fifteen years ago, but you may have met him as a child."

"Of course I met him as a child," enthused Sally. "Yes, I can see the resemblance. He came to the Parochial School for assembly." She remembered and laughed. "Your uncle holds a special place in my family history. There's a story."

"Involving temperance?"

"Yes."

"I see. Was someone's name read aloud in church?"

"My father's, although it was before my time. How did you know?"

"My uncle had half the town converted to his cause. I was reminded of it when they carried me out of the saloons. I made a mockery of the temperance conversions the first time I fell. There was no shortage of folk to remind me of the fact."

"How many times did you fall?" asked Sally, enlivened by the exchange.

His voice was soft. "I'm an old man, my dear. I've fallen many times, but only ever for the drink twice. More of a drowning, you might say."

"My father was a drinker," said Sally. "A swimmer. I wonder sometimes if the drink gave him more years than it took away."

"The drink was like lead for me. My uncle said it was a family trait three generations back — hence the temperance." He was silent for a moment before turning his head towards Sally. She wished she could see his features clearly. "Are you certain you don't know me?" he asked.

"I don't believe I do," she said light-heartedly. "Why?"

"I noticed you bathing a few times," he replied. "Alone. I was worried you'd drift away one day and I sat here until you came back to shore. On another occasion, you went in fully dressed."

"You saw that?"

"Yes, you wore a green coat and a red beret. You hung up the coat and the beret down there on the railing. I didn't think you were going to drown or anything, like the girl in today's newspaper. You made me smile."

She located the day in her mind. It was soon after losing her second baby. She didn't realise anyone was watching.

"Do you live around here?" she asked.

"I lived on Curran Road," he said. "I'm in Belfast now with a cousin. My only daughter went to Chicago with her husband a few years ago. My wife followed this year."

"Oh." she said, curious, yet unwilling to pry for any information he wasn't willing to impart of his own accord. She remembered the woman she had seen at the chapel in the powder blue dress. "Did your daughter marry a naval officer?" she asked, "on all Saint's day a few years ago?"

"Yes," he replied. "How did you know?"

"I saw the wedding and heard the groom was from Chicago."

"The saddest and the happiest day of my life," he said. "It was hard to see her go. And thanks be to God that she only ever saw me sober. You don't read the papers, do you?"

"I do sometimes. What was in the papers?"

"I could keep talking to you and you'd never know that you're in the presence of someone like me." He sat back. "I can be who I once was for today."

"What do you mean?" she asked.

"I did a bad thing. You can know the person I was or you can know the person I wish I had been."

"Could I know the person you are going to be?" asked Sally.

He nodded. "I don't have long left to be that person."

She looked at him. He was gaunt despite his strong build and she felt the spirit of something between them. "You're dying?" She knew the answer as she said the words.

"Yes," he said.

"We share something in common then." Silence followed. "Cancer," she added.

"We share two things in common," he replied. "Perhaps the cancer invited me to sit down beside you. I'm heart-sorry for you."

"If cancer were a person, what would it look like?"

"A soldier with no purpose," he stated flatly.

Sally forced her eyes to focus for long enough to see his tired face. And she realised that she would never wear that face. Know his lines. See the contours carved by a story in a newspaper.

"I will die with no lines," she said. "I'll never get to sin and to seek forgiveness or start a new chapter. I'll try to love God. I won't betray my husband. I won't steal. I'll never take the Lord's name in vain, unless I speak in my mother's tongue. I'll keep the Sabbath holy. I will honour my father and mother for they are both in heaven and easily honoured. I won't kill for I've no taste for it. What else?"

"Bare false witness?"

"What is that? Lying?" Sally reflected for a moment. "I don't think I have anything to lie about. I will miss the decadent decade of secrets. What else is there?"

"Coveting your neighbour's house?"

"I've been guilty of that in the past," laughed Sally. "But not anymore. Besides, it's hardly a worthy sin when you envy a kitchen house over a castle. What have I left out?"

He looked her straight in the eye. "Thou shalt have no other gods before me...Thou shalt not bow down thyself to them, nor serve them: for I the Lord thy God am a jealous God, visiting the iniquity of the fathers upon the children unto the third and fourth generation of them that hate me."

The verse rolled from his tongue in a rhyme.

"Your uncle taught you well," she smiled, and she remembered the words she had once spoken to Jamesina. She said them again. "All things become new." Her face was to the sea. He too was looking straight ahead, down past the path and to a far out place in the distance.

"All things become new," he said. "Even when I did wrong, I always had my faith. Always asked for forgiveness."

"Your uncle was a good preacher."

"Yes, he was. He broke the mould. He wasn't from a wealthy family. He was a soldier from a long line of soldiers. A self-made man. You may also have met my cousin from Belfast, Miss Filly."

"Miss Filly," whispered Sally. "Yes, I did. What became of Miss Filly?"

"Too sad a story for today," he said. "She didn't have enough hope to make it in this life."

Sally understood and felt a solemn sadness for the teacher.

"Your bathing in the sea reminded me of someone I once knew," said Sally's companion. He lifted his hand to his face. "The first line on my face."

"Which commandment did you break?"

"I fell in love."

"With someone else's wife?"

"No," he smiled. "But someone else was in love with her."

"Why didn't you fight for her, like a soldier?"

"A soldier knows his place. Besides, she deserved more than to be a military wife."

"What happened?"

"I served in France and then stayed on in England after. I thought I belonged there for my father and his family were English, but the land of my mother never left me. I came back. I was curious. I was drinking heavily. And then I waited a long time to be put on trial."

"You were put on trial?"

"I did a bad thing. And I fell for the drink again last year when a ghost of the past came to haunt me, and thanks be to God he did for I needed to be punished. But you said you didn't want to know that man."

"I like this man sitting beside me in a quiet corner between life and death," stated Sally.

The wrongs of the man's past were as irrelevant to her as a pharmaceutical store with a thousand cures. Knowing his crime wouldn't make anything better.

"I'm allowed to know you though, am't I?" he said. "Past, present and future."

"I suppose you are," smiled Sally. "What can I tell you? I was a good child, but aren't all children good?"

"Yes."

"I won lots of prizes for music, sat in the front row at school, lost my mother too young, went to technical college, married a doctor who paid for the green coat and the red beret, lost two babies and here I am on the cusp of a new life with diminishing vision and a constant yearning for kippers and ginger ale. What if I had lived to see the lines on my face?"

"Are you yet thirty?"

"Yes. Thirty-three."

"I had seen two wars by thirty-three and had the stomach for it. I'm proud of the soldier I was. Not fond of the man I became."

"You were a good soldier?"

"Yes and a good soldier is made up of many good men."

"Just as a good daughter is made up of many good women," she said, thinking back to all those who had mothered her.

"I had a comrade called John," he went on. "He was my compass when I was lost and I had the strength to carry him when he was shot down. They say I saved him. They don't know that he saved me."

Sally thought about Mary Beth. She knew Mary Beth when she was a young child. She travelled on the train to see her until she was four. She saw pictures of her when the tin box was brought down from the top of the wardrobe. Yet, she had forgotten all of it. At least, she had not understood the significance of it. Perhaps Mary Beth had been her compass when all the good people of the Waterloo Road had carried her, and it pained her to know that she would not live long enough to find Mary Beth and Clara and to know them all over again. If only there was a way to know them all over again.

"I couldn't tune into the civilian way of life," said Sally's companion.

"Wrong radio frequency?" she replied, wondering if there was some way she could tune into the world in which Mary Beth and Clara lived.

"Wrong radio frequency." His voice smiled. "I came back here in my early forties. 1926. I walked, trailing my stick along every old stone wall until there were no more old stone walls. And then I resolved to drink myself to death."

"The temperance preacher's nephew!" she gasped.

"I lost weeks of my life," he said.

"I heard recently that you can remember your own infancy if you're alone long enough."

"I've been alone on many occasions and I've remembered my own infancy, but I don't remember what happened to me when I drank. This cancer, it's like an extra part of me that will lead me back to my master. The drink, it's a lost part of me that lent me to the devil. Anyway, I don't know if I was saved by God or if He too put me on trial, but I found a wife."

Sally didn't know what to make of the last line.

"I love my wife," he said, providing the answer. "Now. Too late. She was young. No lines. I didn't carry her. She wasn't my compass. She wasn't the woman who filled my dreams in the fields of France in the Great War. And she had reason to hate me even as we lived together peacefully. The hatred simmered beneath the surface and the one day it exploded. She said I had another daughter."

"How did she know?"

"She said my two daughters were born around the same time."

"And what will you do about your daughter?" asked Sally, thinking about her own father, the blood father — the one who had wronged Mary Beth in 1914.

"Pray for both of my daughters and for my wife. I can't do anything else in this life."

"I see." Sally's eyes weakened. "I told my husband I'd walk home," she said, "but I don't think I can. My vision comes and goes."

"I'm still strong enough to carry a soldier," he offered, standing.

"I can walk," she said, but if you could be my eyes, I'd be glad."

She stood up and found the crook of his arm. They walked in silence, the green lawns of the town parks coming in and out of focus, the crunch of dead leaves familiar on the path.

"I live at Dalriada," she explained.

She felt his elbow tighten on her hand.

"The Andrews family?" he said.

"I married into the Andrews family."

"I see," he said quietly. "What's your name?"

"Sally."

"And you?"

"Nathanial."

"Nathanial, the soldier," she said softly. "That's what you'll be in the next life. You'll be a soldier when you meet your daughters again. You won't be the man in the paper."

They walked slowly through the park, Nathanial holding her steadfast and strong in the secret space they shared between life and death. But Sally was soon reminded that death was not a straight line. A searing pain tugged at her temples. She could see the outline of the gatepost of the town park. She stopped and held onto it with both arms to support her trembling body. She felt herself fall. And then she was weightless.

Nathanial had lifted her into his arms, and she remembered Kenneth Higgins lifting her and carrying her next door when her father was drunk. She remembered the wind slicing her legs through her nightgown.

"Why wait until the next life," said Nathanial, "when I have one more chance to be a soldier?"

Sally's cheek fell against his neck. He rang the doorbell of Dalriada and stood back.

"Mrs Andrews," he said.

He must have known her. Recognised her from the social features in the newspaper, perhaps.

"Thank you," said Margaret. She called for her son.

Sally could hear Alfie's steps on the stairs and then his arms were wrapped around her. Her weight was shared by a healer and a soldier as they carried her to the settee by the bay window.

"Thank you," she said to Nathanial. She caught the quick beauty of his eyes as he lowered her across the settee. "Will you get home alright?"

"The next train to York Street Station leaves in half an hour," he replied, "Time enough to get to the station."

"I'll drive you there in the motorcar," said Alfie.

"No, I'd prefer to walk," said Nathanial. "But thank you, all the same."

"York Street Station," murmured Sally, her mind drifting as Alfie walked towards the window. "I remember the soldiers coming home. It was like an earthquake."

Margaret was crossing the room to get a blanket and Alfie was pulling down the blind behind her.

"York Street Station. First line." he whispered, pointing to a line on his face. "A place for long goodbyes."

He stood up and walked towards the door.

Sally felt mournful for the conversation that was about to end. "Take care of yourself, Nathanial," she said.

Nathanial turned at the threshold of the door and raised his hat.

"Don't forget your stick," said Sally. "I'll keep an ear out for it on the other side of the wall."

He laughed in a voice that was not accustomed to laughing. "You make death a promise and not a curse," he whispered. "I'll watch out for you in the turquoise seas above. Goodbye and God bless you, Sally. You've given an old man hope."

***

Sally awoke at eight in the evening with a start. She had been dreaming of Nathanial. He was in his soldier's uniform and she was seated beside him looking over the sea whilst rocking a banjo case. She called Alfie's name, but there was no reply.

She half-skipped down the stairs. Her limbs were sturdy. Her eyes were strong enough to read. She opened the banjo case and laid out her father's manuscripts on the floor. Hughie had been playing with the banjo a few weeks before. He must have spotted the postcards from Mary Beth to Winifred and moved them to the postcard collection in the attic.

She fingered through her childhood photographs and some paper documents. And then she realised that there was not a single photograph of her mother. One day soon, Winifred Ramsey would exist only in name.

There were no more postcards, but her hands fell upon a brown envelope. She carefully opened it and saw the words, "Dear Sally." She looked up to the heavens. "God bless you, Hughie," she said.

26th May 1940

Dear Sally,

My time has come and I want you to know that I am grateful for the years I have had, and hopeful that you will rejoice in my passing.

As you read the following words, I pray that you will think of yourself as the daughter of James and Winifred Ramsey. Weep only with the change of seasons for I believe that God placed you at our hearth and that God gave your mother the milk to feed you.

Our Winifred did not bring you into the world, dear Sally, but let that not be cause to make you heart-sad or heart-sorry, for she was your mother in all ways but one. I write this letter to you knowing that you are strong of heart and spirited of mind, and I pray you will understand. It may bring relief to your own soul, for I am sure that you have always known that something set you apart from us.

The winter that you were born was cold and harsh, but we were happy in our own way and we counted our blessings as we took care of the Dalriada for Captain Andrews and his wife. When our baby was born sleeping, your mother cried herself to a peace so deep that I thought she would never awake and be like herself again.

Your mother was alone in the kitchen at the back of Dalriada the night that you came. She heard some noise and found you swaddled in a shawl in the bathtub in the yard. When I got home she pleaded with me not to take you away. She said she would pray every day of her life for the lie. When I heard her sing an old song to you as she nursed you to sleep, I was torn. The lawful thing to do was to deliver you into the hands of the Board of Guardians, but the right thing to do was to allow you to stay with us.

Mary Beth Clarke was the name of the woman who gave life to you, but weeks passed by before it was known to us for certain. She had been raised in a hamlet near to Glenarm that is now abandoned of all its people. She received her education as a maid in big houses where she was quick to learn. I know that you have much of her in you.

When Mary Beth fell on hard times and had no home to shelter her, your mother sent her clean blankets and food and helped her. They were both expecting at the same time. Your mother offered to hide Mary Beth in Dalriada, but she wanted to stay where she was at the shore.

Martin Andrews was fond of Mary Beth. She had been teaching him Gaelic and they had spent many hours together. When he found out she was courting a soldier, he wielded the hand of his class. He made trouble for Mary Beth, staging theatrics that led to her sacking from Dalriada.

Word spread through every saloon in town that Mary Beth had been seen birthing two infants, and a legend was born that is still alive to this day. I am sure you will have heard tell of the mermaid whose second baby swam away into the sea. It was a convenient legend for me and your mother.

Mary Beth's plight was reported in the newspaper. They said she was in the workhouse with a baby. We did not know what to think, for it did not occur to us at that time that there were two babies. Little Clara was lodged with a dance master and his wife in Belfast. Mary Beth had chosen us to be your loving parents.

Your mother left Dalriada as a maid, but kept scrubbing laundry to pay for train tickets to Belfast. She took you to meet Mary Beth and Clara on the first Saturday of each month, but when the war darkened and influenza came to test us all, the visits became further apart. Your mother took you to Belfast only one time in 1919, and that was to say goodbye, for Mary Beth and Clara were bound for a new life in Canada.

I want you to know that Mary Beth held you on her knee. She taught you skipping rhymes and songs and took you by the hand and walked you *around the streets of our great city. She and your mother became close friends, separated not by an ocean, but only by death. I wrote to Mary Beth after your mother passed away, but the letter was returned to me. The address was unknown. I have tried several times to find Mary Beth, but to no avail.*

May it comfort you to know that you shared a place in the womb with your sister more than it saddens you to know that you were parted. And I pray that you can forgive us all the path that led to your separation.

I enclose among my music scores some postcards that went between your mother and Mary Beth. I leave it in God's hands to decide when you should know the truth.

Yours Affectionately

Your father,
James Robert Ramsey.

***

Sally picked up the photograph of Clara and all her father's documents and ran to the front door, collecting her coat from the hall as she moved.

She slowed to a speedy walk as the energy subsided in her limbs, but still, she felt strong. *Strong of heart and spirited of mind.* She smiled.

She tapped the door of number thirty-three and called out, "Maisie! Are you there?" before opening the door.

"Dear dear, what's the matter?" said Grace, who was seated on the armchair by the fire.

"What's wrong?" followed the voice of Jamesina from the scullery. "Is it one of the weans?"

"No, just me!" said Sally.

Maisie and Lily followed Jamesina out of the scullery with tea and a tray of buttered wheaten bread.

"Och, come in," said Maisie. "Take a seat."

"Ye leuk like ye just seen a ghost," said Grace.

"I don't know about seeing ghosts, but I just read a letter from one," said Sally, sitting on the chair by the window. She didn't know where to start. "Remember you said you'd met old Martin Andrews."

"Oh aye," said Grace, winking. "He's no ghost."

"He told us the other night that he was the man who had wronged Mary Beth Clarke," explained Sally.

"He said as much to us forbye," said Maisie.

"Grace," said Sally, "how did you know that Mary Beth had a baby?"

"It was in the papers," said Grace. "The whole town knew. She was in the workhouse and the Reverend Greer helped her find a place for herself in Belfast."

"And the baby?" enquired Sally.

"The wean went tae a family in Belfast," said Grace. "I don't know who. What makes ye think on it?"

"The old legend has some truth in it. There were two babies." She looked around the room. She could trust all of them. "But don't tell a soul."

She had their attention.

"She had twins," she said. "Mary Beth had twins, but she didn't throw one into the water."

"Twins!" exclaimed Grace. "What in the name o—"

"She put one child into the care of someone before she got to the workhouse. Grace, you said you'd seen my ma when she was expecting?"

"That's right, dear."

"And who was her midwife?"

"I dinnae know."

"And did you see her right up til the birth?"

Grace looked into the fire. "No dear. I went tae stay wi my ma for my confinement wi Maisie. Twas a rough winter."

"Martin Andrews is a liar," said Sally.

"Everybody knows thon," nodded Grace. "He gien his da terrible trouble."

"Mary Beth wasn't in love with Martin Andrews." Sally had no evidence to support what she was saying, but she needed them to believe it, even as it dawned on her that she was talking about Alfie's new-found uncle. She hadn't told Alfie any of this. *The decadent decade of secrets.* She smiled thinking back to what she had said to Nathanial.

"Martin made the whole thing up," she said. "Mary Beth was seeing a soldier, and if I don't sound like a mad woman already, I think I met the same soldier a few days ago. Mind the day I collapsed?"

"What on earth has Mary Beth Clarke to do with you?" said Maisie.

"Everything," said Sally. "Everything," she stated. "Winifred Ramsey did not give birth to me. She lost her own baby." Sally looked around the room to four identical expressions of astonishment.

"What in the name of—" said Grace. "I can barely hear masel think," she added, her eyes welling up from staring so intently at Sally. "Boyso. I feel like I've just seen a ghost."

"Mary Beth might still be alive," said Maisie.

"She's alive alright," said Grace, "God's honest truth, I never seen it my whole life til nu. Mary Beth was a plain girl and no like ye in leuks, Sally, dear. But I tell ye somethin for nuthin, she had an air aboot her — a sort o distant air — and I swear tae God I can see it in ye nu. Mary Beth is right in front o me."

"Mary Beth might well be alive in this room," laughed Sally, "but I have a feeling that she isn't on this earth today. You think I'm mad already so I may as well say that I think she's been by my side."

Four blank faces greeted her remark. She held her hands out. "In spirit."

"Lord Almighty," said Grace.

"You have a secret sister," said Lily, who was on the edge of the settee, Sally detected a look of envy. Perhaps every girl dreamed of having a secret sister.

"Yes," said Sally, "I have a sister. And I've been staring at a photograph of her most of my life. Her name is Clara."

"Clara frae the wee brass frame?" said Maisie. "The name o my wean."

Sally laughed. "Yes, Clara from the frame, and if you had looked very closely at that picture of a four year-old girl, you would have seen another four year-old girl you knew well."

"I didnae notice it when you showed me it," said Maisie. "Twins too."

"I didnae know me own self," said Sally.

She took the photograph out of the envelope and handed it to Grace, who squinted and concurred. "Shure, it could be any wean wi curled locks. But tell me this dear, how did ye find oot aboot all of this?"

"Look, here," she said, handing the letter over. "My father wrote a letter to me before he died. He explained everything, but he didn't predict that I'd stop playing music. He left the letter inside the folder with his music manuscripts. Jamesina, read it til your ma there. Maisie, come on into the scullery a minute. Ye'll hae plenty o time to see it later."

The moment the door was closed, Maisie exclaimed, "Good Lord, Sally. First the one thing and now the other. I cannae take it all in!"

"I can. I've been taking it in my whole life. I never did tell you this, Maisie, but Alfie had been sending me to his doctor friend. They thought I was insane. And maybe it was worth it for the hypnosis sessions brought it out of me in the end. Then I met Martin Andrews and I wasn't convinced by him. And I was right. It was his fault that Mary Beth Clarke ended up homeless! A woman doesn't end up living at the shore unless she's trying to prove a point to someone about something. I've always believed that all things are made new, but I wonder now if some memories are handed down to us."

"What do you mean?"

"I'm not sure. Could we know some things naturally — the music we play, the way we dance or draw or sing? I feel things sometimes. I imagine things that turn out to be true."

"Like Cathleen Carmichael," said Maisie.

"Who?"

"The healer. She gave you the potion."

Sally remembered what Maisie had said about the meeting with Cathleen. "She said Mary Beth was looking for a cure."

"Och dear, it could hae been a cure for any ail," said Maisie. "Living oot in the cowl like thon! Shure, any lesser woman would hae caught her death. But tell me, how did ye end up with Winifred and Jimmy Ramsey? "

"Mary Beth left me at Dalriada. I swear I've seen it all in dreams, Maisie."

"And this soldier? Who was he?"

"I don't know his name."

Sally wasn't entirely sure why she lied. It felt right to keep it to herself.

"Will ye try tae find out for sure — aboot the solider?" asked Maisie.

Sally could have easily tracked down the Greer family by doing a tour of the Anglican churches in Belfast. The Reverend Greer had a son who was a minister. There was also a Greer who worked at the Regal picture house in Larne as an usher.

"No. I know all I want to know about him," she said. "And my heart is glad." Whatever sins Nathanial had committed, Sally didn't need to know.

"What about the sister?" asked Maisie, eagerly. "What about Clara?"

"That's what I wanted to ask you. Maisie, I'm full of life, but it won't stay like this for long. My da said he couldn't track down

Mary Beth, but I know that she lived in Smiths Falls in Canada. I want you to keep my personal things in case Clara ever comes to look for me. An envelope. Some photos and things. Not much."

"What about Alfie?"

"I don't want to tell Alfie. I don't want Alfie to live his life with a ghost, looking out for me beyond the grave. I want him to marry and have children — to get on with his life. I dinnae want you to live with a ghost either, but I doubt ye'll hae the time wi thon yins clockin in your kitchen every night o the week!"

"I'm quare an gled ye noticed," laughed Maisie, "for they've my heed turned!" She laid her hand on Sally's. "If Clara's a sister o yours, Sally, then she's a sister o mine. I'll find her. One way or t'other, she'll know you."

Part Two

The Devil's Churn
June 2009

Len embraced the movement of the water. He rested the weight of his body and his heavy rucksack against the railing, inhaling the wind to quell the sea sickness that had engulfed him in the belly of the ship. As the grey sea swelled and the low hills of Scotland faded, he imagined his father — a four year-old boy — leaving his birthplace behind.

He watched three seagulls flurry above the boat, their primitive legs dangling gracelessly. A flash of red occupied the left periphery of his vision. He turned. A girl in a raincoat was looking out to sea, her dimples folding tightly around her lips as she acknowledged him. He looked away, deterred momentarily by the force of her presence, but found himself smiling idiotically into the tide. If his senses were correct, the girl beside him was smiling too.

He faced her, the weight of her beauty pulling his sea legs a notch closer to the deck. Underneath layers of waterproof garments and a tangle of untidy hair, stood a strong silhouette.

"You're not from around here, are you?" he said.

"No, I'm not from around here," she replied, mirroring his accent.

"Ain't that a thing!" he exclaimed, echoing his father again, the man whose dialect was that of Ulster, but whose expressions mimicked the movie scripts of his youth. This was the first girl he had spoken to on his journey, and his disappointment that she was neither a Scottish lass nor an Irish colleen was diminished by the familiarity of home.

He held out his hand as her dark eyes inspected him. "Len Gibson," he said. "Off to seek out the Irish ancestors?"

"How did you guess!" she said, a smile raising the dimples ever higher in her bunched up cheeks. "I'm Kim Craig."

"Where's your family from?"

"County Antrim, but what with direct flights going into Glasgow, I find myself here on a ferry with Len Gibson from Toronto."

"Toronto? How did you guess?"

"You've got a giant maple leaf on your rucksack. And I take it you're musical."

"You can tell that from a maple leaf?"

"No, I can tell that from the box by your feet. What's in it?"

"Bagpipes. I'm doing a solo in the Ulster Hall. My aunt is organising a charity gig."

"I'm impressed!" she exclaimed.

"Do you play?" he asked.

"No. My claim is being mediocre in all aspects of life — except making sure children are safe in the water. I'm afraid I didn't inherit my family's talents and don't play anything at all."

She was not mediocre to the eye, but Len thought better of saying as much. He craned his head backwards. She turned to reveal her own rucksack. "Impossible to tell," he said. "You're either a well experienced traveller or a woman of no fixed abode."

"I borrowed the rucksack and the only badge that matters is this." She pointed to a small maple leaf on the strap. "I'm from

Smiths Falls, Eastern Ontario, where a woman from Ulster went almost one hundred years ago in search of her fortune."

"And what did she find?"

"A frozen canal and some seriously cold Canadian weather."

"Speaking of seriously cold weather, if you haven't been to the UK or Ireland before, there's an important cultural reference that needs to be explained."

"Uh-huh?"

"You're wearing too many layers."

Kim laughed.

"They'll know you're Canadian even if you haven't made it obvious on your rucksack."

"The girls, my acquaintance Len, can be as half-clad as they please. I won't be parting with my Gore-Tex jacket, fleece liner or thermals, for that matter."

"I think I'm more of a friend than an acquaintance now that I know the fabric of your undergarments," he teased. "And this," he added, holding out his arms to the gathering clouds, "is summer time in Ireland or Scotland, or whichever land claims this strip of water."

"Just my luck to meet a Canadian," she smiled. "This trip sure ain't going to plan."

"It got a whole lot better in my mind," replied Len, unashamedly. "Are you doing Europe?"

"No, I'm not doing Europe. What does a person do when doing Europe?"

"Paris, Barcelona, Rome, Berlin, Amsterdam."

"Well, while you're doing Europe, I'll be exploring County Antrim and my past."

"Let's sit," said Len, who was relieved by the encounter and buoyed by the flirtation. "It's seems we're both Irish, and County Antrimers at that. "Tell me, where will you be staying?"

"I'm staying here," she said, removing a crumpled map from her pocket. "The Dalriada Hostel in Larne."

Len scrutinised the map and pointed to the road running down the back of the hostel.

"I'm staying there," he explained, indicating the Waterloo Road. "We'll be neighbours."

"Well, I dunno about you," she said, a country timbre infusing the inflection of her words, "but this travelling ain't all it's cracked up to be. After two days without a bed, I can't wait to get to that youth hostel."

***

Dalriada was a hospice for cancer sufferers and Len felt the wrench of Kim's disappointment as he gathered up her rucksack and morale from the front door. The receptionist made a quick call to a nearby hostel, but it had no vacancies; he knew that Kim was travelling on a tight budget, and not one that facilitated a hotel.

"Dinnae worry," he said, placing a reassuring hand on her shoulder.

"Dinnae worry," laughed Kim. "Is that one of your dad's sayings?"

"Och aye. I'm warming up for the next leg of the journey. Listen, I've only known you for a short time, but I've been thinking about something since you stole the water on the boat— "

"I didn't steal the water! Water is free!"

"It was hot water from a coffee machine in a restaurant on a ship. I think there's an unwritten rule that you need to pay for it."

"Because it's hot?" she exclaimed.

"Yes, because it's hot."

"Well, you can go around Europe paying four bucks for hot water mixed with ground coffee beans if you wish, but a good Smiths Falls girl always has a flask and ready supply of dried, instant coffee."

"You're a woman after Granny Gourley's heart. I was going to ask you — that's if it's not too forward — would you like to stay with me and my granny for tonight? Most of her family lives in Canada, so she's used to catering to travelling Canadians."

Kim was sitting on the wall of the steps and appeared to be contemplating the facade of the building more than Len's proposal. He followed her eyes towards the turret with its three satellite dishes pointing to space.

"How far do we have to go?" asked Kim, running her hand along the stone wall of the steps.

"A short walk."

"And won't your granny be nervous about taking in a stranger?"

"You have a way of becoming a friend very quickly. Besides, she enjoys company, what with her children living so far away. My aunt Clara is in Belfast and my dad is in Canada."

Kim looked back at the building again, her eyes deep with sadness.

"Don't look so glum!" he said, elbowing her to reawaken her spirits as they began to walk through the front garden. "Granny Gourley makes a mean pot o broth."

"Hey, I'm happy to take you up on your offer. A shower and some hot food would be good, but I kinda wanted to see the inside of Dalriada. My great grandmother had a connection with it. "Look here," she said, showing him a postcard. "This was among her things. Not the usual happy image of Ireland."

Len looked at the postcard. There were ladies in fancy hats on the hill to the left, and, in the foreground, a wild looking woman leaning on a wall covered in seaweed.

Kim explained. "On the back it says, 'Memories of Dalriada, Larne.' There's no other message or address on it."

"It looks like the promenade," said Len. "If you walk across the road and through those gates, you'll be there in minutes. I can take you there in the morning. Why do you want to find it?"

"My grandmother, who, like your aunt, happens to be called Clara, died when I was fifteen. She had no father that we know of, but there's a bit of a family mystery. She told my mum about a sister in Ireland. The sister died apparently. We don't know the name or any details, but we think Clara's mum, Mary Beth, was from County Antrim."

"I'm sure you have above mediocre talents in matters of genealogy," said Len, "but can I ask if you checked the census?"

"I can confirm that I did," she smiled, "and there isn't a sign of her."

"I see."

"The residents of Dalriada in 1911 were George, Victoria, Martin and Alfred Andrews. I feel like I know them, I've stared at their names for so long. George was the head of the household and a captain. Martin and Alfred were both scholars. They were Church of Ireland people. No sign of my ancestor, Mary Elizabeth Clarke. She left no birth certificate, but she had to have one, otherwise she wouldn't have been able to travel. In Smiths Falls, word was that Clara's father had died in the Great War."

"So Mary Beth went to Canada alone with her daughter?"

"Yes. My grandmother was four at the time. There was something modern about Mary Beth — the way she raised Clara on her own. My mom's afraid I'll unearth something she doesn't want to know about in Ireland, but what's the worst I'll find? Some sad story about a woman getting pregnant and fending for herself?"

Len stopped and looked in front of him. "Number fifteen," he said.

"Your granny's house?"

"No, this is where she was raised. I don't know who owns it now."

"And the little plaque next door on the lamppost?"

"That little plaque is for wee Hughie. And Granny Gourley will tell you all about wee Hughie."

"Hughie McNeill, 1939-1949," read Kim, running her finger along the letters on the plaque. "I swear my heart just sank to the bottom of the ocean."

"Strong to the finish," smiled Len as he read the inscription. "Like Popeye the Sailor Man."

***

"Ye never seen anything like it in your puff, Clara. Skinny Malink Melodeon wouldnae hae a leuk in if ye seen the size o the boots he brought through the door. I had tae put them in the yard!" "Isn't that right, son?" exclaimed Maisie.

Len looked at Kim, who had been sleeping off her sea sickness while Len had been catching up with his granny. Kim's eyes followed Maisie's every move.

Maisie's slight weight moved from hip to hip as her torso, arms, legs and face all conversed with Clara on the other end of the wire. It was a one-woman-show that silenced Kim.

Len caught a memory of his childhood. "Are ye in or are ye oot?" Granny Gourley was hollering, and "Keep thon deur shut or the buns'll no rise!" And then he was in the present looking at Kim's reflection in the old Art Deco cabinet, her bronze cheeks gleaming in between a porcelain shoe and a crystal trinket, her long, dark hair let loose down her shoulders to dry.

"He's as like our Daniel!" Maisie went on, peering at them both through the mirror above the cabinet, her pink lips gleaming. "A Roman nose! And thon whispy hair. God love him for he's bound to go bald like his da."

Len's leg was tight against Kim's on the two-seater settee and he could feel laughter course through her knee.

"Och, she's a lovely girl," said Maisie, turning and winking theatrically in the direction of Kim. "Sez I tae our Leonard, she's a face like a goddess. They'd make a quare handsome couple, but who am I tae say?"

Kim's knee was now shaking as they both stared at a spirited fire with embarrassment.

"See ye soon, Clara. Night night, pet."

"You should get a cordless phone, Granny," said Len when the call to Clara ended.

Maisie wiped the receiver with a cloth. "Not-tat-tall," she said, punctuating the sounds like a whistle. "And sit up gabbing tae Canada all night long! Naw, I can end a yarn with Iris in seconds by sayin I hiddae sit doon."

"Good strategy!" said Len.

"Them mod-ren washing machines is the same, dear. Sez I til the wee girl next door, the twin tubs have served me well for forty years so there's no sense in changing them now. The young yins dinnae like tae empty the wet clothes in til the rinser, ye see! They dinnae like tae get their hands wet!"

Len smiled knowing that Kim was concentrating hard on every syllable uttered by his grandmother, whose face was radiant from the low summer fire.

"Maisie, would you sit down whilst I fetch you a refreshment?" offered Kim, and Len was sure she got up to escape the inferno between them.

"Thank you, dear," said Maisie, reaching over and squeezing Kim's hand. "I dinnae like til drink alone at my age, ye know, in case I fall doon the stairs. The sherry's in the corner cupboard o the scullery. I took my first drink when my ma died and I'll take the last when I'm a hundert."

"Why quit at one hundred, Granny? You could be here for another twenty years." He addressed Kim. "Granny's ninety-four and still walks up and down Larne Main Street every day."

"Walk? I think hirple is the word ye were leukin for, son. Granny Gourley hirples up and down Larne Main Street ivery day."

Kim stood up, rising up to imposing heights beside Maisie.

"There's beer in the fridge for Leonard," said Maisie, "And you take what ye like, dear. There's a wee bottle o gin the Canadians brought one time. And some tonic forbye."

"Kim saw the little plaque for uncle Hughie," said Len when they were settled by the fire with their drinks. He knew he was in safe territory and that any excuse to talk about Hughie would be gladly received.

"Och aye, our Hughie," sighed Maisie. "The street was black wi folk the day our Hughie was laid tae rest. Black wi folk and black wi umbrellas. It was a wet day." Her diminutive frame sank into the armchair by the fire. "Sez I tae masel, it was a powerful sight. A sky of black umbrellas with rain lashin that hard that I knew that wee Hughie was cryin in heaven for he wasnae meant til die — he was only playin on a swing."

Len glanced at Kim. If she hadn't been transfixed before, she was spellbound now, her eyes glimmering as the story unfolded. Len had heard it a hundred times from his father and Hughie's sisters in Canada, but he had never truly experienced grief for Hughie until he saw it in the eyes of the girl from Smiths Falls.

"The men went oot thon night," Maisie went on. "Every man and his son, some o them wi hatchets, others wi knives, and they went roon the Fectory cutting ropes off every last tyre swingin frae lampposts. And if there hid been blood pumping through them tyres, they're would hae been a bloodbath on the Waterloo Road."

Maisie sipped her sherry before her voice emerged evenly. "When we opened the windows, we could taste the scorchin rubber in the air."

Her words came more slowly as her voice lowered. "There wasnae the colour o fire in the night sky. No orange flames. Just black ones. Black flames and black smoke risin up frae the bonfire t'ward the moon. The black smoke dyed the moon."

Len's father had told him the very same story, that the smoke had travelled so fast and so high, they had sworn Dalriada itself was on fire.

"Tragic," said Kim. "Tragic that wee Hughie died so young."

"Tragedy's what ye see amang the livin," said Maisie with glassy, distant eyes. "For Hughie had a sowl that flitted from one world tae the next. What happened amang the livin was tragic."

Maisie told them about her sister Lily who had huddled by the fire night after night until her husband bought a television set and *Coronation Street* broke years of mourning.

"Wee Hughie," she smiled, pulling the words of his memory up and over her like a warm blanket. "'Och och a nee,'" she added. "That's what Lily used to say when she was dying, 'Och och a nee, take me to wee Hughie.'"

The fire was low, the coal reduced to small glowing jewels that mirrored the words of Maisie.

"Hughie's sisters all live in Canada now," interjected Len to keep the conversation going after a wistful lull.

"Och aye, they all went tae Canada in the end," said Maisie. "But life went on. The streets were filled wi weans playin and leuk ootside nu, on a warm summer's day, not a wean in sight."

Len could see the past glimmering in her eyes.

"Things were different then, love," she said, addressing Kim. "There were characters aboot the place, ye know? *Coronation Street* couldnae compete wi the goins on on the Waterloo Road. By Jove, there was an oul boy at the corner used tae make Daniel and Clara laugh. 'Ho, ho, ho,' he would go the weans passed him by, and they fell for it every time as the yeuchs and laughs poured out of them like rivers. Folk used tae pay til see the mechanical laughing clown in Barry's amusement park in Portrush, but we had the oul buddy at the corner that gien us laughter for free. I wonder nu if wee Hughie sent him wer way."

A raw and breathless noise came from Kim, whose voice cracked without a coherent word. "Sorry!" she exclaimed, "The kid's breaking my heart even though he's sending in a laughing clown. So sorry, Maisie! Can we blame the gin? One gin and I'm an emotional wreck."

Maisie spoke tenderly, "Och dear, it would take a cowl heart no tae fall for the memory o Hughie. I aye believed his spirit was aboot me. "Hello Hughie!" she said, toasting him. "Here's til you and the laughin clown o the Fectory!"

She laughed gently, her eyes misting over as the last jewel of coal turned to black.

***

Kim was a different soul walking the next morning. Len was taken aback by the transformation. She held his hand on the promenade as if she had been holding it for a lifetime, and he felt the spirit of something pass through them both, a simple chemical reaction that unsteadied him for a moment as he adjusted to the newness of Kim.

She pulled him back to the railing and looked up towards the Chaine Memorial Park. "Imagine living here on the rocks, wild and free," she said. "Wouldn't you love to do it for a day? To see what it was like?"

"Like the woman in the postcard?"

"Exactly like the woman in the postcard."

He looked down at the lean hand clutching his and took in the long, misshapen fingers.

"Man, you've got weird hands!" he said, as he ran his hand across the most crooked finger.

"You really are hopeless at romance, aren't you? Here I am flirting with you and you're assessing my fingers for flaws."

"This is flirting?" he smiled, lifting his hand to her cheek. "You're different today."

"No, I'm the same girl with the same crooked fingers as yesterday."

181

Her face remained bronze in colour, but her dimples chastened into a white fold.

"Last night, you were perfect, albeit a little morose. Today, you're charming, albeit imperfect."

"And which do you prefer?" she asked.

"Let's see. I wanted to kiss you on the boat despite the slightly green tinge off your face. I wanted to kiss you when you stole the water, despite your criminal ways. I wanted to kiss the disappointment clean off your face when you saw that Dalriada was not a youth hostel, and more than anything, I wanted to kiss you as you fell under the spell of Granny Gourley. And as I lay on the camp-bed beside you and listened to you snoring, I could have kissed you."

"I did not steal the water and I do not snore. As for spellbound, I was rendered speechless trying to learn Larne language. I will admit, though, I sure did fall for your granny."

Len kissed her. It was an easy kiss, a soft and long kiss. They stopped, and Len looked at her. "I wish to do that again," he said.

"You may do that as often as you care. But first of all, I'd like to walk somewhere with you. It's a place that Maisie mentioned this morning."

They walked along the promenade hand-in-hand, following a path up a hill towards the coastal road. Len stopped and turned and looked behind him to admire the Irish Round tower emerging from the shallow rocks, whilst Kim's attention was fixed on a row of three cottages at the end of the promenade.

"Man, if I had a million bucks," she gushed. "I'd buy that pretty little one on the right. Corran Cottage."

"The one that is so close to the water that it is likely to be consumed by coastal erosion in the next ten years?"

"Oh ye have so little faith," she said. "Thon wee house, as Maisie might say, will be there for a long time, and when I make my fortune, I'll come back to Ireland and buy it."

"Your fortune would not need to be great, and your purchase might prove to be a poor investment. My dad once told me that Larne is the cheapest place—"

Kim turned on her heel and cut him off mid-sentence. "Of all the unromantic sentiments I've ever heard! What's the use of an expensive location? What's the use of a whole group of people living together and not a single laughing clown among them?"

Len was stunned by the change of tone. He had been speaking mechanically and knew that his best tactic for the next mile was to say nothing at all.

They walked towards an arch hollowed out of a cliff that sidled out across the road and into the sea in a series of giant black rocks. "The Black Arch," he said after a long silence, recalling the name from the summer he had spent in Ireland as a boy. "My dad brought me here. Granda Gourley had flowers with him."

"Maisie mentioned this morning that there's a place beside it called the Devil's Churn," said Kim. "She told me the legend of the lonesome piper who rests there and how you can hear the echo of his lament if you sit on the steps and listen carefully."

Len knew Kim well enough after a day to understand that she supported and believed every superstition she was likely to find in Ireland. She was the most impressionable individual he had ever met, and he needed to be on his best behaviour lest her impressions of him dwindle any further.

"Here we go!" she said, gazing down into the slurping sea around a cave of basalt.

There was music, Len realised, a tune that ebbed and flowed and turned the tide. As he held onto the railing at the top of the steps, he was enlivened by the wide eyes of Kim and refreshed by the spray of water that spurted into the air as the sea glugged back and forth in its cave.

"Maisie said he was a wandering piper who lost his true love to the sea," said Kim. "His ghost now plays the same lament over and over. Come on. Up and over those rocks."

"No way," protested Len. "The sea is wild. It's dangerous. What if the tide comes in and we're stranded with no way back."

"It won't turn so fast. The minute we see a change, we come back."

She was gone. He found her moments later tucked into a secluded ridge facing the sea. The June sunshine was strong by Irish standards, but a swift turn in the wind could spell danger for them both. He crouched down on the rock. She turned towards him and a wild expression came at him so fast that he had no time to consume it. She stood up and raised her arms, and he employed every morsel of strength to hold her back when he understood what she was about to do.

"Stop," he warned.

"What's wrong?" she said, and looked at him with perilous eyes.

"You can't go in there. You can't see what lies beneath. You can't dive off this rock. Trust me. It's dangerous."

"I can swim like a fish!"

"You can't swim there. Believe me, Kim, you can't go into that water. We can go back to the promenade where there's more shelter. Please don't do it."

Her face was long as she stared into the sea.

"I think we should go back," he said reluctantly, cognisant that he was out of his depths against the force of the sea and the tornado of moods. "It's dangerous."

She led the way up the ridge and onto the plateau, her long, muscular legs striding easily across the rocks.

She was up the steps and on the footpath when he caught up with her. He gently took her hands in his. "I promise I'll find you somewhere else to swim," he said, placing one savage kiss on her morose lips. "Let's start again somewhere safer than the Devil's Churn."

Horseshoe Cottage

Maisie was radiant in the garden in her peach knitted top and flowery skirt. "Is it your first time in Ireland?" she asked.

"Sure is," said Kim, who was so drawn to Maisie that she decided to stay at home with her while Leonard went out for a run. It was the first time they had had the chance to speak properly, and Kim was curious to know if Maisie could provide any clues to help her find out more about her family. "It's my first time travelling outside Canada."

"There's two types o folk if ye ask me," said Maisie. "Them that stays at home and them that goes away."

"And those who go back and forth?"

"Them's jist homing pigeons, dear."

"My family went back and forth from one side of Canada to the other. My granny settled out west in Vancouver for a while, but she brought the entire family back to Smiths Falls in the 1960s."

"Smiths Falls," said Maisie.

"Yes, Smiths Falls. You've heard of Smiths Falls?"

"Oh I've heard of Smiths Fall, alright," said Maisie. Smiths Falls is the reason I live here alone."

"You've got family there?"

"No dear, my son, Daniel — well, I sent him tae Smiths Falls yince. I was leukin for a woman called Mary Beth Clarke. He didnae find her, but he was that smitten wi Toronto that he flitted there."

Kim froze. "You knew Mary Beth Clarke?"

"No, dear, but my ma did. It's a long story. I had a friend, Sally. She died. She found out that her mother was Mary Beth Clarke and that she had a sister, Clara. I promised I'd find her sister, but I never did."

"Clara was my grandmother!" exclaimed Kim. She knew Larne was a small place, but did not imagine for one moment that she would find such a link to her past at the first house she visited. "Clara is the one who moved out west and came back to Smiths Falls."

Maisie looked up and back to Kim. "God bliss and save us," she said holding her hand up to her chest.

"She passed away when I was fifteen — nearly ten years ago. She told me a story about a sister once. My mum said it was probably a whole load of nonsense. She said Granny had a vivid imagination."

Maisie took Kim's hand. "I never thought I'd see the day. After all these years. And Clara knew she had a sister?"

"Mary Beth died of a heart attack when Clara was only sixteen, but she always talked about the sister to Clara. Then, when Clara had her own children, she had vivid flashbacks."

"Flashbacks," smiled Maisie.

"I know. It sounds crazy. She was a little eccentric, I guess."

"Did she no try tae find her sister?" asked Maisie.

Kim could see that the old lady was concentrating hard, trying to take it all in. "The only thing she possessed of her childhood was a little photograph taken in Ireland," said Kim. "The name Sarah Ramsey was on the back. Is Sally a nickname for Sarah?"

"Aye, it is," said Maisie, shaking her head, tears glazing her eyes.

"Granny met a man from Belfast when she was living in Vancouver in the 1950s. He went to Larne on her behalf and found out that Sarah Ramsey was dead. At least, that's the story she told me. I can't help but wonder if it took this guy as long to establish that Sarah was dead as it has taken me to meet someone who knew her. I can't believe you knew Sally."

"Like a sister," said Maisie. "Like a sister, dear. God's truth, I cannae believe it."

A long silence followed. Kim had a million questions to ask about Sally and Mary Beth, but it seemed that they both needed time to take something in.

"I like it here," said Kim, surveying a long line of skinny back yards. "I like the shore and the wild ocean too. Mind you, I took Len to the Devil's Churn this morning and he didn't like it one bit."

Maisie looked into the distance. "Dear dear," she said, shaking her head. "Len's Granny Esther was found at the Devil's Churn. She drowned. It was daft o me no tae think on it."

"Does Len know that she was found there?"

"I doubt it. Daniel niver spoke o Esther."

"When did she die?"

"Och, t'was one funeral after t'other that winter. Esther was first and I'm terrible ashamed for she was deed a week before we know'd."

"That's so sad."

"A quate sort o sadness, love. When my nephew Hughie died after Christmas, sadness poured oot o the very heavens. And then there was Sally. Come on in oot o the cowl and I'll tell ye all aboot Sally."

***

"You don't look like you've broken a sweat!" said Kim when Len arrived back from his run.

"That's because I haven't been running," he replied with an idiotic grin. "I've been busy. Follow me."

Kim could see that Maisie was tired. She'd relived her entire childhood in the last hour and was beginning to appear more fragile. Kim noted the laboured gait as she got up to see what Len had in store.

He was beaming as he pointed to a silver Mercedes Saloon parked on the street. "How do you like that?" he said.

"I'm not one for motors, son," said Maisie, "but she's a beauty."

"What's this for?" asked Kim, clutching his elbow and resisting the urge to kiss away his silly grin. They had made such a big deal about not being a couple when they had arrived that it seemed like too much effort to explain to Maisie that romance may or may not have blossomed that morning.

"It's for our trip around Ireland. I calculated—"

"You calculated!" teased Kim, "Why doesn't that surprise me? Maisie, did you know that your grandson calculates every last detail of his life? He sat on the boat yesterday and tried to calculate how much money P&O would made from the freight. You and me, we're mere fractions."

"Well if I'm a quarter, you're a half, for I've never seen long legs like it in my puff!" said Maisie. "And what's this aboot a trip? Are ye leavin me already?"

Len explained that he had been planning to go around Ireland on his own, but had invited Kim along. There was no way Kim was going to leave Maisie now. She couldn't be apart from this place. She needed to stay and explore. Besides, she felt nervous about the travel arrangements. What if they disagreed and were stuck together for a week in youth hostels with no diplomatic way to escape each other's company?

Maisie looked at Kim and Len and then to the car, and as she turned her head, Kim could see that she had made her own calculation about the two of them.

"There's no point in hiding, for it's plain til see that there's romance in the air," she stated, her arms folded. "I seen it from the minute the pair o ye walked into my hoose. Oh if Sally could be here now."

"Sally?" said Len.

"You've a bit tae catch up on son, but Kim here is connected tae someone I loved dearly."

"That's great!" he said, placing one arm around Kim. "She kissed me down by the shore, Granny, and what's a man to do?"

"Young yins," sighed Maisie. "Ye've no idea"

"I got the car a couple of days early to take you on a few outings. So, tell me where you'd like to go?"

Maisie looked up and down the street. "I tell ye where I'd like tae go," she said. "I'd like to see my freen Maurice. He has something he wants to show me about an old lady I once knew from the Glynn. I need tae gie him a ring before we go."

***

"Howl on til your hat!" cried Maisie from the back seat as the car coughed up the steep hill.

"Go down a gear!" hollered Kim in exasperation. "You've never driven stick-shift, have you?"

"Kim," said Len calmly as he changed gear, "there have been times in the last two days when your voice has been music to my ears, but right now, I'd prefer it if you'd quit yackin and let me drive the car!"

Kim pressed her lips together tightly and turned to the back to look at Maisie, who was smirking like a naughty school girl.

"Son, ye hae yin slate aff and yin slidin," said Maisie. "Ye must hae got your temper frae your mother's side."

Kim noted the crooked line of cottages on the left side, tiny abodes in white limestone with bottle green paint around the outside of the windows. "How quaint!" she exclaimed, pointing to the old bikes leaning against the window sills.

"My God," said Len, as a sharp bend took them scaling up another vertical climb. "Howl on tight again!"

"It's like a helter-skelter," laughed Maisie, but ye'll need to slow down love and pull in there to the right hand-side.

"I can't pull in there!" exclaimed Len, who kept driving up and beyond the cottage to which Maisie was pointing. "There's nowhere to park!"

Kim thought it best not to speak until he had resolved the parking issue, which he did by turning dramatically into a private driveway, the indicators blaring as he made a u-turn on yet another blind bend. They were all silent when the car passed by its destination, rolled down the hill and finally came to a stop.

"These roads were made for donkeys," said Len. He turned to Maisie in the back. "Having fun?"

"Youse young yins," tutted Maisie, "I tell ye! I walked tae Glenoe in my Sunday court shoes one time, and ye cannae even make it in a motor."

Kim got out of the car first and was immediately struck by the sound of water falling and the colourful scent of vegetation. She helped Maisie out of the back of the car. She looked smaller and more frail out in the open, away from her kitchen house.

"This is the life!" exclaimed Maisie. She held out her arms and inhaled the mountain air.

"It sure is," smiled Leonard, a shaft of sunlight colouring his pale skin. "Where to, Granny?"

Maisie pointed up the steep hill.

"Will you be okay, walking?" said Kim, offering her arm to support her.

"We'll stop half way," said Maisie.

She climbed slowly. Kim felt Maisie's determination in her bony arms. She pulled over at a dry stone wall after a few minutes, took off her bag and patted the stone to indicate that Kim should sit.

"Now, my dear, I need tae tell ye a wee yarn."

"Go on!" said Kim.

"My husband did a bit of roving in his youth. And when he roved, he roved to great heights. Do ye get ma drift, dear?"

"Erm, not really," said Kim. "What kind of roving did he do?" She looked up to Len for help and he gave her a knowing smile.

"He had roving eyes, my dear," said Maisie.

"Ah! I see."

"He had a son. His name is Maurice. A great man and an engineer by trade."

"And you were all friends?"

"Not quite, dear, but his ma, Ellen, came tae Leonard one day and said she couldnae cope. She was terrible afflicted wi pains. The wean stayed a year wi us from he was three year oul. The oul granny wouldnae support the idea of an illegitimate wean, so Ellen hadnae any help. When Ellen was on her feet again, Leonard brought Maurice tae see us the odd Sunday."

"What a story!" said Kim. "Not many women would take in, well, you know—."

"I was no martyr, dear. I had no choice. The wean had naebody. God knows we'd little til werselves, but we'd enough tae feed a wean."

"And does Maurice know he's Leonard's son?" asked Len.

"Maurice has brains tae burn but he's no one for understanding the ways of the folk aboot him, so he doesnae know about Leonard bein his father despite inheriting his very face. He called him Uncle Leonard."

"How incredible!" exclaimed Kim.

"He'll be nervous when he first sees ye, so relax and he'll relax too. If he says it like it is, it's because that's how he sees the world."

"Sure, no problem," said Kim, pulling Maisie to her feet.

***

Maurice opened the door to Horseshoe Cottage. His smile rested easily in soft eyes that betrayed the innocence described by Maisie. "Och hello there, Maisie," he said. He clasped his wrist and stared at Len.

"This is our Daniel's son," said Maisie to Maurice. "You met him when he was a boy. He's called Leonard efter his granda."

Maurice nodded. "God bliss us and keep us, Maisie, for isn't the wean the mirror image of Daniel."

"Aye," said Maisie, winking towards Kim, who was baffled at how Maurice had never found out his true parentage. A man of great intellect, it was clear from the rows of books flanking each side of the hallway, and yet this lie thrived profusely right underneath his statuesque nose, its innocence contorting moral lines, its beauty compelling.

Maurice led them all to the scullery at the back of the cottage. Kim peered into the two rooms en route and saw that order reigned among a riot of flowers, patterns and textures.

"What's all this?" said Maisie as she rifled through a pile of typewritten journals on the table.

Maurice pointed to the box. "The folk historians are to do a talk on my ma's scribblings."

"These couple o tourists in our midst might enjoy her work," said Maisie.

"What's a Corran?" asked Len, reading the name of the journal.

"Sickle in Irish," said Maurice, who was preparing tea. "Part o Larne looks like a sickle from up in the hills."

"I see," said Len. "And your mother wrote stories."

"Aye, folklore and legends and the like. A great imagination, she had!"

Kim looked through each index studiously. "Here's one about faeries," she said, scanning the page. "According to Oul Bessie from Crooked Row, the waterfall is filled with faeries and healing waters."

"Did ye ever?" smiled Maisie. Kim noted a smile widening across her cheeks as she looked up.

"What's yours about?" said Kim to Len.

"The one I'm reading is by Ellen McDowell."

"Ellen was my mother,' said Maurice, who now joined them with four cups of tea.

Len spun the journal around. "This article is about an old healer called Cathleen Carmichael," he began. "It says she was born in 1857 and lived til the ripe old age of one hundred and one." He pointed to the middle of the text and read aloud.

"'When she was almost one hundred years old, Cathleen told me about a maid who came to her before the first war. The woman said she wanted a cure, but Cathleen became aware of the presence of two souls. She said it was the first time that she had ever felt the presence of any unborn child. She offered the woman some ginger to help her in the weeks ahead and then lay down for three days with fatigue, praying hard that there would be no healer with a better cure.'"

"My God!" said Kim, "I just got a shiver right down my spine!"

"Oul Cathleen," said Maisie, looking into the distance. "I met her yince. I didnae know Ellen knew her. Dear dear, leukin at these oul journals filled with characters frae the past, the only thing we can be sure of is that we should all number wer days."

"And people should write things down," interjected Kim, who wished her great grandmother, Mary Beth, had written something down.

"You'd only write something down if you wanted someone to read it," said Maurice.

***

Maisie had recommended a swim in the waterfall. Kim waded into the river, internalising yelps of pain as the shingle sliced her feet and cold water scissored her stomach.

"Come on!" she called.

"You're crazy!" returned Len, who stood stooge-like on a flat rock.

"But it's safe! And look at all those millions of faeries dressed in glitter dancing around the fall. Oul Bessie said they will shower you with good fortune and bless you with a long life."

"Still not coming!"

"Oul Bessie said that he who stands on the rock will tread upon the faeries at work there, and that he will have many years' bad luck."

"You made that up!"

"I did," she laughed, tipping her head back.

"You're crazy!"

"I've befriended these guys and they're helping me get you into the water."

She pinched her nose and lay down so that she could feel the beat of the fall on her back. She flipped over onto her back, freeing her hair from its elastic, allowing it to fan across the pool. She was invisible to the world, alone in a space as small as Maisie's kitchen, and then she was in the arms of Len and he was kissing her and pulling her close to him.

He moved away, smiling and wrapping her hair around his hand.

"So you believe in faeries?" he said.

"Och och anee," gasped Kim, imitating Maisie. "The faeries can hear your very thoughts."

Len laughed, held her hands and twirled her around. "Perhaps you're among own folk," he said. "My Smiths Falls faerie, what you need in your life is an aerospace engineer to ensure your wings are in good order."

"Aha, this is how Leonard Gibson charms the ladies, I see," teased Kim.

They floated for a while until a cloud masked the sun and Kim felt the chill of the water.

"You know, I don't think I should take that trip," said Kim. "I think I can find more about my family if I stay here for a while."

"I don't think I should take that trip either," he said.

"Why?"

"I'll miss out on moments like this."

***

Kim had spent the day wandering around the town, walking aimlessly for hours, imagining she was her great grandmother. Alone. Desperate. Carrying a baby.

She knew how that felt, at least.

Kim's baby had not made it, and at no other time had the confusion of that period of her life haunted her more than when she retraced her great grandmother's footsteps around Larne. The student in Kingston. Her dad's downcast eyes. The first scan. The hope. The second scan. The endometriosis diagnosis. *The likelihood of infertility.*

Life, fear, hope, death — all in four short moons.

She had blocked it all out. Figured she could think about it all when the time was right. Was now the time?

She had tried to picture what Larne would have looked like when Mary Beth walked through it, but other than some well-preserved historical buildings, most remnants of the past were hidden. She realised that the past was never far from old stone walls, and so she followed them along the periphery of graveyards, churches and grand houses. And she became lost not only in Mary Beth's story, but also that of a town and of an island that belonged to two types of folk — those who stayed at home and those who went away.

"What's the latest wi the big trip aroon Ireland?" asked Maisie, settling into her armchair after pouring a bucket of coal onto the fire. It was twenty degrees Celsius outside, but the cold was a constant threat at number thirty-three.

"I'm not going," said Kim. "I'd like to see more of the Glens around here instead. Glenoe was pretty cute."

"Why don't you stay on here?"

"But I couldn't do that." She said it out of politeness, for she would have given her right arm to stay with Maisie a while longer. The carers who had been there that morning said they thought it would do Maisie good to have company. She also needed to ration her time with Len. It never took more than a day for her to recognise a good father — it never took more than a few days to let him go.

"You're tae stay the week." stated Maisie, and Kim took it to be more of an instruction than an invitation.

"Well in that case, I'm going to do some chores to earn my keep."

"No need, my daughter Clara owns the place and has it all sorted. She says if I lift a hand, she'll put me in a box in the Ulster Folk and Transport Museum where folk'll come and listen to me for a coin. Like the laughing clown at Barry's."

"I'd sure pay to see that," said Kim, "but they'd need to take this wee living room with you forbye. Everyone should start using the word *forbye* forbye. Tea?"

"Och aye, ye have me spoilt! I got the carer tae go up to the attic when ye were oot walkin. We could take a keek at Sally's things before Mrs Greenlees gets here. She'll enjoy the rummage through the photos forbye. *Forbye.* Did ye ever?"

"Mrs Greenlees?"

"Aye, love, she calls in every Friday night at seven o'clock.

"I can go for a walk to give you peace for a while."

"Not-tat-tall," she said. "Mrs Greenlees is a freen."

"You mean she's a friend? Or family?"

"Kind o baith."

"Kind o like Maurice?" suggested Kim, preparing for another roving adventure.

"Kind o t'other way, for she's a wean til my sister Jamesina. She was reared by my aunt in Ballymena."

Kim tried not to smile, but couldn't help herself. "So, she's your niece."

"Jamesina got hersel in tae trouble up Pauper's Loanen at the age of sixteen, but I shouldnae be talkin of such things, dear, for it was never mentioned."

"Mrs Greenlees doesn't know?"

"Oh, Grace, I'm sure, knows rightly. Every sinner in town know'd it when Jamesina was alive, but we were heart-feared o her knowin that we know'd. By Jove, I can feel Jamesina shaking her fist as I speak. I'd better shush or the heavens will open."

"You all knew, but no one said a thing? The British Secret Service would do well to recruit your family."

"Grace was fond o Jamesina. And I doubt she would hae been so soft on her if she had been her daughter and not her cousin."

Kim helped Maisie prepare a small supper. Corned beef sandwiches made from plain bread were stacked on the bottom tier of a cake stand, thick pancakes fresh from the griddle were lathered with butter and positioned on the second tier and fresh strawberries from the garden were placed alongside fairy cakes on the third. She set the cake stand and matching cups and plates onto the top table of a nest of three.

Maisie pulled out a wooden box from underneath her chair. She lifted out some old photographs and selected one particularly dour depiction of the Higgins children to show to Kim. She explained who they all were: Jamesina standing tall and conscientious with a little boy resting on her right hip; Maisie with a height of curls on her head, an identical little boy on her hip; and Lily, a picture of innocence with one long plait gracing her shoulder.

Maisie breathed life into each piece of thick card. There was the ordeal of Grace Higgins scrubbing the children raw in front of the fire, as they squirmed and squealed in a tin tub of boiling water. There was the misery of wearing old army remnants transformed into thick, itchy Sunday School clothes. And then the tension and excitement of avoiding puddles on the walk to a pharmaceutical store in which oversized shoes were placed upon the feet of barefoot children.

Kim thought about her slim iPhone with its unweighty memories snapped in seconds —a reel of digital pixels that was not worth handing down.

Maisie rifled through portraits of each of the Higgins girls. First came a handsome side profile of Jamesina, her large, intelligent eyes looking over her shoulder — a farewell glance back at a childhood after the encounter up Pauper's Loanen, perhaps. Next came a full length image of Maisie in a loose dress with a dropped waist, her face alive with the confident smile of a woman fit to conquer a future husband's demons. And then there was Lily, hair undulating in finger waves around a cap, a smile masking teeth that were apparently all pulled out and replaced with dentures before she was twenty.

"Och och anee," rhymed Maisie. "I niver thought I'd be the last."

"You must miss them all," said Kim.

"Och aye. It's quate here at night. I seen a time when I couldnae get rid o them, but folk dinnae sit up the way they used tae. Ye hiddae make an appointment nu tae see a freen. Here we are nu. Sally's envelop."

"What became of Sally's husband?" asked Kim, curious as to why he didn't have her things.

"He had two boys and a girl tae his second wife, but they all moved away. He turned Dalriada over to a cancer charity when his second wife died and moved tae the cottage doon there at the foot o Waterloo Bay."

"The kids didn't want Dalriada?"

"Och sure naebody wants tae live in a castle surrounded by a moat o fectory folk."

"Is there anything left of its contents?"

"Maist o the furniture is still in Dalriada." She pointed to the cabinet that served as a telephone stand. "Thon cabinet," she said, "belonged tae Sally and Doctor Andrews. The doctor gien it tae me along wi a porcelain shoe and some wee crystal trinkets. I think it's right that ye take the trinkets hame tae Canada."

"Oh I couldn't."

"We'll sort ye oot wi a suitcase, so ye can keep them safe."

Maisie emptied the contents of the envelope and spread them across the small table.

"Wow, look at the hair!" exclaimed Kim, lifting the first photograph. It was a teenage girl. Long, thick hair, tumbled over a dark, velvet gown, and rested on her thighs. Sally could see the air of both her grandmother and her mom.

"Glory be tae the woman wi lang hair!" said Maisie.

Kim cocked her head to the side.

"It was a sin to hae short hair in them days, dear."

"I see."

"My sister, Lily, was the first sinner in the family for she cropped her hair into a bob at the age of twelve and broke her daddy's heart. These photographs are all of Sally. And there's her birth certificate. Sarah Ramsey. Born 4 January 1915, daughter of Winifred and James Ramsey."

"I'm so intrigued about how Winifred and James became her parents."

"Ye'll see in the letter," said Maisie. "And ye'll need tae go back to Dalriada tae see Sally's garden."

"I will. A cute photograph of her from 1935," said Kim. "How chic she is with the little beret on the head!"

Maisie studied Kim's face for a moment before showing her a sepia photograph of Sally as a young woman. Her hair was sculpted into waves, a fur shawl set around her shoulders.

The doorbell rang and Maisie got up slowly from the chair, picking up a tin of hard candy on her way. Kim could hear children speaking, candy jangling and a man saying he would be back at nine.

She shook hands with the old lady, who was like Maisie in frame and build. "A pleasure to meet you," said Kim.

"Kim's frae Canada," said Maisie. "She's tracing her family tree. Maisie lifted an excerpt from a newspaper and placed reading glasses on the end of her nose. She read, "'*Miss Clara Clarke stole the limelight with a sprightly jig whilst her mother, Mary Beth, per-formed an old Irish step dance called 'The Blackbird' and accompanied Dance Master Peter O'Reilly in a two-hand reel.'*"

"Let me see that," enthused Kim "'Oh my goodness. It's my great granny and she's doing 'The Blackbird'. What the heck is 'The Blackbird?'"

If Kim was surprised by the existence of the newspaper article, she was stunned when Mrs Greenlees sprang to her feet.

"What are ye leukin at me all agog for?" said Grace to Maisie as she heeled and toe'd. "I was in the senior championship of the Ballymena Musical Festival. And the Glens Feis. And the Newry Feis."

"You've an amazing memory," said Kim.

"My memory's in my feet, dear, for I'm eighty-three years old and couldnae tell ye what I had for my breakfast this mornin. But I do mind Mrs McConnell learnin us 'The Blackbird' in the Protestant Hall in Ballymena. I practised it for weeks to get it right. And Mr O'Reilly, he was the adjudicator when I won my first medal."

"Small world!" said Kim. "I can't believe Mary Beth was up on that stage in the Ulster Hall. I mean, my granny was shy and private. My mum can't get over me having a Facebook account."

"Och ye should add me as a friend," said Grace, pulling a brand new smartphone from her bag. "I've got three generations! Kim what?"

"It's Kim Craig," she laughed. "You're fast on that thing."

"Check your phone tae see if it worked!"

"I can't," said Kim. "I didn't pay my provider for roaming, so I'm travelling unconnected. You're so hip with your dancing and your technology!"

"Our Grace was aye very mod-ren," said Maisie. "Show Kim thon thing wi the oul newspapers."

"Wait til ye see, love," she said, selecting a number of options on the screen and calling out words as she sat down and performed another dance with her fingers and a small, rubber pen. "Advanced search. Grace McKay. Irish Folk Dancing. *Ballymena Observer*. 1936-1948. Dee de de de de. See! It's me!" She showed Kim the list of articles with the name Grace McKay on the screen.

"That was easy," said Kim.

"I used tae buy the daily newspapers," she explained, "but found the oul yins mair newsworthy, so got masel a subscription tae the past."

"Could you look up Clara Clarke and Mary Beth Clarke?"

"Ye need tae be a bit mair specific, dear. Alright. Let me see."

Another series of clicks followed in tune to Grace's words. "Advanced search. Mary Clarke. Clara Clarke. Irish Folk Dancing. *Belfast News-Letter*. What years? Let's try 1914 to 1918. Here, take a keek."

A list of nine references to Mary Clarke populated the screen. At the top was the Ulster Hall one that Kim still held in her hand, but this version was a full page long with more photographs included.

"Hang on," said Kim, taking the phone. "It's a picture of Mary Beth. Look at her standing there with her hair flowing down her shoulders and her foot pointed. And beside a man in a kilt too. There's little Clara as well!"

Kim studied the face of Mary Beth and saw the warm smile of her granny Clara. She flicked back a screen and selected the next article, the title of which indicated another feis. It was 1909 in Belfast and Mary was winning a reel.

"Nothing in the years between 1911 and 1917, said Grace. "Mibby she was in Larne at that time. Let's hae a leuk. I'll change the publication place to Larne."

Kim enjoyed Grace's enthusiasm and the encounter with her past.

"Hey presto!" called Grace. "One article. 28th January 1915."

"'*Homeless Woman Rehabilitated*'" read Kim. "'*The weekly meeting of the Board was held on Wednesday. The Master's Weekly Report showed the following details - since last week 26 admitted, 1 born, 1 died, 27 discharged, number remaining 146, as against 148 for corresponding period last year. Average cost of a pauper 5s 1 ½ d. Board considered the case of Miss Mary Elizabeth Clarke and infant, who were moved by the corporation from unlawful shelter at the shore. Miss Clarke, who heretofore held positions of responsibility, was deemed to be capable of independent means. A motion was carried by Rev. Greer that she should be rehabilitated as a governess at the Girls Friendly Society Lodge in College Street Belfast, where she will teach piano and physical exercise. The fate of the infant is under review.*'"

"You'll want to read this letter," said Maisie when Kim had finished reading the article on Clara's phone. "Away and take it up to the back room, dear," she added. Perhaps she understood that Kim needed some space to digest the information and suppress the large knot lodged in her throat after reading the report from the newspaper.

The Business of Humanity

The pigeons pecking the dirt crumbs scattered when Kim stepped off the train in a long, green dress. She walked towards Len, bringing the hubbub of Yorkgate station to a confounding hush.

Len caught the eye of an elderly man, who gave him a nod of approval, the sort of crafty expression his father often accorded him in the secret confines of his newspaper.

"Like my new dress?" smiled Kim, holding out the clingy fabric in a curtsy.

"It maximises your looks, that's for sure" said Len, conscious of another shift in Kim's mood. Maisie said that Kim had cried a river after reading the letter from James Ramsey to Sally.

"Why thank you," said Kim. "I had a little browse around the shops yesterday. What a girl saves on coffee, she spends on pretty dresses."

"May Costa weep! You look amazing."

"Yorkgate," said Kim. "Maisie said this station replaced the one mentioned in the letter, where Winifred brought Sally to meet Mary Beth and Clara. Imagine them all saying goodbye each time." Her eyes filled with tears.

Len looked around. It was a utilitarian station designed to welcome the traveller with a cursory handshake and not to host romantic trysts or poignant farewells. He caught Kim's reflection in the glass and was struck by the realisation that this romantic tryst would end in a farewell too soon. He kissed her again.

"That's the kind of kiss that should be hidden behind a waterfall in Glenoe," she smiled. "You're taking advantage of knowing not a sinner in town."

"Not a sinner! I see Maisie's been rubbing off on you."

"I cannae help it," said Kim.

Len took her hand and walked towards the city centre. "So, you read a letter that made you cry for an hour and you drank sherry with two old ladies until half past nine. I think we need to get out in the city for a night out."

"I did all my partying in college," said Kim.

"I didn't know you went to college. You told me you didn't have a degree."

"I went to Kingston for a few months. Anyway, these old ladies are entertaining enough for me. Grace Greenlees was up dancing and all sorts. And that was before she had the sherry! I'd like to take both Maisie and Grace home with me!"

"You'll probably want to steal my aunt Clara too. She's a musician, although she works in the education authority now. She's taken a bus downtown and will see us at City Hall."

They walked in silence until Len spotted a couple looking through the window of a jewellery shop. Without thinking, he led Kim to the window.

"Why are we looking at our own reflections?" she enquired.

"I'm going to bring you back here in precisely two years," stated Len.

"Two years!" she coughed, her eyes wandering around the blue velvet shelves. "You're a little confident."

"I've been touched by healing waters. See you here on 15 June 2011."

"We've only just met!" she laughed. "We absolutely have no concrete plans for 15 June 2011, and certainly none that involve a jewellery store."

They continued walking and Len knew that Kim was more buoyed than put off by his outrageous statement of intent. She was gliding along Royal Avenue in her maxi dress like an Egyptian Pharaoh, and Len couldn't quite believe that she was holding his hand.

"The faeries promised me," he asserted playfully, "that I could rescue you from Smiths Falls and take you back to Toronto. He who steps off the rock and into the Glenoe waterfall pond will be blessed."

"Oh, I don't think that's how it works," said Kim. "Some other guy could be waiting for me at home, and I could do something wonderful in Smiths Falls."

"I'm sorry to say Ms Craig, your destiny was written long before you were born. I was meant to bump into you on that ship."

She smiled and squeezed his hand.

"I called my dad last night and told him all about you. He said he remembers Sally. He was fond of her as a young boy. He also said Smiths Falls is pretty nice."

"Your dad knows the way to a girl's heart in that case. He perhaps understands its position as the centre of the universe. He could teach you a thing or two"

"I guess he could," laughed Len.

***

Clara didn't waste any time on introductions. She led Len and Kim straight into the City Hall with a swing in her stiletto-heeled step and began telling them the history of the place. It seemed she enjoyed history as much as gossip. Len had discovered her enthusiasm for family secrets the night before over dinner. He had been too young on previous visits to have any real adult conversations with his aunt, and he still felt a little childlike when she revealed some surprising information about the past.

Jane Gourley, Clara's paternal grandmother, was also the mother of Esther Gibson. There had always been a loose, undefined blood connection between the Gibsons and the Gourleys — the reason Esther had left her little boy with Maisie and Leonard one Hallowe'en night — but everything was now a little clearer.

"Well, Kim, I can't wait to get to know you," enthused Clara, who did not look anything like sixty years of age. She was trim, fit and never stopped talking. "I've been intrigued by Sally Andrews' story my whole life," she went on, hooking arms with Kim.

They moved along the corridors of the museum swiftly, until they reached panels of the *White Star Line* exhibition. Kim was nodding and Clara was pointing at a model of a ship, and Len was wondering how it had come to pass that Kim had been on the ship between Cairnryan and Larne beside him, not knowing their connection — not knowing that their families shared so much history.

"Mary Beth could have been on a ship just like this one when she went to Canada," said Kim, pointing to the miniature vessel. It was *The Olympic*, the sister ship of the infamous *Titanic*. "Mind you, now that I know about the workhouse, I guess Mary didn't have such a pleasant journey."

"You don't know that," said Clara, who had the air of an efficient tour guide. "She became a governess. I bet she made her mark on the Girls' Friendly Society."

"Why would they have sent her there?" asked Kim, who had formed a bond with Clara that delegated Len to the role of usher. He held the doors of the cafe to allow the conversation to continue.

"It seems that this Reverend Greer on the Board of Guardians was protecting her," said Clara. "Maybe there was a connection."

"Maybe," replied Kim pensively.

"You know, organisations like the Girls' Friendly Society, the Girl Guides and the Girls' Brigade were revolutionary in their day," she said, reverting back to an informative guide. "Men were suspicious of what might happen if women were left to their own devices."

"So the GFS was run by women?" said Kim.

"Churches were behind the scenes," said Clara, "but wealthy women took charge. They tried to help young women when conditions in factories were bleak. Tried to pull them up and make ladies of them. They were the feminists of their day. Your great grandmother was an interesting character and a strong woman. Tea and scones for everyone?" Clara didn't await a response. She had the tray filled and was paying for the order before Len had the chance to request coffee.

They were seated when Clara reached over the table and placed her hand on Kim's arm. "My name comes from the little photograph of your granny, Clara."

"I know," said Kim. "It's incredible."

"My father told me I was named after his clarinet," laughed Clara, "but my mother said he was full of nonsense. I was named after the picture on Sally Andrews' mantelpiece in Dalriada." "My mother is very precious about Sally's memory," Clara went on. "And Sally became a friend to me through the photographs in the big wooden box. There's nothing more enthralling than finding a piece of your mother's childhood. To know that there was more than guldering at weans!"

"There's a thing," said Len. "I always think of Granny as warm and funny."

"She softened," said Clara. "I suppose she had her reasons to be stern when we were children. Kim, I understand you met my half-brother?"

"Yes," said Kim, her cheeks reddening. "I met him in Glenoe. He looks a bit like this Len here."

"He does," said Clara, smiling at Len, who made another adjustment to a family tree that was increasingly overripe with

DNA. If Esther and Leonard were brother and sister, then his father and Maurice were first cousins on the blood tree.

"My mother threw all convention to the wind when it came to looking out for Maurice," said Clara. "I'll never understand why she didn't just pretend we were distant cousins."

Clara turned her attention to Kim again. "Enough of my family. Yours is much more intriguing."

"Oh, I don't know," said Kim. "I'd love to be a member of your family for a day. Do you think it's okay if I stay with your mum? I don't want to confuse her."

"It would make me happy," said Clara. "I'm planning to retire this year and move home to stay with her. I've one daughter in France and one has just moved to London. No excuse for me to stick around in Belfast anymore."

"Have you read the letter from Sally's father?" asked Kim.

"Yes," smiled Clara. "My girls were always obsessed by what they called 'the mermaid story.' I phoned my eldest daughter this morning to tell her about you and she said, 'Och Mammy, it's like the mermaid has swum back into Larne Lough.'"

Kim smiled. "What about the father of Sally and Clara," she asked. "The soldier. Did anyone know who he was?"

"Clara and Sally were conceived during the Great War," said Clara, "so there were plenty of soldiers around, but Sally apparently once met an elderly gentleman in the park. She believed he was her father."

"I'd love to figure it out," said Kim.

"There's always DNA testing," said Len. "There are a few cool websites you could check out."

"Maybe," said Kim. "We'll see."

"When you think about it," said Clara. "You two both ended up in Canada because of Mary Beth Clarke."

"See!" said Len. "Aunt Clara, I did tell Kim that it was all meant to be. She's not quite convinced and is now talking about staying in Larne instead of going on her travels with me."

"Plenty of time for romance later, young man," said Clara. "A girl needs to get to know herself before committing herself to any man."

***

Len held Kim's hand as they walked along the promenade in Larne. The shoreline was like a mosaic of shapes pinned onto a flawless sky, the old round tower and chimneys of the power station silhouetted in straight lines on a grey horizon.

He recalled what Kim had said when they first visited the shore, that she'd like to live there, wild and free, and it was feasible in the mosaic in his mind to cut out a place for her on the smooth, white shingle. But Mary Beth had lived on the shore, and it seemed that she had given birth there in a wilderness of unfettered freedom.

The chimney stacks of the power station would not have been a feature of the landscape when Clara and Sally were born. In their place, steam funnels from great ships would have populated the grey panorama. Len pieced together the view from what he had read. There would have been a long prison ship permanently anchored in the lough and emigrant ships destined for America in the bay. There would have been dozens of small boats moving back and forth, bringing exotic fruits and cheap cotton and departing with Brown's Irish linen and rope. There would have been travellers leaving for America, and travellers arriving to build ships on the docks.

What would Mary Beth have seen on the night that her children were conceived? Had it been a night for thieves, or a night for lovers?

They climbed up the steep path. It was covered in tarmac, but Len was able to picture a woman alone on a dirt path, two babies strapped around her with a shawl, one destined for Dalriada and one for the workhouse.

Kim was in front of Len as they climbed up the hill. She turned and tugged at his arm playfully. "Come on Casanova!" she said. "Get into first gear!"

"You've changed again!" he smiled. "You've been so quiet. I thought you'd left your spirit in Belfast with Clara."

"I'm re-energised walking in my ancestor's shoes — that's if she had any shoes when she walked to Dalriada holding two babies. God, can you imagine?"

"Maybe she walked down that lane." Len turned to the left and pointed. "Bankheads Loanen. That old wall goes all the way down to the Glenarm Road."

"Oh, I wish we knew what had happened," said Kim. "Was it day or was it night? Was she alone? Did anyone see her or help her? And what agreement did she make with Winifred?"

"You might never know," said Len, trailing a stick along the old stone wall.

Kim smiled and fell into a dream-like state again.

The gates to Dalriada were open and patients were dotted around the lawn. Len observed the building from the front path, a childlike cutting on nature's mosaic. "Let's go look around the back this time," he said. "They said we were welcome to explore."

"It would have been impossible to look after two babies during a cold, harsh winter," stated Kim. "I mean, without a pushchair, how would she have even carried them? Maybe Clara liked Winifred and chose her to care for her child."

"Maybe," replied Len, sauntering towards the garden pond, stopping to look at the small white statue of a little girl playing a flute. He looked closer and read the inscription. "Sally's garden. In memory of Sarah Andrews, 1915-1949."

Kim touched the white stone. "Maisie said there was a garden. I wonder why it's a sculpture of a child."

"There's more on the column," indicated Leonard. "Mother of two souls." He paused. "I didn't know Sally had children."

"No," whispered Kim. "There were no children. Only souls." She held out her arms and turned slowly.

Len stood up straight, his arms hanging heavily by his side. Kim had a way of reacting to the mysteries of loss and the mysteries of the past. He walked around the pond, studying the white heads of the water hawthorn and the yellow tips of golden club.

Kim pointed towards the old wall backing onto the Waterloo Road. "Imagine Sally coming from over that wall to live here in this grand house when her friends were only a stone's throw away." She stopped and allowed her words to settle. "Maybe in some subconscious way, she missed her sister." She turned to Len. "Twins have a way of knowing things. An intuition."

Len smiled and took her hand.

"I want to stay," she said, her spirit flowing again. "All the way from Belfast, I couldn't shake the idea from my mind. You'll think I'm crazy."

"No. Nothing this week seems crazy to me." He watched her move around the pond. "What are you thinking?"

"I'm thinking of staying here to work."

"Work? What would you do?"

"I don't know." Kim touched the plinth holding up the sculpture of the girl with the flute. "There might be work for a sports coach. I could do a little massage on the side."

"And my ambitions of taking you to Toronto?"

"Those ambitions are admirable."

"Man, you're gonna break my heart," he said. "Let's sit down a moment, so I can recover."

Warmth glimmered in Kim's brown eyes, but Len was struck by disappointment, the inevitable consequence of falling under the spell of someone like Kim.

She joined him on the grass by the pond. "You know you're turning out to be a romantic, right?"

He smiled.

"I'd like you to take me to Armagh," she said. "Look at this." She took a book from her bag.

"It's a book," he said.

"Yes. An old-fashioned concept indeed. An old travel book. See, the Antrim Coast is on the cover. It was on the bookshelf in the back room. Look at the inscription inside."

Len read the words, "To Leonard, With fond memories of your music at the McNeill Hotel, Richard Hayward, 1950."

"The writer must have heard Granda Leonard play," he said.

"Listen to this," said Kim. "The beauty of Armagh is the beauty of an old woman who has aged gracefully. Beauty is there, and dignity, and a deep understanding which comes from more than three-thousand years of intimate connection with the business of humanity."

"The business of humanity!" repeated Len. "I guess if you knew about the business of humanity for that long, the goings on of your family and my family wouldn't surprise a single soul."

***

Len led Kim back towards the factory area, retracing the steps Mary Beth would have taken to the workhouse.

"Is the workhouse near Pauper's Loanen?" asked Kim as they passed the redundant red-bricked funnel of the Brown's Irish linen factory, a structure that had yet to be lifted from the crooked mosaic of the land.

"Granny told you the story about Jamesina?" said Len.

"She sure did."

"Pauper's Loanen is to the right." Len pointed when they got to the end of Factory Row. "The old workhouse is the other way. It's some sort of medical centre now. Not far to go."

They were soon in front of a large stone edifice with green copper-topped towers. "Granny Maisie worked in an office there when it was a hospital," said Leonard. They were standing underneath the canopy of a fruitless blossom tree.

"It looks like an old private school," observed Kim. "Kinda pretty. In the same way that Dalriada is pretty. It lures you in."

Len looked at Kim. There was something about her that seemed older than her years.

"It's hard to imagine this place once symbolised destitution," she said.

"It's one thing standing here," said Len. "I guess they wouldn't have wanted people to get too comfortable on the inside."

"Granny Clara's first home," sighed Kim. "Man, these chills down my back!"

"They're spreading." Len smiled.

"Don't you want to know the whole story about your family?" she asked. "You said your dad never knew who his father was."

"No," he replied, turning towards the building. "None of us needs know the whole truth. The people of Armagh will teach you that with their three-thousand years of intimate connection with the business of humanity. But you want to try to figure out who Clara's father was?"

"I think I do."

"You might end up sad," he said.

"I don't mind sadness."

"Of course you don't," smiled Len. "Granny Maisie would say you've been here before."

Life Everlasting
Toronto, June 2011

It was the safe side of Len that mattered when fear consumed Kim on a turbulent flight. She pictured him walking around an aircraft hangar or sitting at a computer or whatever it was that he did as quality control manager of aircraft wings, and felt reassured that there were people like Len Gibson who could hold planes up in the air.

It was tempting to kiss him there and then at the gate, but she didn't know the etiquette attached to seeing a circumvented lover for the first time in two years.

"Welcome home!" he said animatedly, taking the handle of her wheelie case.

"Thank you for meeting me," she replied. "I think I may need to lie down before you show me the wonders of the city. I'm still a little queasy from the flight."

"Change of plan," he said, directing her right towards the exit as she wandered aimlessly left at a junction. "We're going to Smiths Falls. Can you nap in the car?"

"You're coming with me to Smiths Falls?" she exclaimed. It was a little forward, even for someone who had hinted at nuptials four days into a holiday romance, but she understood that he would have every detail of the journey planned with military precision.

In fact, she was comforted after the frenzy of the flight to be in the hands of someone so meticulous. And safe. Len was safe. Everything about him, from his smoothly shaven face to his shiny brogues, was reassuring.

"I'm driving you to Smiths Falls," he said with confidence.

"No way, it's too far," she protested half-heartedly, knowing well it was a course that had already been decided. "I can't ask you to do that."

"It's all sorted."

Kim was surprised when Len took her hand.

"I've been waiting two years to hold your hand," he said in response to her thoughts. "We're stopping in Kingston for lunch, so I reckon you'll be with your parents in five hours."

"Is this the Toronto version of Len?"

"What do you mean?"

"You're even more organised than you were in Ireland!"

"I was on holiday in Ireland," he said. "I was in a relaxed state. Besides, a man has to impress a woman if he's about to meet her parents."

Kim hadn't been in the company of her parents since Christmas when they had arrived in Ireland with her brother to see for themselves what Kim had come to know as home. Kim and her mum had walked side-by-side with the ghosts of Mary Beth and Sally. They had even bathed in the sea on New Year's Day with some local women who lived beyond the artifice of modern life. Kim could still feel the laceration of water on her skin, the crunch of shingle, the connected dots of her heritage — four generations of a female line that might end with her.

"Hey," said Kim, "I'll need to warn my mum and dad."

"The spare room is ready for me. I've been in touch with them already."

She stopped in the middle of the corridor and looked at Len. "How on earth did you find them?"

"Facebook. I found your sister and she gave me your mum's number."

"Oh boy, she'll think there's romance in the air. And I've never told her that we had a thing."

"There is romance in the air, and we do have a thing. You just held the pause button down for a little too long!"

"Leonard Gibson, a true romantic? I cannae get over it!"

"You have spent too long in Larne, Miss Craig! As for the romance, if you keep a guy waiting two years, believe me, it's possible."

"But you were dating, weren't you?"

"Now and then. Here and there." He smiled coyly.

"Casanova, you weren't all that heart-broken! And by the way, you stood me up for our date!"

"What date?"

"The one by the jewellery store in Belfast."

"But you told me you didn't want a long-distance relationship," he said, his face colouring. "I assumed—"

"I'm kidding!" She kissed his cheek and watched his green eyes brighten. She thought back to that moment, standing at the window of the store on Royal Avenue. She hadn't even seen what was on display. All she had seen was the reflection of a couple holding hands, and when she dreamed of Len, it was that image she saw foremost in her mind. "You're right," she went on. "I didn't want a relationship. But your social media content is so dull that I had to come to see for myself if you're real."

"You're gauging whether a person is real by their social media posts? Yours aren't so revelatory either. If it weren't for the guy who tagged you in the bar in Belfast, I wouldn't have known a thing about your fling."

"I didn't have a fling!" she protested. "The photographs covered up a terribly dull night. The real party was at number seventeen."

"I still can't believe you went to live there," he said.

"I liked having neighbours. I could hear them snore. It was a great comfort."

"And the guy kissing you?"

"It was a peck on the cheek from a colleague. Were you jealous?"

"Yes, I was jealous."

***

A pillow of warm air cushioned Kim's senses when she stepped out of the air-conditioned car. She had slept the moment they hit Highway 401 and awoke when the car began to slow on its way through the carpark.

Len had chosen Kingston Mills lockstation for his picnic, a place where the strong metal arms of man intervened with nature in such a sympathetic way that it was unclear where man's intervention ended and nature began. Kim breathed in the stout scent of canal and inhaled the swell scent of home.

"This heat is incredible," she said, stretching out her arms, allowing the sun to smother her skin.

Len placed a picnic blanket and supplies onto the grass. His grocery store picnic was a contrast to the freshly boiled eggs, homemade sandwiches and fruit that Clara provided on their 'Richard Hayward tours' — monthly day-trips with Maisie that revolved around an old travel book and the formula of reading the relevant chapter and then expressing dismay that so much of Hayward's Ulster had disappeared.

Kim lay down and ran her hands across the grass at the side of the picnic blanket. "Am I almost home?" she asked. "Or is it a dream?"

"It had better not be a dream," he replied, and she could tell he was sitting upright studying her face. "I'm not used to seeing you at this angle."

Her eyes remained closed. She smiled.

"All those nights in Maisie's," he went on. "I could never see your face from my camp bed. All I had were your soft snores."

She grabbed a handful of grass to propel at him, but let it fall through her fingers. "I'm too at peace to protest," she said.

A shadow blocked the sun from her eyelids. A kiss touched her lips.

She sat up and looked at him. "You were right, you know?"

"About what?"

"You told me I might find out something I didn't want to know."

He squinted at the sun.

"I took one of those DNA tests," she ventured.

He spoke carefully. "Science can be a wonderful thing. It can produce feats of engineering like this canal, but it can also disrupt the natural ecosystem."

"I guess I almost upset the natural ecosystem of one family," she lamented. "Your freen Grace Greenlees is my freen too, but the topic is strictly off limits as long as she is alive."

"You're connected to Jamesina's daughter?"

"Grace Greenlees is my great aunt by blood," said Kim.

"Wow! I didn't expect that."

"The guy who fathered Sally and Clara also fathered Grace. And one more child that I know of. And I made the mistake of telling Grace."

"How did she take it?"

"Not well. I don't even know if she understood what I was saying because the conversation ended so abruptly. Even now in this heat, my blood is running cold thinking about it."

"Oh dear," said Len.

"I bounded up that road like an eejit with a print out from the ancestry site and thoughts of stars aligning. I didn't use my head at all."

"I see," he said.

"In her whole life, Grace Greenlees had never heard anyone discuss the issue of her true parentage. That was my first insult. 'Hey look, your dad is a relation of mine.' Well, I swear to God the fire went out in Maisie's living room."

"Oh man!"

"I almost took the next flight back to Canada, and believe me, I would have taken it if it weren't for the fact that my mum and dad had booked their flights to come over."

"But wait a moment," said Len. "Why was Grace even on that DNA site if she didn't want to know who her father was?"

"She likes family history and her son thought it might be a nice gift for her. He lives in Canada and is happy to meet me some time, but I guess Grace didn't understand what she was signing up for. She thought it was another great subscription to the past, like the old newspapers she loves so well. If I'm honest, I didn't realise there would be a whole web of connections either."

"Imagine if that kind of science had always been available," said Len.

"Well, you'd wonder what impact it would have had on the business of humanity."

"What did Maisie say?"

"'God bliss and keep us for nu I've seen it all.'"

Len laughed. "I guess at ninety-six, there's little left to see."

Kim lay back and relaxed. A veil of sleep covered her eyelids.

"Tell me about the man behind your female line," said Len.

Female line. Could he read her mind? "The father was called Nathanial Greer," she said. "A decorated soldier."

"Sounds promising," said Len, whose enthusiasm was such that the balance of her feelings about Nathanial shifted in his favour.

"I thought so too," she replied. "I found a DNA link to him through a family in Chicago. In 1911, Nathanial Greer was living with his uncle, the Anglican minister, Reverend Greer — the same guy who spoke up about Mary Beth at the workhouse meeting."

"Go on..."

"He was born in England," explained Kim, "but I guess he was a sort of Ulster prototype in his allegiance to crown and country. He served in the Boer War in 1890, signed the Ulster Covenant against Irish Home Rule in 1912 and continued his military career in the British army after the First World War. What made him less predictable was the wait to walk down the aisle. He was in his early forties when he got married to Margaret 'Betty' Hamilton. Their daughter was born in 1926, the same month as Grace Greenlees and eleven years after Sally and Clara."

"Maybe Nathanial and Betty were in love," said Len. "Maybe Nathanial and Mary Beth were in love."

"I'm confident that Nathanial was in love with Mary Beth. The letter from Sally's dad said as much, but then I stumbled across a court case. I looked up Nathanial's name in the old newspapers."

"And?" said Len.

"And I cried."

"Oh."

"I didn't even get a chance to catch my breath and get into the article because the headline read in big bold letters, *HE WAS CRUEL*. Those were Betty's words in 1948 about her husband of twenty-odd years. Hey, you've gone all quiet."

"I have, haven't I? I had an inkling, but remained hopeful, not just for you, but for the memory of my old aunt, Jamesina."

"I was hopeful even as I read the court case," said Kim, "but women in those days did not take their husbands to court for abuse. Women accepted the cuts and bruises doled out to them. I've lived in that community and even today it would be a shock to read an article like that about a neighbour. He must have been bad. The court case was probably the reason Betty moved to America."

"I see."

"I saw his picture. I'll show you." Kim reached into her bag for her phone. She scrolled the images and stopped and looked again. She could see her own reflection in the two military photographs of a man in command of his six foot, five inches frame. "I see myself a little around the eyes," she said.

"And the dimples," observed Len, pointing.

"'It won't happen again.' That's what he said." It was the one line in the blow-by-blow account of physical abuse that gave Kim hope. "I need to believe that it never happened again."

"Was he a drinker?" asked Len.

"Yes. That was clear. He had been drinking heavily. I also thought about shell-shock. Perhaps the boundaries of violence had become distorted in his mind after the terror of the Great War."

"I'm beginning to figure out why people look back," said Len. "Aren't they trying to find that little snippet of information that gives them reason? There is one relation of mine who intrigues me."

"Who?"

"Granda Leonard's brother, Tam. A forgotten soul, although he fought on the beaches of Normandy. I'm in the army reserves, you see."

"I'm not in the least bit surprised," said Kim. "You have a military persona."

"I'm not sure what to make of that."

She kissed him.

"I'll take that as a positive response," he beamed. "I almost went to officer college when I came back from Ireland."

"Full-time military!" she exclaimed.

"Yes, but I didn't go through with it. It was a couple of weeks after a girl from Smiths Falls broke my heart. I thought about officer training and I thought about Tam."

"The girl did not break your heart," stated Kim. "The girl was a sports coach who could see that it needed a little work out. Tell me more about Tam."

"My granny Esther was a sister of Leonard and Tam. Tam would have been my great uncle, but I didn't know that before I met you in Ireland. I have three photographs of him in uniform and a military record of his endeavours. That's all that remains of him. He held his rifle in the air to protect it from the water when he got off the boat at Lion-Sur-Mer and he was gunned down in seconds. A waste of humanity. I'll keep his things in the same little tin that my dad kept them in and I'll hand them down, but there's nothing more to know."

Kim was silent. *Handed down.* Loaded words.

"Hey, don't cry for Tam," said Len, wiping a tear from her eye.

"I may as well," she smiled. "No one else has shed a tear for him lately. It's a shame that he's been forgotten."

"I'm pretty sure that Granda Leonard shed tears through his music for his brother. I've seen you cry over ghosts you've never met twice. Remember Hughie?"

"Wee Hughie is always on my mind," smiled Kim. "His plaque was right outside my door for two years. This Nathanial Greer character, I read his military records from the First World War."

"And?"

"An exemplary disciplinary record. No cases of drunkenness. No bad behaviour, at all, in fact. His employment sheet said he was a strong leader and a hard-working man."

"Interesting."

"It was something to hold onto. If you know that someone has been violent towards a woman, can you ever forgive them?"

"Every person has to be forgiven," said Leonard, "otherwise what hope is there for any of us?"

"Maybe," said Kim.

"None of us know what's ahead of us. Imagine life got difficult and you turned to drink and did something terrible. If you didn't forgive yourself, you'd stop being." He took her hand. "I don't think my granny Esther drowned by accident," he said. "I think she jumped off those rocks."

"Why do you say that?" asked Kim, recalling how inviting the sea had been beside the Devil's Churn.

"Maisie said she had a cruel childhood. How would she have known how to save herself if she had never been shown compassion?"

Kim looked away. "I was pregnant once," she said.

Len sat up. Kim followed.

"First term of university."

"I see," he said, his voice barely audible.

"Miscarriage at four months."

"I'm sorry."

"I could run." She looked down at her legs. "So, I ran."

Silence.

"They said the running was good for the baby. But that doesn't matter when you know what you wanted."

He stood up and pulled Kim to her feet. "Let's walk," he said. He lifted a stick from the water's edge.

"I have this condition," she said. "Not something you talk about if you're about to start dating someone. I may never get to do what you said."

"To do what?"

"To hand something down. You need to know that."

They walked a few steps in silence.

"Didn't you meet my Granny Maisie?" said Len.

"I did."

He turned to face her. "Who do you think made the man behind the man standing before you?"

Kim knew the answer.

"Maisie took in a little boy called Daniel and raised him as her own. She handed her heart down to him. She taught him how to be a man. There are no blood ties between them."

Kim smiled. They walked on for a while.

"I wonder why Sally thought she had met Nathanial."

"You seem drawn to him," said Len, twisting the stick in his hand.

"Maybe I am. I hope he had a good second life."

"A good second life," sighed Len. He tossed the stick into the water. "Maisie told me that life is like the pictures with two shorts and a long feature with a happy ending."

"That's funny," smiled Kim. They walked slowly under the heavy sunshine. "Maybe the long feature with the happy ending comes after this life," she said.

Len spoke after a long pause. "My dad so loved the movies when he was a kid. He said that the first time he went to the old Regal Picture House in Larne, he thought he was in heaven — red, velvet heaven."

"I know the site of that old picture house," said Kim, recalling the derelict spot that she had passed on her walks. "Maisie frequently laments its demise — that and the hotels that once flanked the entire route between the harbour and the Head of the Town."

"You must have walked every inch of that place."

"I sure did. I ran a fair bit of it too. One day, I was sitting on the summer seat at Bankheads when this old guy pulled up beside me. 'Move up! Two deep! Standing room in the back stalls only! Have your tickets at the ready, please!' That's what he said. We got talking and he told me he had worked as an usher at the

Regal all his days. He must have been ninety, if he was a day. A great character like Maisie. Made me laugh."

"Don't they say a church is its people and not the buildings?"

"True," reflected Kim, thinking of the children walking home from school with their instruments in hand.

"Have you finished digging?" he asked, snapping off another branch from an overhanging tree.

"I think I have," she said. "Tell me the thing about the shorts and the happy ending again."

He laughed and tossed the stick in the air, catching it and then twirling it masterfully. "Life is like two shorts and a main feature with a happy ending."

"And where exactly are we?" she asked.

"Still in the first short, I guess. About to go into the second if you'd allow me to accompany you."

"That would be just fine," smiled Kim.

"My dad's favourite shorts were 'Popeye' and 'The Three Stooges,'" he said as the car came into sight. "Plenty of opportunity for mishaps in the shorts!"

"You're promising me mishaps?" she laughed, noting how adeptly he twirled the stick around in his fingers.

"I sure am."

"You'd be getting involved with someone who will never be able to justify fancy coffee," she said.

"You'd be getting involved with someone who will never have the sense to bring his own flask."

"I can live with that," she smiled.

They both looked back down the canal. Kim observed how the two banks came together, parallel lines running into one indistinct horizon. She took Len's hand and allowed herself to hold on.

Epilogue
March 2020

Maisie looked out towards the chimney stacks and back-to-backs of Little Ballymena and beyond the factory area to the sea.

She hated the wheelchair, but it was the only way her two decaying hips could make it up the hill. She sat at the top end of the McGarel Cemetery, holding a petunia plant in a plastic pot, while Clara fussed over the family plot with a trowel, muttering that Maisie belonged at home in isolation away from the new silent killer. The schools behind them had all closed down already. There was talk that cemeteries would be next.

Maisie had enough experience of killers, silent or with bombs, to know how long they lingered on. Her plot was ready.

It was her first venture beyond the front garden since her birthday party. Every year was worth a decade now. They would gather in the Pigeon Club and she would enter the room, all done up like the Queen.

No longer was she the girl in the second row.

She would tell them not to make a fuss, but she enjoyed the way the children looked at her — the same way she had once looked at Cathleen Carmichael. The young were mesmerised by every line in her bark, not least the nurses who frequently took photographs of her on their smartphones.

Maisie often asked why God had granted her such a long life. Daniel had met his maker already. Clara was strong, but she no longer needed Maisie to hold her tight against her chest. Maisie laughed thinking about her daughter framing the fifth card from Elizabeth R, complaining that they were running out of wall above the fireplace.

Maisie turned to the headstone. "God bliss ye and keep ye, Hughie, Ma, Da, Jamesina, Lily, Rab, and Leonard." She smiled thinking about Leonard, her quiet companion, and her eyes misted over as she read the inscription on the stone. *Sleeping under a braw, bricht moonlicht nicht.*

If ye can say, 'It's a braw, bricht moonlicht nicht,' Then yer a'richt, ye ken.

"You tell them, Hughie, for they're feared today. They don't know it'll be a'richt."

Inches away was a large plot, that of the Reverend Greer. Maisie's eyes roamed over its obelisk to the wall by Pauper's Loanen — to Jamesina, a sixteen year-old girl walking home from a dance. Nathanial's name was etched in one small corner of the obelisk. No one had ever figured out what happened that night between Jamesina and Nathanial Greer, but Maisie had seen enough to know that it did not matter. Grace Greenlees had been a gift to Jamesina, and when Sally Andrews had died, Grace Greenlees had been a gift to Maisie.

Grace too had been called. She had never asked more about Sally being her sister, but when Maisie had leaned into Grace's coffin to kiss her goodbye, she had seen Sally's small Irish dancing medal around her neck.

Clara wheeled Maisie to the second plot, a few feet away, and began to pluck weeds from it. There lay Winifred, James and Sally. Maisie pictured the scene from a March day long ago — the dark hole in the freshly dug ground, the sodden earth covered with hessian sacks, the gloss of a coffin that held her best friend.

Sally had called her cancer a soldier with no purpose, but it had a purpose. Grace Higgins was right, after all. Death had brought peace. And here they were, Nathanial and Sally, father and daughter, the dust of their bones sharing this space.

There were no family plots where Sally, Nathanial, Mary Beth and Clara resided.

Maisie lifted a handful of soil from the plant. It trickled through her fingers and fell rhythmically onto the stone below, where a line of bluebells grew through the cracks of stone. She felt a breeze and a hand upon her shoulder.

Tippa rippa rapper on my shoulder
Tippa rippa rapper on my shoulder
Tippa rippa rapper on my shoulder
I'll be your master

"In and out go dusty bluebells," said Maisie.

She pictured Sally's thick, long hair meandering down her back as she tippa rippa rappered on the shoulder of the girl in front, and she recalled singing and dancing and playing at the corner for hours on end between factory bells, school bells and dusty bluebells.

She recaptured that time for just one moment, and as she watched the dust dance across the bluebells, peace fell upon her like the cool touch of Brown's Irish linen.

It was time to return to her master.

Author's Note

Dusty Bluebells is a fictional story based on a mill community in Larne, County Antrim. The community is close to the Town Parks, and its main artery, Waterloo Road, is a long line of small kitchen houses and parlour houses that sweeps down to the Antrim Coast Road. Many of those who worked at the Brown's Irish Linen Mill in the late 1800s were migrants from the Ballymena countryside, hence the old moniker "Little Ballymena." The Brown's Irish Linen Mill comprised a flax dam near the Victoria Road and a weaving mill on the Lower Waterloo Road. A large and rather sturdy old stone wall separates the kitchen houses from the "big houses" on the other side.

Many of the sights and sounds in this novel — skipping rhymes, songs, yarns, idioms, expressions — were handed down to me by family, particularly my beloved great aunt, Nancy Hewitt (née Ross), who lived at 82 Upper Waterloo Road; her husband, Dan, and her mother, Mrs Ross, make an appearance in the novel.

I also learned a great deal from the Doey family, who, early on in the process of writing this novel, provided me with access to the diary of Martha Doey (née Taylor). Martha was raised on the Waterloo Road and was a contemporary of my great aunts and uncles on the Ross side of my family. Through the diary, I was able to find the kind of detail that would not ordinarily be recorded in history books. Stunning photographs of Martha as a young girl inspired the character Sally Ramsey, although I should stress that Sally's story in the novel is fictional.

The people of the factory community in Larne speak a Scots dialect that is comparable to anything found in the Lowlands of Scotland. However, owing to the fact that English and Scots are mutually comprehensible, all we knew as children was that we did not speak "proper English." I have endeavoured to ensure that the dialogue of the novel is written in such a way that it will be understood by the widest possible audience of readers.

Larne, throughout the second half of the 1800s and up until the 1960s, was a popular tourist resort, and Henry McNeill, tourism pioneer, made a significant contribution to the global tourism industry when he created package holidays for English tourists to the Larne area. One character, Mary Beth Clarke, was inspired by Jean Park, a widow who lived on the shore at Bally-gally Bay. She sold dulse to tourists travelling along the Antrim Coast Road and was washed away in a hurricane in 1894 at the age of 71.

The story of Maisie and Sally is fictional. Dalriada, Horseshoe Cottage and Corran Cottage are also fictional, but the rest of the locations in the novel are real. If the people living in houses 33, 15 and 17 during the specific timeline of the novel experienced any of the events in the novel, it is purely coincidental.

Many anecdotes and historical details in the novel are based on reality: hallowe'en was, and remains, an important celebration in this community; the fiddle, flute and melodeon tradition was widespread in Larne; the tourism trade fuelled the entertainment genes of the town; Larne linen was said to be strong enough to dam a river; my great uncle Norman King served during the Berlin Airlift and worked as a driver for the padre; my great aunt Peggy and many other Larne women married American soldiers stationed in Larne in the 1940s; Mrs Ross, was a local midwife;

Martha Doey was whipped until she bled at the Parochial school in the early 1920s, and she also saw the premature departure of her favourite pig; there was rationing from one world war to the next and this is also described in Martha's diary; the short-term contract employment situation was a reality for the men who talked socialism at the corner in the 1920s and 1930s, while the women scrubbed linen for a pittance; many left Larne in the 1950s, and beyond, to live in Canada; the poor house report, with the exception of Mary Beth Clarke's plight, is real; lots of people on the Waterloo Road would have been proficient step dancers, a tradition continues to be strong in Larne today through the Festival Tradition of Irish dancing —as recorded in detail in my book, *Irish Dancing: The Festival Story.*

Acknowledgements

A world of thanks goes to Martha Doey's family: her daughters, Irene, Jean and Margaret; her son, Bobby, whom I had the pleasure to meet before he passed away; and her granddaughter Barbra Cooke, who has been a fantastic help to me.

I am grateful to my granda's brother, Norman King, who told me all about his time serving with the RAF in Germany during the Berlin Airlift. Likewise, my granny Rossborough's sister, Jean McCullagh, brought the period or her childhood to life for me. (Jean celebrated her 105th birthday in 2019).

Most of all, I appreciate family, friends and acquaintances in Larne who helped me either wittingly or unwittingly — from the elderly gentleman I met in an Argos queue one day, who rang out a soliloquy from his long career at the Regal Picture House, to the dozens of people who posted unique details of past life to Facebook group, Memories of Larne. In many ways, this book is an ode to Larne.

As I reached the final furlong in this tale, I turned to a fellow Women Aloud NI member, writer, film maker and poet, Angela Graham, who has an interest in languages of Ireland. I am indebted to Angela for investing so much time in my work. Her insights were invaluable. Thanks also goes to Dr. Frank Ferguson, Director of the Centre for Irish and Scottish Studies at Ulster University and historian, Dr. David Hume.

The joy of publishing books is that readers can sometimes become friends, so when Canadian reader Susan Graham visited my home during a holiday to tell me in person how much she enjoyed *Snugville Street* and *A Belfast Tale*, I knew that she would be a great beta reader. Thank you Susan. Your feedback was wonderful.

I am grateful to reader Mandy Ross for assuring me that the novel would pass the Waterloo Road test, and that it would mean something to the people of my hometown. I am also thankful for the encouragement received from Heather McCrudden, Glenyss Glass, Marie Mitchell, Liam Logan, Ian Hooper and Caroline Johnstone.

Final thanks goes to the Arts Council of Northern Ireland for providing a *'Support for the Individual Artist Programme'* grant, funded by the National Lottery in 2016/2017.

Book Club Questions

1. Discuss what family means in Dusty Bluebells.
2. Would you prefer life at Dalriada or life on the Waterloo Road?
3. Is Sally ill or is she afflicted by memories?
4. Why does Leonard believe that Maisie has the blue blood of a prince?
5. The character of Mary Beth was inspired by a real woman who lived on the shore. Why do you think such a woman would opt out of conventional society at that time?
6. Why is Kim so intrigued about her family's past? And why does young Leonard not explore DNA testing?
7. What is the importance of reflections/mirroring in the novel?
8. There are several incidences of cruelty in the novel. What is the impact?
9. What difference would it have made if the author had written the entire book in Standard English?
10. Is the town a character in this novel?

About the Author

Angeline King, Writer in Residence of Ulster University from September 2020, is the author of contemporary novels *Snugville Street* (2015) and *A Belfast Tale* (2016). Angeline was selected as one of Libraries NI three emerging authors in 2017 and received the Arts Council of Northern Ireland SIAP award to write this novel in 2016. Angeline has written essays for the *Irish Times*; a history book, *Irish Dancing: The Festival story* (2018) and an illustrated children's book, *Children of Latharna* (2017). She also edited *Shaped by the Sea* (2020) and oversaw Women Aloud NI's *North Star* collection (2020). Angeline, who has worked in international business for 20 years, lives in her beloved hometown, Larne, with her husband and children. She has a BA Hons in French and Modern History from Queens' University Belfast, and an MA in Applied Languages & Business from Ulster University.

Printed in Great Britain
by Amazon